Lisa Lueddecke

a *shiver* of *snow* and *sky*

■SCHOLASTIC

For Dad

Scholastic Children's Books
An imprint of Scholastic Ltd
Euston House, 24 Eversholt Street
London, NW1 1DB, UK
Registered office: Westfield Road, Southam, Warwickshire, CV47 0RA
SCHOLASTIC and associated logos are trademarks and/
or registered trademarks of Scholastic Inc.

First published in the UK by Scholastic Ltd, 2017

Text copyright © Lisa Lueddecke, 2017
The right of Lisa Lueddecke to be identified as the
author of this work has been asserted by her.

ISBN 978 1407 17403 7

A CIP catalogue for this book is
available from the British Library.

Printed and bound by CPI Group (UK) Ltd, Croydon, CR0 4YY
Papers used by Scholastic Children's Books are made
from wood grown in sustainable forests.

1 3 5 7 9 10 8 6 4 2

www.scholastic.co.uk

Though my soul may set in darkness, it
   will rise in perfect light;
I have loved the stars too fondly to be
   fearful of the night.

SARAH WILLIAMS

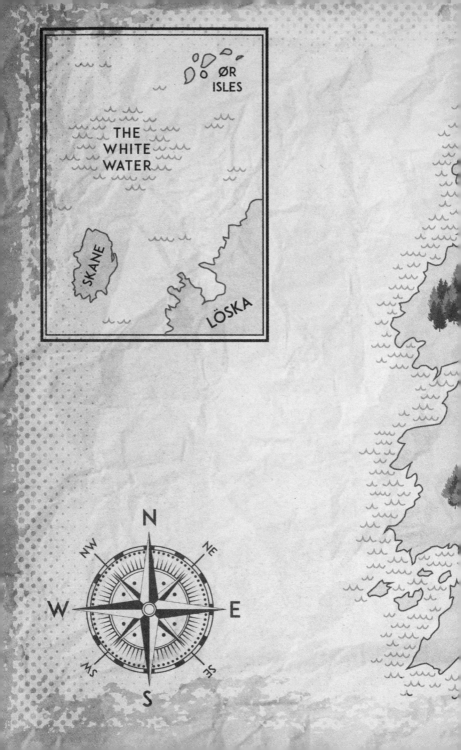

Chapter 1

Skane was built on superstition. Always enter your home right foot first. When you sneeze, someone who bears you ill will has just spoken your name. Don't whistle while looking towards the sun or you might bring on rain.

But mostly, the superstitions were about the lights. Bright, colourful lights that danced for us in the clear night sky.

Green was common. It meant the Goddess was happy, and everything was as it should be.

Blue meant snow, and lots of it. Best round up your sheep and haul in some firewood before those first few flurries started to fly.

And then there was red. Red was different, rarer.

Red was a warning.

*

The lights danced. The lós, most called it, a word given to us by the old rune singers who translated it from symbols and pictures etched into cave walls. They waved and morphed and rippled like the sky was a lake into which someone had dropped a pebble.

"What are they?" I would ask my father every night as a child.

Every night he would answer differently. "They are the last remnants of the setting sun dancing for the moon." "They're the light of the stars reflecting off the sea." "They just . . . are." Eventually, I realized he didn't know. No one knew. The Goddess could change their colour; that was the only certainty. What they were, why they were there – those were still mysteries to us. Perhaps they always would be.

Between those of us who were staring up at them now, the air grew still, charged, as if we were on a mountaintop and the breeze had stopped.

I'd joined a few other villagers who were seated on the large rocks that fell away into the sea. On nights like this one, when the lights shone so vibrantly that they lit up the snow in vivid greens and blues, groups of us would gather to gaze at them. When the sky demanded our attention, we obeyed.

"They're changing," Ivar said beside me, but his words were a fading echo, distant and hollow. My eyes were fixed on the sky, and I didn't miss the subtle shifts here

2

and there as the bright blues became pinks and purples. They were deep too, reminiscent of a sunset.

My skin prickled, hairs standing on end, but not from the cold. This hue was dreadfully close to another, drawing ever nearer to a shade none of us in Skane wanted to see again.

It had happened seventeen years ago, the sky glowing crimson only days before a fever outbreak had ravaged our villages. Once it set in, nearly two hundred people died in a matter of days. I was born, and lived. My mother birthed me, and died. They said I was lucky. One quarter of those who perished were children.

Lucky. I'd never know her. Lucky. I'd had to be passed around other mothers who'd recently given birth – mothers whose children would know them, know what they looked like. How they sounded. Have memories of them to cherish. I was nursed to health by strangers.

Lucky.

Seventeen years was a long time, but no one had forgotten. Whenever the lights in the sky shifted away from green, even for just a few seconds, the villagers held their breath.

"Ivar," I whispered, but his name felt strange on my tongue. Meaningless, foreign, as my throat began to constrict. His presence usually grounded me, was my guiding point of comfort when life tried to smother me, but tonight, it did nothing. I may as well have been alone on a boat in the middle of the sea.

He drew in a long breath, one mitten-clad hand just barely touching mine.

The edges of the tendrils were changing. Shifting. Deepening. One particular whorl high overhead, waving like a scrap of cloth in the wind, was almost wholly crimson. It seemed to bleed out from there, infecting all the nearby branches with its blood-red disease. My body went cold, as if the colour had been stolen directly from my veins. Mist from the crashing waves stung my eyes, but I couldn't close them. I raced to find parts of the lights that hadn't changed, that were still uncorrupted, like I could singlehandedly prevent it from progressing.

It took mere minutes. Minutes for the entire sky to stain red. It bore down on us, a presage, a desperate but wordless warning we had no way to translate. *It's coming*, it screamed. *The plague is coming*. It was always the devastating plague, haunting us every few decades since we'd first arrived in Skane. But *why* it was coming was as knowable as how many snowflakes would make up the next storm, or how many raindrops it took to fill the sea.

I clutched at the icy rock beneath me, my fingers long since numb through my mittens. I suddenly felt keenly conscious of the scale of the lós, and of my own fragility in comparison. What does one tiny, useless form matter in a world where such dark things can happen? How many of these poor souls around me would be dead within days? Weeks? A wave of confusion and sickness came over me, and I couldn't tell the sky from the land. Doubling over, my head spinning as though I were falling through the dark places between the stars, I closed my eyes and forced cold, crisp air into my lungs.

Breathe in. Breathe out.

I recovered my orientation slowly, gripping the rock and setting my eyes on the stars that managed to shine through the cursed red lights. I expected fear to take hold of my heart and mind, paralysing me after all the stories I'd heard about the blood red sky, but it wasn't fear that gripped me. Instead, anger surged to life like a springtime river, refilling my frozen veins. Anger, because I didn't know why it was happening. Anger, because I knew the sky didn't portend that a handful of fishermen would drown at sea or a child would get lost in the woods and be found days later, buried under the snow. Anger, because when the lights glowed red, it meant the lives of everyone I knew and loved were at stake, and I had a greater chance of thawing Lake Hornsträsk in midwinter than stopping it.

Anger, because when the red lós shone, it meant that somewhere in Skane the plague was brewing once more and it was hungry for bodies.

Somewhere nearby, but just far enough away to be distorted by the breeze, someone began to chant the

5

words. I'd heard them innumerable times before. Knew every word and nuance by heart, forward and backwards. Without looking away from the sky, I let my voice join in.

> *"Green, green, the lights glow green*
> *Happy is our gracious queen*
> *Blue, blue, the lights glow blue*
> *A vicious storm nearby does brew*
> *Red, red, the lights glow red*
> *Beware the dangers up ahead."*

Chapter 2

Fear hung like shards of frozen mist in the air. Not just the quiet, inward fear that left one wide-eyed and anxious, but the kind that brought tears to pale faces and cries to the lips of those who could no longer hold it in. Families huddled together in tightly-woven embraces, savouring these precious moments of peace and calm before the plague came back with a bloodied vengeance. Children, young enough to not have been alive last time but old enough to know the stories, wept into their hands. Grown men tried to stay stony-faced and silent, but their eyes glistened with secret tears that would fall when no one was looking.

Despite the crying and embracing and whispering that passed around the people like rustling leaves, we all made our way towards the centre of the village. We acted on instinct. The red lights show. Then comes the bonfire. A large circle of stones had long ago been formed in the village, and it was our gathering point, our place of congregating at various times throughout the year: midsummer, the new year, and it was where we gathered to talk about the red lós. This would be my first time doing so, and the heaviness of that fact made every step a struggle.

On other days, the gatherings were a happy event, causing excitement amongst the children as it meant food and games and stories told by anyone who had one to tell. On the warmest day of the year, we'd sit around in nothing but our thinnest wraps and sip cool drinks, all thoughts of winter fading away into nothingness. This time, though, that excitement was nowhere to be found. This time, I ignored the knot in my stomach as I watched the wan faces of the villagers gathering together to discuss the unspeakable.

Log upon log had been piled within the stones, dripped here and there with oil and stuffed with bits of smaller sticks and twigs for kindling. It was just as I was arriving, rolling with me the round stump of a tree to use as a seat, that a sombre-faced woman sent sparks flying on to the pile, and flames kindled to life.

I stared into the growing blaze, red lights dancing before my eyes. I watched a few sticks catch fire and burn away, and couldn't help but wish that we could be that way. Not the sticks, the fire. Catch on and consume our doubts, our worries. Overcome whatever lay before us with a power that could not be quenched. If that sort of will could catch on, if we could all add fuel to the fire, then perhaps we'd fare better than the last time. Perhaps a few more lives could be saved.

A stump thudded to the ground beside me. Ivar. "All alone?" he said, seating himself and extending his hands towards the warmth. He wasn't wearing mittens and his hands bore callouses where he'd spent so much time writing, and blisters from shovelling snow. Ivar was from a long line of rune singers, men and women trained in the art of translating the ancient language and the corresponding images into Agric, the language we spoke today. It had made me jealous as a child, the way he could scratch out letters quicker than I could read them. I did everything slower than him, reading and writing in particular. But those were his life blood, his meaning. I could fish and shear sheep, if I cared enough to try, but it was my desire to do something, to *know* something others might not, that encouraged me to learn the stars.

"Early comers get the best seats," I replied, watching a small stick go up in flames.

More and more villagers gathered, some bringing wooden chairs from their homes, others bringing boxes, and still others bringing stumps like our own. The oldest man in our village, Ymir, was helped to the fire by his wife and grandson. They placed him in a large wooden chair, and tucked blankets around his shoulders and legs. I'd heard Ymir was nearly one hundred years old, but by the lines on his face, the weight he carried in his eyes, I sometimes felt as though he'd watched the island of Skane itself be born from the waves. He'd taught me about the stars so many years ago, taking me on as a pupil after finding me on a rooftop staring up at the sky. I'd been tracing out their shapes in the snow, learning where to spot them and at what times of year they showed. He told me the stories of the constellations, of the maps they painted and how to use them to find my way when lost.

Móri, Ivar's little cousin, came to sit at our feet, some sticks in his hands. Whittling was a favourite pastime of Ivar's, when he wasn't reading runes, and he'd passed it down to some of the children. I tugged at a blond wisp of his Móri's and he swatted me away like a fly without bothering to look up.

Across the fire, Father sat with my sister, Anneka. Her face was deathly white, shiny patches on her cheeks where tears were drying in the heat of the fire. Her eyes caught mine for a heartbeat before she looked away. I watched, through the licking flames, the light dance in my father's eyes. When compared with Ymir, he could be a child, but on his own, lines formed from years of worry, from fighting the wild sea, crossed his face. Anneka said that some used to call him handsome.

Maybe he had been, once upon a time. To me, he was just my father. A symbol of strength, of respect, and sometimes of fear.

Once as a child, I'd heard Anneka ask him if he couldn't perhaps be a bit softer. Why he insisted on that harsh exterior that sometimes frightened us to the point of tears. His response had been unyielding, yet even so young, I'd understood it.

"Our ancestors didn't come here, didn't sail an unfamiliar sea to start a life for us that would be easy. They knew it would be hard, and hard it is. It's the weak ones who fall, Anneka. It's the frail who succumb. I won't let you be weak. I won't watch you fall. It's not in my blood and I won't let it be in yours."

A new understanding of him had dawned then, and while there were still times when he frightened me, still times when anger at him burned so hot I feared it would come out in some unforgivable action, that understanding remained.

"Tonight," Ymir began, "we saw the red lós."

All our eyes turned obediently to him, a chill settling into the air despite the fire. Ymir's age and presence demanded respect from everyone around him. When he spoke, people listened.

"Many of you younger folk" – he looked to me and Ivar, who sat near him – "won't remember the last time they shone in the sky. They were the same, back then, starting out so simple and ... unthreatening, but transforming. I was younger, perhaps not *too* much younger" – a faint smile – "but young enough that the lights made me angry."

I looked to the ground, recalling the fire that had run through my veins when the red lights bled in the sky.

"But the one thing we all, every single one of us since the first of our boots landed here, have had to accept is that we cannot understand it. The Goddess sees fit to warn us, to put us on our guard, but not to give us an explanation. That'd be meddling. Meddling in the affairs of mere mortals, and that's crossing a boundary that's been in place since the dawn of time."

A few whispers passed around the group and the fire crackled. People leaned in, eyes glistening with curiosity and reflections from the flames. Móri carried on whittling, as though he wasn't listening, but I could sense the straining of his ears, the way his hands paused in their work every few seconds to hear better.

"Seventeen years ago was the first time I saw the red lights," Ymir continued softly. "It still seems like yesterday. Before that, I'd only heard stories from my father. When he was a young boy, they'd glowed once. It was ten days before they knew why. Days before a villager followed a trail of blood through the trees to where a body lay in the snow, raging with fever and bleeding from their eyes and nose. It caught on like kindling, sweeping through the village and taking one life after another. By the end, only half of them remained. The oldest was a mere forty, the youngest was ten."

The youngest was ten. Maybe I *was* lucky. Lucky to have survived as a baby when so many before me had perished.

Not a noise could be heard in the cold night air. Mouths hung open, but we had all forgotten how to breathe. An unexplainable urge gripped me. I wanted to reach over and take Ivar's hand, to squeeze it until my own hand shook. Not out of fright, but a desire to know I wasn't alone.

"And again, seventeen years ago," Ymir continued, softer. "Again, it happened, and again it took so many of our lives. Again, husbands were torn from their wives, and children were separated from their mothers by the unforgiving boundary of life and death."

I could have sworn he glanced at me.

"It should be different this time," someone shouted from the group, a middle-aged man I barely knew. His eyes blazed as he spoke, fuelled by a passion born from fear. "Anyone who shows signs of illness, anyone at all, should be quarantined. We know what will happen if we don't."

A few nodded, and a few shook their heads. I did nothing, only stared at the man, turning his words over in my mind. I'd seen the fever caves before. Crept in the early

13

morning hours to the caves north of the village, where horrors had been etched into the very air around them. It was where some of the ill had been herded, left to die alone, away from their families, cold and feverish. Some died quickly from the plague, others froze to death. Some families, like mine, wouldn't let their ill be taken. My father wouldn't part with my mother until she'd passed, and her body was moved to one of the fever caves to be burned. The ash had long since disappeared, but some bones remained, those that had defied the fire out of will or sheer luck, refusing to be taken from Skane. That was all that remained: the charred shards of bones that even the animals wouldn't touch.

No one was meant to go there, but tell a child not to do something and it creates a burning desire so intense that nothing else can quench it.

I wished I hadn't.

The moment I saw the bones, I had emptied my stomach into the snow. They could have been my mother's.

Such a blanket of darkness had been cast over the group that, noticing it, Ymir turned to me.

"Ósa. Perhaps you could tell us a story about the stars." He smiled weakly and I couldn't say no. We were all a part of this, but the children didn't deserve such evils.

For a long moment, I gazed into the fire, sorting through my roaring thoughts. There were so many stories, but they'd fallen from my mind and vanished at Ymir's words. All I could remember were vague hints, unclear shapes.

A long breath of cold air and my thoughts returned to me. It couldn't be a dark tale, not after what we'd just heard. The red lights brought with them shadows and darkness enough, yet so many of the stories were tragedies or horrors; finding a happy one was next to impossible. Blocking out the fire with a hand, I craned my neck to look up and the story stared back at me.

"Once," I began, keeping my eyes on the stars, "there was an immortal princess who roamed the world, forever heartbroken, for all those whom she loved had died. Many men had fallen for her, consumed by her otherworldly beauty, but one by one they'd passed on, taken from the world by their mortality. Yet on the princess lived, one lifetime of despair after another. So one day, while weeping from her heartbreak and unable to bear it any longer, she begged the Goddess to remove her from the pain she was doomed to endure for eternity. And, taking pity upon her, the Goddess pulled her from the earth and placed her as a constellation in the sky, beside the Warrior, so she wouldn't be alone. And at long last, the Immortal had found a love of which she would never be robbed, one she could cherish for ever. The Warrior loved her so fiercely, he placed a ring of light on her finger, so she would for ever be reminded of his love. And that is the brightest star in the constellation, there to the right." I pointed to the brilliant, glistening star overhead, and it warmed my heart. No matter what happened here in Skane, no matter how bleak our future looked, that love would live on, until even the stars crumbled from the sky and the universe around us went dark. There was beauty in that, and hope. On days like these, hope was a welcome friend.

Now the children's eyes were wide as they stared up into the heavens, and seeing it brought me a small spark of happiness. Some of the cold from earlier had been chased away. It was just a story, they were just words, but there was a comfort in it.

The time for stories had to end, and when it did, that chill settled back into my bones. Several girls offered to walk the children home for bed, but nearly everyone else remained. Once again, all eyes were on Ymir, though mouths stayed silent. Everyone burned with questions, but we waited for Ymir to speak first.

I threw a small twig into the fire.

"I know what you all want to hear," Ymir said quietly, but with that sense of firm understanding that begged respect. "You all want to hear that this time, we have a plan. That we know what can be done about it. That we know how to save everyone. I might as well tell you

16

right now, it isn't so. I don't know how to prevent it any more than you do." He looked into his lap and played with the corner of the blanket. "But what we can do is be extra vigilant. Last time it came within days. It could start in any one of us."

His words filled the air around us with a hopelessness so heavy it was a struggle to breathe. I pulled at the wraps around my neck to alleviate some of the pressure, but it did nothing. Beside me, Ivar's gaze was firmly on the ground, his mouth set in a thin line. Good. I was glad to see him as angry as I was.

"Don't let this lack of understanding dampen your resolve to survive," Ymir went on. "Many of us have lived through the red lights once before, and hopefully, many of us will do so again. Stay watchful. If you feel unwell, if something strikes you as out of place, tell someone. Tell me. Tell anyone you can find. Do not prolong our ignorance. Perhaps with some cunning and forethought, more of us will survive this time."

Though many of us will die.

My mind finished the thought for him, and I ground my teeth so loudly that Ivar shot me a sideways glance. I shook my head and he looked away.

Waiting and watching wouldn't save our lives. Sitting by and hoping wouldn't give doomed souls a few extra days. I looked around the group. In a few weeks, some of these faces would be gone. Some of these friends and family members would die. I could lie in my bed and hope for their salvation until they were taken one by one, or I could fuel this anger inside me and use it to find a way to help them.

Chapter 3

Sleep was elusive that night, for what remained of it. I caught small, dozing snatches through dawn and into the grey morning, the wind that whistled outside the earthen-and-wood walls of my family home acting as both a lullaby and a hindrance. Sometimes it was soft, gentle, easing my restless mind. And sometimes it was shrill, harsh, like someone screaming just outside our door. My broken dreams were dark, full of bones and skin and a blood red sky that retained its colour even in the daytime. When I awoke to a snapping fire and low voices, my eyes were blurred, my neck stiff.

"Snow's coming," my father said, his scratchy voice muted with my head pressed into the blankets. A lifetime of fishing on the harsh Grey Sea, where winds were high and raised voices were the only way to communicate, had left his voice gravelly. But it was still somehow comforting to hear him speak. One too many times we'd thought he'd been lost, consumed by a squalling storm that blew in with little or no notice. Each time he came home was a gift, Anneka said.

"We'll watch the sheep," my sister answered. Anneka was always up before me, before anyone. Something in her blood made her rise before the sun. "Ósa's good about bringing them in on time." Then, under her breath, "And little else." I could tell by the way her voice changed that she'd turned her head to say it in my direction, in hopes that I'd hear her.

If I were to let the sheep die, the lack of wool would drive her mad. Knitting was her one pastime, the one thing she did from sunrise to sunset. And as tempting as it was to drive her mad, sheep were essential, here in Skane. Sheep meant wool, and wool meant warmth. Warmth meant the difference between life and death in the winter.

"You won't go out today, will you?" Anneka asked. When there was a pause, she added, "After the red lós, I thought maybe—"

"Life goes on after the damned red lights, Anneka," Father snapped. "We still require food."

A long pause. Anneka stayed silent.

"We're short one man on the boat," my father said, changing the subject. I could hear him shuffling around, preparing to leave. "Klas's baby came last night."

"Bless that little babe. And what a night to be born." The way she again fell silent told me that Father had sent her a look warning her not to mention the red lights. "You can't be out long, anyway," Anneka said brazenly. Few people were brave enough to speak to my father in such a way, but she got away with more things than most. "Not if a storm's coming," she added, softer.

"I'm a fisherman, Anneka." His voice carried the edge of a freshly-sharpened blade. "And you are not." He stood and grabbed a fur cloak from a peg on the wall by the door, but paused before leaving.

"Ósa."

I blinked at my name from my place in the corner. "Father?"

"You come."

"But, Father—" Anneka rushed to say. He stopped her.

"She's been on the boat before. She has her sea legs and she can fill in for Klas. It'll give us a better chance of a good catch. We'll come back when the waters start swelling."

Seventeen years as my father's daughter had taught me not to question his authority. And, contrary to what we wanted to think, his authority hadn't yet led us astray.

I emerged from the warmth of my furs, the relative cold beyond my cocoon biting my skin. Soon, I'd be out in the wind and snow, fighting the sea with my father, and Anneka would be here, warm and knitting by the fire. So it went.

21

I took the chunk of bread Anneka was holding out to me. It was stale from drying near the fire. I knew there was some fresh bread she'd made yesterday, but I didn't bother asking her for it. She'd tell me I should get up earlier or make it myself.

"Don't turn your nose up at it like that," she spat. "Digestion'll keep you warm." Every bit of her tone screamed that I wasn't worth the time it took her to speak. It had always been this way, ever since my arrival in this wretched world had taken away her mother. Our mother. It was like she'd forgotten that it was my mother who'd died too. As if, because I'd never truly known her, I had no right to mourn her loss. As if I didn't already feel guilty every day that I lived and breathed and my mother didn't.

I could fight back when she treated me poorly. Sometimes I did, but mostly I didn't. There was always a tiny voice in the back of my mind, a distant whisper that she was right to be angry with me.

I bit my lip, my mind still thick with a lack of sleep, and donned my boots and cloak. Father waited by the door. As I tried to cover my curls with a warm hat, I said to Anneka, "Ivar may come for me. Tell him—"

"Tell him she can play after our work," my father finished, and my sister smirked.

Better his word be the final one. We said nothing more as I finished wrapping up and we left the house.

The wind was sharp. It cut my face and eyes, and the clouds were so low I was certain I could reach up and touch them, if I hadn't been clutching my wraps so tightly. When we were younger, Ivar said he'd heard that the soft appearance of clouds was deceiving, and that they were made of tiny shards of ice, so we'd slice our fingers open if we tried to grasp them. Maybe it was true, maybe it wasn't. He liked to spread fairy tales, back then. But given how biting the cold wind and snow were, I was inclined to believe it.

By this time tomorrow, our little earthen village would be buried beneath metres of snow, appearing as no more than white mounds in the land. We'd all be inside, warm under piles of furs and knits and taking turns to tell stories until we fell asleep, lulled by the whistling wind just beyond the walls. It would be the kind of storm the sky would have warned us about, if it hadn't been bleeding red.

I blinked my eyes against the wind, knowing full well it would be far worse at sea. We were fools to go out now, yet I'd rather be a brave fool than a cowardly one. Rather show my father I had more of a place in Skane than staring up at the stars and traipsing to caves with Ivar. Show my sister that I was earning just as much of a right to exist in this world as she was.

This wouldn't be the first time my father had seen fit to embark on the boat during the onset of a storm and thus far he'd always come back. Try as I might, though, I could find no comfort in that.

"Remember," my father said as we neared the docks, "follow my orders. My word is law on my boat. We don't come back until I say we come back."

"But your promise to—"

He silenced me with a look that could freeze the sea. I said nothing more.

The clouds were so oppressive I couldn't see the docks until we were upon them. The waves crashed beneath us, so hard that spray hit my boots and froze there. I stomped frequently to break it up, or else the cold from the building ice would seep through my boots and I'd lose feeling in my feet. That would be one dangerous step towards losing them completely. I'd seen that before. Seen the blunt stumps of arms or legs where hands and feet had once been. Cold was an unforgiving intruder. One either respected it or succumbed to it.

"Albrekt."

I looked up to the man my father addressed. He stood on the boat, bobbing around on the waves while securing crates that would, with any luck, soon be filled with fish. His legs remained steady despite the movement, a gift earned over a lifetime at sea.

"Eldór. Heard about Klas?" Albrekt returned to his work with barely a glance in our direction. His hands moved quickly despite the cold, though whether he was always so deft or if it was due to the impending storm, I couldn't tell.

"I have," my father replied, motioning for me to climb aboard before him. He offered no hand to steady me, but I didn't require it. I'd boarded in rough waters enough times before to do so without plunging into the freezing depths. I held fast to the crude mast and eyed the near-ragged sail affixed to it. My father notoriously cut corners when it came to repairs, and every day that passed made that fact increasingly more evident. One day, I feared, he would forego one too many repairs, and the results would be disastrous.

"Waste no more time," my father instructed Albrekt, and the tiniest flame of hope kindled within me. It was the first mention he'd made of being aware of the impending storm. Until now he'd appeared to be feigning ignorance.

Albrekt pulled the ropes and cast us off the dock. I held fast to the edge of the boat, the swells rocking us like a babe in a cradle. My right foot caught on a patch of ice on the floor and I lost my footing momentarily, clinging on with all my strength. I didn't meet my father's eyes; I knew the stern look I'd find there.

The skies were angry. They pressed down on us, urging us back, yet onwards we sailed. Everything nature had within its power seemed to be sending us a message, a warning, which we merely ignored. I forced my eyes away from above and fell into a sort of rhythm as I helped Father and Albrekt drop the nets off the back of the longboat. With any luck, before too long, we'd pull them up again teeming with fish. Some we'd keep for our families and some we'd sell or trade to the local villages, who would then dry it for the winter. Sometimes, when the winters were especially long and cold, salted and dried fish was the only thing that saw us through. If I wasn't so entirely grateful to have enough food to survive – something of which Anneka never failed to remind me – I'd say I oft grew tired of the repetition.

The first net was less than half as full as any of us wanted to see. We placed the catch in the wooden crates tied to the edge of the boat, and then cast it out again. I knew my father was hoping that a successful catch would counter the foolhardiness of going out before a storm such as this one, but it didn't look like that was to be. And I couldn't help but wonder if the fish had been mostly frightened away. A rough sea like this must make even them want to take shelter.

As the winds grew, Father spent more time fighting with the sails than aiding Albrekt and I in unloading the nets. The boat rocked and swayed and sometimes we were forced to stop our task in favour of gripping anything we could reach for stability as it crashed headlong into a wave. Between hauling in nets and bracing against the swells, the crates slowly, slowly began to fill.

A solitary, indignant fish flopped out of a crate and

on to the deck. I crouched to pick it up and toss it back, but as I rose to replace it, something in the waves caught my attention. I froze for a moment, no longer aware of the fish in my hand or the rocking of the boat. I narrowed my eyes, trying to separate the oppressive fog from the white waves. I was sure I'd seen something – a shadow, maybe. A bit of flotsam on the sea. But whatever it was vanished, eaten up by the roiling waves.

There.

Again.

"Father."

I pointed away over the water, as accurately as I could despite the movement of the boat. A sail? If so, it was a dark one, unfamiliar. All the village boats were at the docks. We didn't get travellers in these parts and no one else from the village was foolhardy enough to go out in a storm such as this.

"I see nothing," Father said.

"Nor do I," Albrekt replied.

Both returned to their work.

Whatever it was vanished once again, and this time it didn't reappear. I dropped my hand to my side. Now, not even my layers of furs and knits kept me warm. Now, the cold I felt came from within.

Chapter 4

Wind tore into Ivar's face where he stood, just outside the door to Ósa's family's house, but he barely felt it as he worked to wrap his mind around Anneka's words.

"She's gone out with our father." Anneka smiled sweetly, too sweetly for the madness that had just come from her mouth and the snow hitting her face. Strands of her usually neat reddish hair whipped around into her eyes, though whether she genuinely didn't notice or was feigning ignorance to continue smiling, Ivar couldn't tell. "I imagine they'll be back soon."

"I'm sorry, what?" Ivar asked, his mouth open in disbelief.

"Ósa's gone out with our father. I imagine—"

"I heard you," he interrupted, and spun around to walk away. "I'm going to take her home."

"Please come in and warm up!" Anneka called into the wind, but ignored her. He just let her insignificant words be carried far, far away and forgotten.

Anneka didn't matter. What *did* matter was that, out of all of the senseless, cruel things Ósa's father had ever done, taking her out to sea in this weather had to top the list. *Ósa was on a boat. On the water. In this storm.* Why hadn't he taken her sister? Why hadn't he risked Anneka's life? There were many reasons, surely, not the least of which was the affection Eldór had always shown for Anneka that Ósa would never receive. Yes, perhaps Ósa was better suited to sailing: lighter, quicker, smarter. The elder daughter was, as far as Ivar was concerned, just shy of useless. She let her chores slide to her sister, she rarely left the house, and the way she spoke to Ósa, the things he'd overheard, made it a constant struggle to bite his tongue.

He marched through the village, the force of his footfalls resonating through his body as he fought the wind. The walk had to be done by heart; the snow fell so intensely he could scarcely see his own feet on the ground. If she was out in the boat, then they'd come back to the docks. So be it. He'd wait through the storm. Hell, he'd wait through the night if he had to. Snow be damned. *Someone* in this world was going to show Ósa how much she meant to them. But every day he could see the lines of pain around her mouth and eyes, see the way the guilt pressed against her like the clouds pressed against the village now. It wasn't fair. It was awful, what had happened to her mother, but it wasn't Ósa's fault.

And one day, he would help her see that.

Chapter 5

As we returned to the docks, riding the writhing waves like a dead leaf in the wind, I remained at the back of the boat, staring out into the fog and mist and cloud. Something had been out there, I'd never been more certain of anything in my life. *Something* had appeared in the fog, a passing shadow, a fleeting hint of danger. My heart beat fast within my chest, warming my core and filling me with energy. Father and Albrekt may not have believed me, but I didn't need them to. I trusted my own eyes. There was something on the water and the shiver in my muscles told me it was out of place.

"Catch, Ósa," my father shouted, tossing me a rope with just barely enough time for me to react. I gripped it tightly with my gloved hands, the joints of my fingers aching from the cold, and helped to pull us to the docks.

The wind howled, as though it came straight from the mouth of an angry goddess. Waves lashed the boat; snowflakes stung my eyes.

"Get yourself home," Father called, while he and Albrekt worked to pull the full crates from the boat. They were two strong men who'd spent a lifetime doing this, and the turning weather acted like a fire beneath them. I'd only get in the way. Without responding, I pulled my cloak as tightly around my frame as I could and made my way up the icy dock to the village. More than once I lost my footing. I was like one of those baby deer I'd seen in the woods, with their long, spindly legs that weren't used to walking. They'd teeter and shake and fall over as they worked to learn how to balance.

Amid the snapping wind and wall of snow, I recalled the folktales some of the elderly villagers recounted at gatherings, when we'd all sit around a giant bonfire and share food and drink while the children played with carved wooden animals. Some of the stories were more like ancient rumours passed down from long ago, of warm lands somewhere far to the south, where the sun shone every day and it never snowed. They said you could swim naked in the sea there and the sun would darken your skin. You could eat the colourful fruit that grew on the trees and there was never a need to stockpile for the frozen months because there was no winter.

As the wind beat the snow against my face, I imagined

lying naked in the sun, falling asleep in its warmth. Anneka would condemn me, probably skin me alive at the very thought of lying out of doors, unclothed for all to see. But the dream of a warm sun, of snowless ground beneath my skin, was too inviting to care about what my sister thought.

A shadow up ahead.

My feet stopped.

Thoughts of that sail – if that's truly what it was – flooded my mind like a broken dam. I stood still, blinking snow out of my eyes while I watched it come closer, closer, cutting through the storm toward me. My heart was a drum. My pulse was thunder.

"Ósa?"

My name reached my ears, though barely. Instantly, the wind whipped it away, dashing it against the wall of a house or the trunk of a tree outside the village, shattering it beyond recognition. Through the furious snow between us, I could just make out Ivar's eyes behind his layers of wraps.

He extended a heavily-mittened hand to me, which I took, and after the loneliness of the sea and the apprehension of what I'd seen on the water, the contact sent a pulse of warmth through my body.

He turned and leaned into the wind, leading me further into the village. Even without being able to see due to the storm, I knew we weren't headed to my home.

33

He didn't have to explain. From where he'd found me, his house was much closer. Within minutes, he was kicking aside drifted snow and shoving open the heavy wooden door.

The wind screamed behind us as he closed the door, and it faded into nothing more than a dull roar in the periphery of my senses. It was jarring, for a moment, having spent so many hours exposed to the elements, to be now suddenly removed from them.

"Perhaps next time your father can tie an anchor to your feet and sink you to the bottom of the sea," he said with a mock cheerfulness that conveyed precisely what he thought of the ordeal. But buried beneath the harsh words was sincere concern. He was angry at my father, that much was clear. I moved on.

"They'll worry."

"I stopped by there to find you. Anneka told me you'd gone out. I let her know I'd take you in until it passed."

Relief tickled my mind, knowing I didn't have to go back out in the storm, though I couldn't imagine Anneka was thrilled with the prospect. As it was, she complained frequently to Father that I spent too much time with Ivar.

"People will start to talk," she'd said.

"I wish they would," I'd answered. I could think of worse rumours than *something* going on between me and Ivar. There was a point last year when it almost had. For a while, I'd told myself that I'd imagined it. That some

34

time over the course of our lives, of growing up together in a world so cold that we were fuelled by thoughts of comfort and warmth, I'd allowed myself to dream it. To create a spark where there was nothing except ice. But it had happened. Or, almost.

We'd gone out with a sled to collect wood from a fallen tree that had already been chopped into firewood. Loading it turned into a snowball fight, and we'd ended up tackling each other on the ground. We'd rolled around, snow clinging to our hair, our clothes, our skin. And then there was this fleeting moment, this handful of seconds where we'd stopped moving and our bodies were pressed together, Ivar's face close to mine. His eyes had never seemed so blue.

I could have closed the distance and pressed my lips to his, and I almost did. The temptation to kiss him, to discover how our lips felt when they touched, was more consuming than the winds of even the strongest blizzard. Then the moment ended and, like one of those stars that streak across the sky and vanish in the blink of an eye, never came back.

I'd thought about it again, on days when the sun was bright and brilliant and the air was crisp and frozen, when his eyes shone bluer than the sea and his cheeks were pink from the cold, I'd find myself watching him for a second too long. Sometimes he'd notice, and when he did, I wouldn't look away. I'd just keep staring until his mouth twisted into a smile that could melt the snow around us, along with whatever anxieties the day had brought with it.

I edged closer to the fire, longing to feel my fingers and toes again. They didn't feel like my own, rather like foreign appendages stuck to my body. I held them out to the flames, dimly contemplating submerging them in the blaze. A burning sensation had to be preferable to this feeling of unfamiliar leather wrapped around bones that weren't mine.

A few scrolls lay around the room, and I stared absently at their partly unrolled forms. For me, I knew the stars. I knew which ones appeared where at certain times of the year. I knew the stories behind the pictures they painted in the sky. I knew the names of the shapes they created. But Ivar's gift was just . . . different. Fascinating. It seemed impossible, the way he could read ancient writings like it was the language we spoke now. Translating was hard work. Language had to change, once the Löskans established themselves in Skane. Not everyone from the continent spoke the same language or the same dialect. Over time, the use of runes had been phased out, until it died altogether. More than once, Ivar had expressed his sadness over that fact. "A lost art," he had called it.

In my periphery, I could feel him staring at me, his eyes on my face like tiny flames.

"Your father is a damned fool."

"And yet he brought me back alive." There was nothing Ivar could say that I didn't already know. He looked away, sourly, the firelight casting half his face in shadow. "There was a sail," I said. I didn't know when I'd realized what it was, but saying it aloud filled me with certainty. The jarring contrast of our two lines of thought caused a brief lull in the conversation. He still stood near to the door, part way through pulling off his mittens. After a moment, he tossed them into a basket, then pushed a wooden stool nearer to me with his foot. I sat.

"A sail." It wasn't a question.

"A sail. Out on the water. No one else saw it."

"No question?"

"No. I only saw it through the fog and waves, but I saw it." I kneeled to be closer to the flames. The tips of my fingers began to tingle as they were reignited with life.

"Could it have been debris from the storm? The trunk of a tree, or a boat torn from the docks?" I cut him a look, sensing how he was attempting to walk a line, to not assume my eyes had failed me but not to take it at face value either.

"Yes, it could," I said, and it was the truth. "But I feel ... certain. Certain like I know you're standing here. Like I know this fire is hot." They were basic examples, ones I might give to a child, but they worked to illustrate my point.

Ivar hesitated, then dropped to his knees across the

fire from me. The flames flicked in his eyes, blue like mine, but darker. He was a shadowed reflection of me: where my hair was light, his was darker. Where my eyes were the blue of the sky, his were the blue of the sea before a storm. "I can't think of anyone else who would have gone out in this. Hell, I'm fairly certain no human being would, no matter where they're from." He scratched the back of his head and rumpled his hair, lines of worry around his eyes.

"They didn't. All the village boats were tied at the docks." There wasn't a chance it was anyone from the continent. It was so far, and the waters so rough, that it was too dangerous to attempt in all but the most dire of circumstances. It hadn't happened in generations. Not since Löska had fallen to the Ør, the barbaric peoples of the Ør Isles, even further to the north than Skane. The isles were dotted into the far north of the White Water like droplets of blood, nearly impossible to access with the wild waters of the open ocean acting like a barrier. No longer content with their small islands, the Ør had invaded the nearby country of Löska, the former homeland of my people, from which some had managed to flee.

And they came here. It was far from the Ør, far enough that, with any luck, they'd never be found.

Thoughts of the Ør reminded me that reading the runes wasn't always a gift. Some of the runes were stories about the Ør, stories of how they wore leathers made from the skins of those they conquered, stories of their jewellery, made from human jawbones and teeth.

"Perhaps the Löskans are fleeing again," Ivar mused. "Perhaps things have only grown worse over there."

Hearing his voice, familiar and calm, chased away all thoughts of the Ør and skin and teeth. But what he said turned my stomach. If things had grown worse, then it was to a level I couldn't comprehend. The stories that had come with our people were so dark, so evil that we were certain nothing could be worse.

"You should eat," Ivar told me suddenly and firmly, rising and moving across the room. I knew him. The change of subject was to allow him more time to think, uninterrupted by my own musings. He placed a slab of dried fish between two chunks of bread, a favourite meal of his, and offered it to me on a wooden plate. I ate, both hungry and not, and we didn't speak again until I'd finished. I wondered, as I watched his face, what thoughts were moving through his mind. Mine were a mixture of worry and frustration and curiosity. Skane was usually quiet, uneventful, save for the weather or local village disputes that were almost always quickly settled. But since last night, the sky had shone red and I'd seen an unfamiliar sail out at sea. So much could change in one night.

"Huh." He broke the silence. "And I thought nothing could tear our minds from the lós."

I saw red again. Sweeping tendrils of blood reached out for me, and in the midst of them, a black sail. My hands shook so hard, I dropped the wooden plate. It clattered to the floor, spun a few times, and then settled.

Ivar said nothing, only watched me until I'd calmed. Shutting my eyes, I breathed in and out steadily, feeling the air as it passed through my nose and into my lungs, then back out again. A strange sensation that only became stranger the longer I concentrated on it, but it worked to distract my tumultuous thoughts.

"Something has to be done," I told him, opening my eyes. "The red lós, now a sail. I can't. I can't just sit by and wait." Tears burned behind my eyes. Never before had trying to be strong made me feel so weak.

"What will you do?" He asked it quietly, uncertainly, but something in his tone made me feel like he believed in me.

I shook my head, pulling all of my curls to one side and gripping them tightly. "I'll start with the Goddess."

"Ósa..." he said softly. I hated the way he said it. Hated the way he trailed off as if I was a child he was about to let down. "I know what this means to you. I understand, you know I do. But we can't... We can't stop it."

"I know that," I said through my teeth. This was our curse. Stay in Skane and submit ourselves to the will of the sky, and lose a few hundred people at a time – not only when I was born, but time and again before that – or flee the island and return to Löska. Return to face the Ør, where we would all die. There was no option where everyone survived. "I know," I repeated. "But I was barely alive last time. I'm here now." Despite the sadness and anger and fear warring within me, a single, tenacious spark found enough fuel to start a fire. "I cannot change history, but the future is still mine to live."

Silence reigned.

Not all of the runes had been translated yet, especially in the further, more remote caves. While Skane had been a symbol of hope for the Löskans, it was also vast and cold and filled with predators. Few people travelled from the villages alone.

"There's a cave a few miles from here, further inland." Ivar tapped a scroll that bore only a few bits of writing. "I've been to it once before but I was forced to return early when a storm came in. I only managed to grab a few snatches of writings." He leaned forward, resting both elbows on his knees. "I don't know what else is in there, and I can't promise it will be useful, but it's the best I can do, short of scouring the countryside for undiscovered caves."

I tapped my forefinger against my chin, thinking. That wasn't the worst idea in the world. Caves we'd never been to might hold writings about things we'd never—

"No."

I could tell by his face that he knew my thoughts. I hugged myself and looked away.

"I'll go with you. To the cave."

He eyed me, as if deciding whether or not to fight me on that point. "It isn't an easy walk."

I tapped my fingers rhythmically against my upper arm and didn't reply. He knew that was a poor excuse for me to not go.

"Even less so with the new snow." His eyes moved to the door, thoughtfully. "Perhaps we should start praying for the storm to end."

"Stop that," I said.

"Stop what?"

"Stop trying to put me off. I'm going with you."

He looked at me for a moment, absentmindedly running a finger back and forth over his forehead as he considered my words, then smiled ever so slightly. My heart jumped with relief. We would do this together.

The creaking and rattling of the door was dying down, each passing minute bringing the smallest amount of quiet. That was the thing about these storms: they came with the fury of a thousand angry goddesses, but left as quickly as a wave broke on the shore. Within perhaps an hour, the wind would be all but gone, and outside dainty little snowflakes would be lazily falling the short distance from the low-hanging clouds to the ground. In its wake, the storm would leave snow drifted so high, our houses would seem small in comparison.

We didn't say more. Not yet, anyway. For now, we both stared into the flames, lost in the wanderings of our own thoughts.

Chapter 6

I slept at Ivar's that night. His mother and father hadn't come home, which wasn't worrying. Many people would have set up wherever they were when the storm came in, unable or unwilling to brave the elements. That was the way of our village. Our homes were always open to our neighbours. We'd planned during the night to head out at first light, and as if my sleeping mind knew the importance of this adventure, it awoke me just as dawn was breaking.

"Ivar." I made sure my voice was loud in the stillness. He started a bit, his eyes opening wide.

"Yes. Right." He shook his head, too-long hair falling around his eyes, and sat upright, pinching the bridge of his nose between his fingers. "Off we go."

I helped myself to a small portion of dried rabbit

he'd showed me last night. After nearly nothing but fish in recent weeks, the intense flavour made me hold it in my mouth longer than usual. Being the daughter of a fisherman meant little variation in diet – not that I could complain, for at the very least it meant a consistent flow of food, which was more than some people could say.

"This walk will be hard work," Ivar said, sighing slightly. He tugged on his boots. "It will take us hours to get there and hours to get back. We'll stop in to see your family on the way out. I'm sure they'll want to know you survived last night."

I donned my mittens and cloak. I couldn't imagine that they'd been worried sick. "You said the cave was inland. Which way?"

"West," he answered. "Near..." He cleared his throat. "Near the lake."

I'd not been in that direction in ages, and after the bonfire, an invisible fist clenched around my stomach at the thought. It was far from the nearest village, and not the sort of place one frequented without company. In addition, if you went that way and then veered north, you'd be headed to the foothills of the Kall Mountains, and that alone was reason to stay away. We were a fearful group, us Löskan descendants. We stuck to the sea and huddled in our villages. We hunted in the nearby woods and we used only local resources. Journeys of more than a kilometre or two, without the express destination of another village, simply weren't done.

Cling to the coast, everyone said. *Then all you have to do is watch your back.* It made sense. With the water on one side, it left only one direction from which danger could approach.

"There's a pack just there," Ivar said, pointing. Supple leather. Ivar had probably made it himself. "We'll need food after our hike."

I filled it with a few chunks of bread and some more dried rabbit, along with a leather pouch filled with water. The other unspoken reason for packing food was for the chance that we got stranded, either in the cave or far enough from home that we wouldn't be able to return. Never leave the village without being prepared for the worst. It was one of the very first lessons all our mothers and fathers had taught us. There were too many stories that could be told of those poor souls who'd left with nothing, and were later found when the snow melted enough to find them, their bodies blue and stiff.

Anneka and Father were unsurprised, albeit mildly irritated, at my overnight absence. When I stopped by our house, my sister had drily suggested that it looked like I hadn't had much sleep, something I knew she didn't truly believe – or desperately hoped wasn't true – and that word would no doubt start to spread. I, in turn,

46

suggested I had other ways to keep myself warm during the night, and slipped back to rejoin Ivar.

Outside the village, the snow was deep and we made slow progress. Manoeuvring between trees and over fallen logs with the wooden snowshoes strapped to our feet made my legs ache, but this wasn't a time for complaining. Whenever I began to grumble inwardly, I'd picture the red sky or the sail out at sea and it would ignite within me a new fire that would offer enough energy to push on even a little bit further. I trailed a few steps behind Ivar, sometimes using his footprints to avoid having to forge my own way through the snow. Now and then we stopped to catch our breath, but mostly we pressed on silently. Any moment, the plague could be bearing down on us. It was enough to make me look over my shoulder more than once, as though it were a physical being that haunted my shadow.

What a nightmare it was, I thought as we walked. Death lurked just hours or days away, but where the plague would start, whose body it would first see fit to consume, we couldn't know. I was angry, but also sad and tired. I wanted to stop it, but couldn't. I wanted to instil hope in those around me, but there was only unease, or a strange kind of calm that spoke of either ignorance or acceptance.

We shouldn't have to accept this.

I surveyed the blanketed land during one of our

pauses, and my thoughts found their way to my mouth. "There's always a beauty in the after-storm stillness."

Ivar watched me for a moment, then nodded and looked away. I wasn't one for small talk. Conversations to no end were often better left unsaid. It was a trait of mine that had irritated him as far back as my memory could go, but one that was bred into me.

The woods were quiet, padded with thick, soft snow, the sun teasing us from behind the scurrying clouds. Off towards the northwest, the sky was still dark where the storm was passing through. If it made it as far as the Kall Mountains before breaking apart, they'd be buried beneath even more snow than we were. "I think Skane is catching its breath," he said, breathing in deeply as if to make his point.

The bare trees shook with distant thunder, a low rumble rolling over the hills towards us. I felt the vibration in my stomach. That happened sometimes, during the bigger storms. The sky would shake and groan, angry. We moved on, the sun arcing its way towards midday before the glistening waters of Lake Hornsträsk appeared in the valley below us. It stretched away for nearly a mile, most of the edge frozen. Its centre was still thawed, but as the season crept closer to winter, it would continue to freeze until the entire surface was one block of ice several metres deep.

Today, the lake looked different. My mind was knitted

with worry and darkness, laced together so tightly they created a sensation of dread that weighed me down like an anchor. Ymir had told me a story once. A story of how, generations ago, a star had fallen from the sky and into the ground, destroying everything in its path. In the years that followed, the lake had formed, and for decades no one went near it. I couldn't see it the same away again after that. As if Ymir's words had come to life, I could see a falling star, a raging ball of fire careening to the ground, destroying a village and the surrounding area and leaving a mark so deep a lake would form. What lay beneath those frozen waters? Bones and broken homes and the remnants of extinguished lives. Hopes and dreams and thoughts of a future, all snatched away and crushed in the flash of a bright light. It wasn't just a lake: it was a burial ground.

"The animals haven't yet stirred, it would seem," Ivar said presently, forcing my gaze away from the water. I eyed the fresh snow along the banks below us. The only tracks in the vicinity were our own.

"I don't blame them," I replied. We weren't making directly for the lake, rather towards a series of cliffs set away from the right bank.

We moved slowly, steadily, the knowledge of how far we were from home encouraging us to use caution. As we walked, I recalled other stories, superstitions, passed around through the villages. Our people, particularly the elderly ones, took pride in the yarns they spun to the younger generations, some of which were true, and some of which were not – deciding which was which was half the fun.

"Those stories," I said, watching as the cliffs rose taller before us. "The ones grandfathers like to tell, about the caves." I knew he understood what I meant. "Do you think they hold truth?"

A moment passed before Ivar answered. "I don't know." A few more steps. "I've never seen it to be true myself, but that means little. My father always said rune singing is too valuable a skill to let it disappear in fear of fairy tales."

People held that some of the caves where writings had been found, and even the ones that hadn't yet been discovered, had been cursed long ago by old gods or rune writers, or goodness knows what else. They said the runes held a darkness that was better left alone. "We should spend our time looking to the future instead of trying to see into the past," one storyteller had said.

That would be easier if the past didn't hold information that could mean the difference between having a future and not.

And besides that, they'd been written to be read. People hadn't spent so much time and energy carving them into stone walls for nothing but the darkness to see, so that they could pass down through the aeons and disappear unread when this world at last turned to dust.

Perhaps it was an art form that we should once again assume. After all, what if many of us lost our lives by the plague looming ever nearer on our horizon since the appearance of the red lós? What if, in the future, someone else discovered Skane, and the cave wall runes were their only way of knowing what had become of us? What if, one day, my life was nothing more than a few markings on a cave wall?

Dark thoughts led to dark feelings and dark deeds. I took in a breath of the crisp air and cleared my head.

When we were finally in the shadow of the cliffs, in front of the maw of a cave ready to swallow us whole, we stopped. I eyed it, unnerved, while Ivar adjusted his bags and withdrew the knife from its sheath, as if to ensure he hadn't lost it on the way. I touched mine gently, praying I'd never have need for it.

"You can help with light," Ivar instructed me. "I'll do the translating if you can hold the candles. It's dark in there."

Darker than a midnight with no stars. I knew that. I'd been into caves like these before.

We each pulled a candle from our bags and lit the wick. Out here in the sunlight, the flames were almost impossible to see, but in the blackness of the caves, they would be blinding. Ensuring our remaining candles and flint were within easy reach – losing our source of light on the inside could be deadly – we entered the cave.

My first instinct was to turn around and seek the daylight again, but this was why we had come. We were here for the secrets that slept in the shadows, that had been stowed away for future eyes like ours to read. Save for Ivar's first visit, when was the last time a human had walked here? How long since these rocks had seen a human form pass by, searching for answers or satisfying some aching curiosity? Had the last souls to enter been those who'd written on the walls? Had other villagers come exploring since then? Some small part of me wanted to think we were the first people to enter this place in generations. It made the very air we breathed seem hallowed.

Our candles sent flickering light dancing around us as we moved through the narrow passageways. The shadows warped and shifted, sometimes growing, sometimes shrinking as our candles moved. The ground beneath us was slick, where dripping water had frozen. I worked to keep my footing, while my senses remained alert. Watchful. The shadows could hide anything, and the stories of the caves weighed heavily on my mind. Around turns and bends in the rock, I strained my eyes to make out anything out of place. But always, there was just more rock, more ice and more shadow.

I stayed close to Ivar. I could feel his body as our clothes brushed together and see his breath that left white bursts in the air. "It isn't far," Ivar whispered. I could understand why. Even the whisper was deafening in the utter stillness. Our footfalls bounced off the walls, echoing back to us, hollow and faint. There was only darkness in every direction. The thought of Ivar having come here alone made my skin crawl.

He turned to glance at me, as though making sure I was still following him. Like I would just separate and strike off on my own. Still, though, I was glad he looked. The way my candle reflected in his eyes was soft, comforting, and my body tingled with a longing to be held.

"Here," Ivar said at last, and our candlelight fell on a wall covered in markings. Scratches, carvings of numbers and letters I'd never understand on my own. What meanings they did hold for me only came from Ivar's translation. Some of them, like the runes in caves closer to the village, had become lodged in my brain like a splinter, the kind that festers and doesn't go away. These etchings were how we'd come to know almost everything about our lost culture and about those who came before us. The warriors, the settlers, the pioneers. But more importantly, it was how we'd come to know anything about the Goddess.

What little scraps of information we'd learned about our Goddess had come from caves like these, where more scratches and shapes told short anecdotes or relayed the beliefs of those who had come before us. Some of our knowledge had been handed down from the generations past, but precious little. Skane was a cold, brutal country, nearly always wrapped in winter. Many of those first peoples so long ago didn't survive to tell stories. It took countless years, generation upon tiny generation, of trying to survive and stake out an existence here before it finally caught on. Before their homes could finally stand the storms, before their hunting skills were enough for survival.

Before they knew which parts of the island to leave alone.

At first glance it was much like the caves closer to Neska, but the unreadable writings could be vastly different. Just like how, to many, the stars seemed vast and senseless, these pictures and shapes seemed nonsensical. Yet they told us far more than the stars ever would.

Ivar set his bags on the floor of the cave, handing me his candle. Wax dripped on to my mittens and I wished I could feel the burn. Cold was seeping into my bones, in here where sunlight never reached. I exhaled while Ivar withdrew a scroll, sending a burst of white into the frozen air. I imagined the burst was smoke from a fire that burned inside me, and the thought sent a faint warmth to my heart.

Removing his mittens and rubbing his hands together quickly, Ivar turned to stare at the wall, as if searching for the place he'd left off. I held the candles aloft, illuminating the wall as best as I could.

Markings lit up, some strange, wavy lettering, some crude images that had been scratched on to the surface with a sharp stone or something similar. They were scattered intermittently, the letters and pictures somehow forming a bigger picture once deciphered. To someone like me, it made no sense. But to a mind like Ivar's, one that had been trained to understand them, they were yet another piece in the overall story of Skane's beginning.

Well, Skane had been here long before us. But it was different, back then, back before our ancestors came on boats, hope in their eyes and fear in their hearts. It was empty, it seemed, devoid of life, save for the animals. Waiting for someone to find it, to love it, to start an existence.

As I eyed the markings on the wall, I imagined them being written, a fur-clad form, alone, scratching away at the stone, desperate to have their story heard. Imagining a future where someone like Ivar would stumble across it, read it, know it. Make the hours of frozen fingers worth it. Be thought about, even just for a moment. Man or woman, I didn't know. Young or old, it was a mystery. Whoever they were, these writings were a phantom echo of their soul, and that fact alone was beautiful.

"I got to here." He touched a rune near the top left of the wall, then retrieved the scroll from the floor. "It's a villager, relaying stories of their travels. So far, they're just talking about an attack. Wolves." He pointed to the faint drawing of what looked like an animal. "They were attracted to a nearby river."

He fell quiet, looking from the wall to the scroll, occasionally jotting down words. Luckily, we had little trouble with wolves. Packs of them would travel by occasionally, and we'd either hear their howls during the nights or find their tracks the next morning. But we humans were far too much trouble for them, unless they caught us alone. I'd seen one in the woods once, when I was up a tree. Its hulking, white-grey form was so large that I couldn't look away until it was long out of sight.

I held one candle up to the wall and a second candle near to his scroll. The shadows kept dancing in my periphery, making me jumpy. I could envision them coming to life, reaching out to swallow us.

"That," Ivar whispered, touching another rune. It had peaks, and even I knew what it meant. "The mountains."

I stared at the rune while he continued to work. It transformed in my mind from a scratching on a wall to one of the dark, snowy peaks of the Kalls. Never before had I laid eyes on them, but from the stories I'd heard and tales Ivar had told me from the translations, I'd painted my own image of them. Tall. Dark. Deadly.

"*I travelled to the mountains,*" he read aloud. Then, after another few minutes of working, "*It is home to the jōt, amongst other things. Territorial. Night dwellers. Their camp was filled with bones.*"

Jōt. The giants. They'd been mentioned in more than one story, passed down to deter anyone from travelling to the mountains. *Bones*. I glanced around the cave, as if the dark words might bring something sinister to life. The shadows suddenly seemed deeper.

Perhaps it was my mind, perhaps it was the curse of the runes, but I was almost certain there was a faint sound somewhere else in the cave. A light padding, similar to a footfall. I glanced at Ivar. He was listening, I could sense it, but there were no more noises. He breathed in, then out, and carried on with the translation. There were many animals that no doubt came to explore these caves, searching for shelter or food or water. If a predator happened upon us, we were armed.

"If you can reach the highest peak, you may hear the Goddess speak."

I whipped my head around and stared at Ivar. He was focused on the wall, as if double-checking the translation. Then he nodded. "They don't elaborate. They just go on to discuss the hunting of a wolf."

"There has to be more," I said, turning my own eyes to the wall, like I could make sense of it myself. "What do they mean?"

"There's nothing else, Ósa," he said gently, like I was too frail to bear a more direct response.

I gripped the candles so tightly they shook, sending wax spilling to the floor.

We searched the other walls for writings, but found none. When at last we'd finished, and exited the cave into the sunlight, there were footprints in the snow.

They weren't ours.

Chapter 7

The footprints approached the cave from the opposite direction of ours. They stopped at the entrance, then picked up again and ended at the face of the cliff. We blinked into the sunlight, searching around us for any sign of life. Nothing. The footprints were strange. Similar to ours, but narrower and longer. They were no one's from our village, of that we were certain. Nor did they resemble any known animals.

"A traveller, maybe," Ivar offered, but his heart wasn't in it. And the question neither of us were asking aloud was, *How did they scale the cliffs?* It was perhaps thirty metres of sheer, icy rock face. There were no ropes or tools, nothing that would enable such a climb. Yet the footprints disappeared at the base. There was no mistaking that.

I stared up, expecting to find a pair of eyes gazing

down, but there was just rock, and then the sky. Yet still I tensed, wracked by that unmistakable feeling of being watched. I'd felt it before, while playing hide-and-seek with the village children. Whenever I was the one seeking, peering around tree trunks and house corners, I could feel their little eyes watching me from their hiding places.

I held my hair in a fist to keep it from my eyes, and gazed at the cliff until Ivar pulled me away.

"We shouldn't waste time," he said, eyeing the direction from whence the footsteps came. "We could follow them, but it would mean hours and the day is getting on. We need to get back to the village."

"Yes," I agreed. Our voices were heavy with a sort of resigned emptiness. There were precious few people in Skane who would wander around a remote area such as this alone, in the wake of a storm. We were an exception. Either they were a fool, or they weren't like anyone we'd met. And regardless of who or what they were, I didn't fancy a meeting with them. "Let's go."

We strapped on our snowshoes, and I followed him away from the cave. More than once we turned to look back, but there was still nothing. Perhaps, despite the prints looking remarkably human, they were those of an animal that could deftly climb the cliff much easier than we could. Whether that was the most comforting answer or the real one, I couldn't be sure. The only thing of which I could be deadly certain was the sudden, burning need to be away from here. Away from these caves. From this lake. The air felt haunted, the snow cursed.

"I know what you're thinking." Ivar's voice filtered to me from up ahead. I blinked at the back of his head, out of breath and confused. I was thinking about footprints and being followed. "You want to talk to the Goddess."

Ah. While, of course, that had filled my mind in the cave, I'd all but forgotten about it since we'd emerged. I had much to weigh – how would we reach the mountains? How would we ever convince anyone to let us go? What if we never made it? – and I needed to be somewhere alone. The image of a jōt camp littered with bones – both animal and human – was enough to deter anyone from going. And the jōt weren't even the worst of it. Who knew what other horrors those mountains harboured. They could be home to almost anything; so much of the range was unexplored. But there was a saying I'd heard countless times, mostly when people recounted the stories of the first continental settlers of Skane. "Better a few lose their lives to save many, than many lose their lives to save a few." So many had lost their lives to give Skane a fighting chance: some on the crossing from Löska, some after their arrival, killed by predators before they'd had a chance to build proper homes. Some had perished trying to reach the mountains. So many had given their all to fight for a new life in a new country. What was the life of one more girl, if it meant giving Skane a chance?

After all, my presence in the village would hardly be missed. Not by my father, anyway, and not by Anneka.

My mouth felt dry and coarse. "I need water," I said, without responding to his previous statement. I didn't need to tell him he was right; he already knew. I reached into my pack as we stopped walking.

Footsteps, not our own, continued on after our halt, then stopped.

We froze.

An echo? Unlikely. The trees were too open here, too far apart to offer such a response. With nearly identical timing, we both kneeled and unstrapped our snowshoes – they could help with walking distances but hindered our agility – ready for whatever came next. Under the semi-shade of the trees, the snow wasn't nearly as deep as it was in the open air. I began walking forward again and Ivar did the same. We took perhaps another five paces, then stopped.

Again, footsteps echoed behind us, and then ceased.

Our knives were in our hands in a flash. We stood shoulder to shoulder, gazing back through the trees. I tried to separate the trunks from the shadows and the snowdrifts, searching for anything moving. The forest just sat there, still and calm and seemingly empty, save for our own presence, our shallow breaths of rising panic.

A feeling crept over me. It seeped through my skin, into my bones. The same one I'd felt at the cliff. The same one I felt during hide-and-seek.

Eyes.

Slowly, I turned to my right, staring into the forest. A form, standing between two trees, and a second one, not far behind it.

"Ivar."

He turned, and froze.

They were tall, taller than either of us, and so, so skinny. Their bones protruded sickeningly from under their skin, which was visible beneath the leather armour covering their midsections. Yet, despite their slenderness, I could sense their strength from the ten metres between us. Flaps of the leather hung down to their knees, where their gaunt legs showed until they disappeared into the snow. Around their necks were slight ropes, dripping with what looked horrifyingly like bones.

Teeth.

And their faces. So narrow and angular, their own teeth large and broken, ragged, wispy hair growing only from the backs of their heads, near their necks. Their bald heads were a map of scars, lines crossing this way and that. In their hands were long knives, carved from what looked like stone. Eyes white as snow. Pupils black as charred wood.

I'd never seen anything like them before, but somehow I knew. *I knew what they were.*

They stood perfectly still, unblinking, staring at us, as we stared at them.

Then they screamed.

As if they were in one another's heads, they erupted in a piercing screech that I was certain would reach the Kall Mountains themselves and lunged towards us. Those long, powerful legs carried them across the distance in seconds, barely giving us time to blink. The world fell away into blinding white light until all I could see were those forms coming towards us, until all I could feel was every hidden store of energy bursting to the surface in a reckless bid for survival.

Ivar growled as he braced his feet in the snow against the onslaught, and I gripped my knife so tightly my knuckles began to ache. Already, it was slick with sweat as my body surged to life.

Now I knew why we'd always been told not to venture so far from the village. No one would hear us out here. They would only find us – what remained of us – perhaps days from now, perhaps weeks from now.

Ivar's knife clashed with stone. I had seconds to take it in before my own attacker was upon me. We'd all learned how to use knives, but only to fend off a wolf, or even a bear, on the hunt. We'd never been prepared for this. Never been trained in hand-to-hand combat.

And these ... creatures. Fighting wasn't an art form for them, that much was clear. They held knives, but they bore down in a way that made it obvious they most often relied on their own brute strength to disable a victim. If they got their hands on our bodies, we would break like a twig on a dead tree.

My own knife met stone, and the force sent a wave of pain through my body. I wouldn't be able to keep this up. I could perhaps withstand one or two more of those before the air left my lungs. I'd have to find another way to defend myself.

They kept screeching as they attacked, as if the noise somehow gave them strength. Thinking as quickly and as clearly as I could in the brief snatch of time before the next blow, I took in my opponent. It was large. Skinny, but tall and bulky. Agile in its own way, though not like me. I could move faster than the monster. Spinning to my right just in time to avoid the next blow – its knife crashed into the snow where I'd been standing a second before – I ducked and lashed out, my blade barely nicking its exposed leg. A wound opened up instantly and dark blood ran into the snow. Its scream changed then, but whether it was from pain or anger, I couldn't tell. I didn't have enough time to decide. It spun, the arm with the knife slashing out in a wild arc, ready to sever me in two. I jumped back, losing my footing and falling into the snow.

At the same moment I realized any breath could be my last – would be my last – Ivar's attacker released a deafening howl and it momentarily distracted my own. I used the second of interruption to roll away and leap to my feet, blinking the snow out of my eyes. Ivar was latched on to the back of his own opponent, whose knife had become deeply lodged in the trunk of a tree. The sight of just how deep into it he'd cut, knowing the power it would take to get it that far, turned my stomach.

My opponent, seeing I'd got away, screamed again and held the knife high over its head with both hands. On a sudden impulse, I ran directly towards it. As I'd faintly hoped, I surprised it, and I stuck my knife into the first exposed skin I could find. It was that place just below the neck, before the chest bone. There were many veins there, ones I knew could kill it if cut.

I didn't have the chance to wait and see. The monster grabbed me by my hair and flung me away from it into the snow, as if I was one of those rag dolls mothers made for their children. Blood poured from its neck as I struggled to find my footing. In the background of my senses, I became aware that now only my attacker screamed. Had Ivar killed his opponent, or had his opponent killed Ivar?

I couldn't stop to think about it, no matter how much I wanted to. Not in this moment, anyway. My attacker was still coming for me, and my arsenal of ideas was all but empty.

Suddenly, the creature lunging for me stopped advancing, and its head jerked unnaturally. Behind it, I could just barely make out Ivar, hanging on to its hair with all his body strength. I knew what to do. Gripping my knife as tightly as I could, I ran forward and put all of my force into burying the knife in the creature's exposed neck. It gargled, still trying to emit that piercing scream. Its arms flailed, searching for any purchase it could find. Finding none, it wobbled a little bit, then fell. Its body thudded into the snow.

Absolute silence followed.

My hands shook violently. Dark blood stained the snow around us. The creature Ivar had engaged lay slumped against a tree, bleeding from its neck as well. They were so, so awful. Large and fierce and grotesque.

I half-sat, half-fell into the snow, my right hand still tightened into a fist where I'd stuck the knife into the creature's neck. Wrapping my arms around myself, I met Ivar's tired eyes. His chest rose and fell with ragged breaths. So much passed between us in that look. So much knowing and thankfulness and exhaustion. This journey to the caves, this fight against the monsters, it meant a great deal. It meant a beginning, and an end. It meant life in Skane would never be the same again.

It meant the Ør had finally found us.

Chapter 8

The shadows were long by the time we returned to the village. Never before had I been so relieved to see the modest little place we called home. Those few souls milling about outdoors stared at us as we passed through, and I looked down at my body. Bruised. Covered in blood that wasn't mine. Bearing the weight of dark news.

"What happened?" My father waited outside our home, his arms crossed. Beside him stood Albrekt, and Sigvard, Ivar's father, approached as well.

"We will need a village meeting," Ivar replied, catching his breath from our long trek. "We bring news."

The three men exchanged a glance, then my father said, "Tell us."

"Not out here in the open." I shook my head. "Not yet."

I entered our home, the others following behind me. My sister sat by the fire, a pile of knitting on her knees. "Oh, you've returned," she said, dropping her hands into her lap. But her annoyance was short-lived when she saw the others entering behind me. "What's this?"

I didn't reply. My energy had been drained and I needed to conserve what little I had left for our long explanation. I let my cloak fall to the floor.

I sat before the fire, across from everyone else. Ivar remained standing by his father, his arms crossed, holding his elbows. It was hard to feel joy at being back safely, knowing our safety now had an all but imminent end. I closed my eyes and drank in the warmth of the fire.

"Tell us," my father said again.

Ivar's eyes met my own. We were both so tired, yet one of us had to speak. I offered my voice.

"We went to the caves at the lake," I began, staring into the fire. Anneka let out a light *humph* from beside me. "We went seeking runes, hoping for something that might guide us after the red lights appeared." I knew how foolish it sounded, and the dubious looks from the men across from me did nothing to quell that. I cut to the point. "But we were followed." In the ensuing pause, the only sound was the snapping of the fire as it consumed the wood. "We found tracks outside the cave that weren't our own. They disappeared at the cliffs. When we made to return to the village..." Though I willed it to continue, my voice trailed off. It was a struggle to even think the words, let alone speak them. "Ør."

Silence.

After a heartbeat, my sister's hand moved to cover her mouth, as tears welled in her eyes. For a moment, I found myself pitying her, the picture of fear. My father, though his face was pale, wasn't so quick to believe.

"Surely you are mistaken. No one alive today has seen one. How would you know?"

"The runes," Ivar whispered, then found his voice. "They are exactly as the runes said. The leathers, the jewellery, all of it." He cleared his throat and shook his head, as if it would erase the memory. "We left the bodies in the woods near the lake. They were too large, too heavy to bring. But we know where they are, should you want to see them for yourself." His words were terse, challenging.

"They were scouts, we think," I continued. "Their armour bore crude badges, resembling some sort of ranking. I ... I think they came in the ship I saw yesterday." I stared at my father, and he stared back. Unspoken words hung in the air between us. There was so much I wanted to say, but this was neither the time nor the place.

Another moment of silence passed. I could understand it. I'd seen the Ør face to face, heard their screams and felt the force of their blows, but even still I could hardly make sense of it. All of us, everyone in this village, had been born into a life of peace. It wasn't an easy life. The winters were harsh, sometimes we went hungry, sometimes we lost lives to the sea, but in our generations, we'd never been under attack. The very notion of danger, danger from a land not our own, was unfathomable.

"They must know," Sigvard hissed. "They must have seen the lights and know what's upon us. It would give them the advantage, when we are at our weakest."

"Eldór and I," Albrekt said. "We'll go and examine the bodies at daybreak. It's too far to go and return by sunset."

"Agreed," my father said. "For now, spread the word. We'll call a meeting in the village centre tonight."

Everyone left, Ivar touching my hand briefly as he passed. My father motioned for Anneka to follow them. She did so, a flash of hatred and triumph in her eyes. She had witnessed the full force of my father's temper unleashed on me before.

"I raised you better than to travel so far from the village without a very good reason," my father hissed the moment we were alone.

My skin flashed hot and my tongue cracked like a whip. "You hardly raised me at all," I replied, my voice deadly low. After the events of the day, the monsters and the fight in the woods, I was in no mood to entertain his cruelty.

His eyes gleamed in a way that was just sinister enough

to make me almost regret my words. "I have given you a home and food on an island where you would struggle for either without me. I could have turned you over to another family when your mother died, but I kept you, against my better judgement."

Against my better judgement.

The words nearly flayed the skin from my bones. I took a step closer to him, gazing into every dark speck of his eyes. "Then why did you keep me when I could have been happier elsewhere?"

"I feared guilt."

Some ruthless part of me wanted to laugh at him, at the very notion of him fearing guilt when every minute of every day of my entire life had been wracked by it, consumed by, driven by it. The only reason he kept me as a part of his family was to avoid feeling guilty. It wasn't from love or duty or tenderness, it was from his fear of how it would make him feel, and that was far from a good enough reason.

"Then that was your gravest mistake," I said finally. "Because guilty or not, you robbed this house of every ounce of love and light and left us to drown in your bitterness. You leave the village every day in your boat, and I revel in the wake you leave behind. I couldn't save Mother's life, but neither could you, and you've let me fall on your sword over it for seventeen years."

They were evil words and I regretted them the

moment they'd escaped into the air, but a part of me had awoken that was vying for control of my mouth. After everything that had happened today and since the red lights had appeared, the calm veneer I'd built over the course of my life disappeared like melting snow. All of the hurt and anger he'd caused me boiled to the surface, until there was so much of it that I lost control. I took a step back to give him some space, to gauge his reaction. He simply stared at me, eyes boring into mine as he considered his next words, but they never came.

The stars winked from above, as though mocking my insignificance in the universe. I lay on a rock by the sea; it was a favourite spot of mine, big enough to lie on and watch the stars, and surrounded by the sounds of the crashing waves. Here, two of the most powerful forces in the world seemed to collide: the sea and the sky. While it made me feel small and sometimes helpless, it was also a reminder that there were forces out there much bigger than the Ør.

The meeting was starting without me. My presence wasn't required, and no one would think to look for me here. Ivar would be there to fill in the story and answer questions as needed. I couldn't stomach hearing it again. After my fight with my father, the thought of seeing him again sent pain shooting through my heart. He'd hurt me and I'd hurt him. There were bigger things to worry about now, but the guilt about what I'd said grew heavier by the minute.

Besides, as far as I was concerned, talking about the Ør and the plague again would get us nowhere. I wanted to act. Between Ivar and I, I'd always been the more impulsive one, the one who spent less time thinking and more time doing. Sometimes it was a blessing and sometimes it was a curse. Right now, I was inclined to believe it was the former. Time was running out, we needed to act fast.

Overhead, I focused on one particular shape in the sky. It was a woman, a crown resting on her head and a cloak on her shoulders. The Goddess. Unlike the other constellations, She never moved. No matter the time of day or month or year, She remained stationary, watching over us. That set of bright, well-placed stars symbolized so much, including the only being who knew why the red lights existed. Why the plague haunted us.

The more I gazed at the stars, the hotter my blood became, boiling beneath my skin. Why should I have to travel all the way to the mountains to speak to Her? There She was, directly above, so close, and yet so infinitely far. Nothing I could say or do would bring Her any closer. If I wished to seek Her counsel, to find out what could be done to save those whom I loved, I would have to meet Her on Her terms. Back in the village, they'd all be planning how to defend themselves, and discussing how to train us to use knives and bows and arrows, pretending that enough of them would still be alive to fight the approaching Ør. Pretending that the plague wouldn't sneak in and destroy us long before the Ør ever reached our shores. If Skane was to have even the smallest of chances, persuading Her to hold off the plague – and the Ør – would be our only real hope.

I thought then, as I stared at the sky, of a conversation with Ymir.

"These constellations," he said, sweeping a hand up to the sparkling night sky, "they are like pictures. They are artwork on a grand scale, there for us to love and admire from below. When we look up, we don't just see darkness, emptiness. We see light."

"Who painted them?" I asked, letting my eyes drift from one bright star to another.

Ymir was quiet for a moment. "I don't know who exactly," he answered softly. "Someone from the past, long, long ago. It's like those cave wall writings your friend Ivar can read. Someone had to write those for us to read now, someone who wanted us to know their story. I think the stars are much like that. They're a story about the universe, but so much time has passed that we have no hope of translating it properly. We can just enjoy the pictures and invent our own stories."

I felt a thrill at his words, at the thought of someone using the sky to paint a portrait of the past. How much time did it take? How much power? One day, I swore, I would find a way to paint the sky.

A neighbour in the sky to the Goddess, the Giant loomed against the velvety black backdrop. It was one of the largest shapes, made up of many, many stars. Our ancestors spoke of the jōt, as did many of the cave wall runes. They're tall, we were told. The size of at least three grown men, though usually more. Stronger than a bear, they almost never use weapons. Some joked darkly that, if they flicked a finger against us, our bodies would shatter as they fell.

In many ways, I supposed, they were like the Ør. Only they didn't invade our lands. And while they would fight and kill when necessary, they didn't seek out war. While that sort of size and power would have at one time been difficult for me to picture, having met the Ør in person helped to bridge the gap between my frail imaginings of the jōt and their reality.

A frigid breeze swept in from the sea. Sitting up, I wrapped my arms around my knees and stared out to the water. It was from there, from where my eyes were affixed to, that the end of Skane would come. From these waters, countless foreign sails would amass, and from the boats would come the Ør. There would be many of them, so, so many of them, and from the moment the first foot touched our land, we could only hope our deaths would be quick. How long we'd sat here, quiet, safe, fighting against a frozen land for a chance at a life that was never to be. How many lives we'd sacrificed, trying to lay down roots somewhere far from the horrors of what happened in Löska. In many ways, Skane was like a sapling, the start of a new life, which the Ør would simply pluck up and crush.

I wasn't brave, or even terribly useful. I couldn't read runes like Ivar or sail a ship like my father, but I would rather be damned to die at the hands of the mountains than sit by and watch my world, my people, be ripped limb from limb and left to drown in their own blood. If we had to die, let us die in a fight. Not on our knees begging for our lives. Let them come looking for their scouts. I'd send their heads out to meet them in boats.

Let no more children grow up without knowing their parents.

I closed my eyes and saw my mother's face – how I imagined it. Hair as light as mine, but perhaps less curly. Green eyes like Anneka's, but more vibrant and beautiful. Happy eyes. A mouth that always smiled. Neither my sister nor my father had ever told me what she'd looked like, refused to on every occasion I'd asked. I didn't deserve to know, Anneka said. There was no point in looking back, Father told me.

I left the coast and made the short trek to the village, my steps filled with purpose. Away from the waves, the silence was deafening. The only noises came from my boots in the snow and even that was muted. The trees seemed to stand taller around me, as if showing their support of my new plan. Behind them hung the ever-watchful stars.

There was a bonfire in the centre of the village, and a crowd – just about everyone who lived here – was gathered around it. My father stood in the middle, beside the fire, along with Sigvard and a handful of others who were generally looked up to as the village leaders. There wasn't much order to how they became leaders; the title tended to fall upon those who were successful in their trade, like my father, or whose skill garnered respect from the villagers, like Sigvard. One day, if he chose to follow in his father's footsteps, Ivar would be a leader too. Rune singers were always respected. I'd heard stories that things were different in Löska, that there was usually one man in charge, and everyone wanted his power. *Power invites disaster*, Sigvard had once said. Things were different in Skane. Women could offer as much as the men – Ivar's grandmother had been a widely-respected rune singer – and the power of leadership was divided amongst more than one person.

Even from a distance, I could tell those gathered were debating. Some voices were raised in an earnest appeal, and others were more calm and rational.

"We can train," my father said, "but the sooner we all accept our fate, the better. Don't fill your heads with foolishness."

"We can offer every last bit of strength we have," Sigvard countered. "We can't lie in our beds and wait to be slaughtered."

"The only reason we are here, Sigvard," my father replied, "is because our ancestors' world was destroyed. The Ør took Löska as easily as a toy from a child. With so few of us, even if we rally every village we know of, we'd make nothing more than a few hours' work for them."

"The only reason we are here," Sigvard shot back, "is because our ancestors fought against all odds and escaped to build a life."

A few voices erupted in agreement.

"With talk like yours, Eldór, we'll never stand a chance!" someone shouted.

"Aye, we'd rather hear Sigvard speak," another added. "We want to hear of hope."

"I am more comfortable with speaking of what is real and of what is to come, than filling your heads with fairy tales," my father replied, so calm it was almost alarming. "Have you all forgotten about the plague in your blind fear of the Ør? How many of us do you think will live to see the fight? I lost more than some of you last time. You can hope for the best, but I'm prepared for the worst."

I stopped moving. Father never mentioned Mother. Ever. His face was blank, but pain pressed behind his eyes, a sort of headache he'd been suffering for seventeen years.

I pushed through the throng.

"I'm going to the mountains."

Eyes dug into me, especially my father's. His forehead wrinkled, a mixture of both confusion and anger. "What nonsense are you on about now, Ósa? We are discussing serious matters." He waved me off like a fly.

"There were runes," I continued, speaking loud enough to be heard. "Runes in the cave by the lake. They said if I make it to the mountains, I can hear the Goddess speak. It's our only hope. We must beg Her to call off the plague, and to help us battle the Ør. We cannot survive both. We could hardly survive one."

My words were met with silence. My father continued to stare at me, perhaps questioning whether I'd taken leave of my senses.

"I can ask Her, I think. Ask Her what can be done."

My father shook his head. "Nothing can be done, Ósa."

From somewhere in the crowd, Ivar stepped up. "You don't know that," he said. "You can risk your daughter's life at sea in a storm, but you draw the line at standing up to the Ør?"

The look that my father gave to Ivar could have turned the world to stone, if Ivar's anger hadn't given him such a resilience. I opened my mouth to say something, to ease the tension, but closed it again.

"At a moment like this," Ivar continued, not the least bit subdued, "we should allow for more than one possibility. Someone carved that rune. Someone who knew something."

I understood how we must sound, but no one else had seen the things we'd seen, learned the things we'd learned. In my heart, I knew that going to the Kalls might be nothing more than a death sentence. But I also knew that, no matter how small, it also offered us some a chance at survival.

"It's foolish," I conceded, more to my father than to anyone else. "It may end in my death, and yes, perhaps we will all die anyway. But if there's anything She can offer, we'll never receive it if I don't try. She cared enough to put the red lights in the sky to warn us. Perhaps She'll care enough to help us through it. Perhaps She can be persuaded to stop the plague, to stop the advance of the Ør."

The fire crackled, warming the right side of my face. I kept my eyes on my father, unflinching. Intimidation was his strong point, and he well knew it. But not this time. This time, I wouldn't back down.

"Where was She seventeen years ago?" he said, barely above a whisper. "Where was She when babies were burning from within, the elderly dying a slow, dragging death? Where was She when your own mother was taken, delirious to the end? She didn't know me, didn't know Anneka. She died a stranger, Ósa. My wife died a stranger to me."

I blinked away the burn of tears behind my eyes. I'd never heard him speak this way. Never heard him utter words that were born from raw emotion and pain.

"The Goddess left us to rot back then. She'll do the same now."

A fist tightened around my heart, and in the edges of my vision, I saw Ivar glance at me. My father's face was calm, stony. He watched me, waiting for me to give in.

"I can fix it," I whispered. My father's eyes cut into me. "I can help this time, try to stop it. I owe you that. I owe Anneka that."

"You can never undo it."

A lump in my throat tried to choke me, but I swallowed it.

"I say she goes," someone said from the crowd.

"As do I," another added.

Before long, everyone was agreeing, nodding and speaking to each other with a sense of affirmation. I met one pair of eyes after another, finding them filled with hope. After so much fright, so much heartbreak and worry, the sight melted my heart.

It was another few minutes before my father replied. "Go if you want," he said, his voice resigned. "But go alone. We can't spare another body that could be here aiding in the preparations. Everyone should be trained with knives and bows and arrows. Everyone will learn to defend themselves. Ivar will see to that."

He paused, and the look in his eyes dismissed me. When he returned to discussing the preparations, a tremor of terror ran through me. While I'd wanted his blessing – though perhaps not his permission – not one part of me thought he'd condemn me to the mountains alone.

Chapter 9

I packed that evening. Anneka sat malevolently in the corner of the room, her words dripping with poison.

"You know the mountains are haunted," she'd told me, instilling her voice with an eerie chill that made me shiver. Then, in a low tone that sounded almost like a chant, she recited a familiar poem we'd all learned as children.

"In mountains tall
Where snow falls deep
The shadows crawl
The demons sleep.

The giants stalk
The misty ways,

Where darkness walks
Through night and day.

Beware the hills,
Beware the peaks,
Where night-time kills,
And mountains speak.

"I know you've heard the stories."

I'd nodded, stoking the fire and willing away the chill of her words. "We all have."

"Then what sort of foolhardy hero's mission is this? Why would you, of all people, choose to go?"

I couldn't tell if her words stemmed from genuine concern or a desire to make me miserable. It could have been either, and I was too exhausted to convince myself that she was capable of sympathy. Anneka didn't do things for me, and certainly not out of kindness. It had always been that way. As I sat, staring into the fire, I remembered a time many years ago, when I'd learned just how deep her hatred of me went.

I couldn't have been much older than eleven. Father was out at sea with some others, and the clear skies spoke of good weather, so we knew he wouldn't be back until late. While Father was gone, the leadership of the house fell to Anneka, as the elder sister. Those were the worst days. Often I could get away, spend my days with Ivar or traipsing through the woods, sitting in the pen with the sheep or climbing up to the rooftop to stare at the sky.

No matter where I went or how long I was out, I always had to return home. Eventually, hunger and sleep would pull at me and I'd be drawn back to the house, my feet hesitating and complaining all the way. It was a clear but frigid night. I'd been lying in a pen with some new lambs, watching and laughing as they unsteadily learned to walk, and now and then looking at a scroll I'd stolen from Ivar, pretending I knew how to read it. Sometimes I thought that if I stared at the markings for long enough, my mind would begin to make sense of them. It never worked, but my unwavering insistence on trying remained strong throughout the years to follow.

I made my way through the streets, stopping to kick stones or glance up at the blossoming stars, or just to stand and hold myself and take in the night. Night held a charm, a power that I often fell victim to, feeling its draw and pull and bidding me stay out for far longer than I should. On this particular night, I longed to stay in the cold embrace of the outdoors until the sun rose once again, but the bite in the air whispered that it would be foolish. On nights like tonight, even my soul could freeze.

The door to my home was locked. I tried again, just to be sure it wasn't the cold making me weak, but it wouldn't budge. I knocked a few times and called out Anneka's name.

When there was no reply, I knocked again. A moment later, the door cracked open.

"Yes?" she asked, barely opening the door wide enough for me to see her face.

I blinked a few times. "Let me in."

She made a show of thinking for a moment and then shook her head. "No. I don't exist to play host to you at your beck and call, Ósa," she said. "I made dinner earlier and you weren't here. I'm settling in for the night and waiting for Father. When he returns, then you may come in. But, not before." And she pushed the door shut.

I stood staring at it for a long moment, keenly aware of the deepening cold. She'd never done this before. She'd never been motherly, but this was something else entirely. For a few seconds, I hoped that maybe it was some wildly unfunny joke, that in a moment, she would open the door with a wicked gleam in her eye and warn me not to be so late again. But the door remained closed.

Slowly, I turned away and looked around the village. I could go to Ivar's, certainly, but then I'd have to explain what had happened, why I couldn't go home, and shame was already settling into my being. I didn't want to tell anyone. Didn't want to share the news that my own sister had locked me out of the house on a night as cold as this one.

So I walked and I walked and I walked until I found a cave out of the breeze. I piled some sticks atop one another and lit them using a flint I kept in my cloak at all times – just in case. I'd rarely ever had need for it, but in that moment, I thanked the Goddess it was with me. When the sticks were crackling nicely, I sat cross-legged before them and held my hands over the growing warmth. Father would be back soon, surely. I could wait an hour or two and then return and tell him what had happened. Although I doubted he would reprimand my sister. He would either tell us to sort out our differences amongst ourselves, or take her side and say that I should have been home earlier.

At some point, my father probably went home and slept in a warm bed by a large fire that had roared for most of the day. But I didn't. I piled more and more sticks on to my little fire, and spent a cold, disturbed night in the cave. He didn't come searching for me and the pain of his indifference stung me sharply.

The intensity of the memory had me on my feet and out of the door. I couldn't bear to be around Anneka's sneering and contempt for a second more.

Very little light penetrated the towering fir trees, yet somehow the snow seemed to glow, illuminating the woods around me in ethereal light. My footprints trailed away, disappearing somewhere far ahead, ghosts of my presence that would vanish with the lightly falling snow.

The village seemed an eternity away from where I stood in the frozen woods, as night crept towards dawn. Out here, there were just trees and snow and quiet, and the white breaths I released into the air. All was still and peaceful, a world of its own on an island consumed by fear. Out here, my sister couldn't talk to me and I didn't have to avoid my father's gaze. There was a solace in a snow-laden forest wrapped in night found nowhere else, a loneliness that made me better acquainted with myself. After all, when it was just me and a hundred thousand trees that could neither speak nor think, I was the only company I had.

"Uxi," I said softly, though it rang loud in the quiet. A pause, then again, "Uxi."

Faint movement fluttered to my right. A white owl landed silently on a low branch. From a pocket in my cloak, I withdrew some paper, inside of which I'd wrapped a small bit of meat, not enough to be missed by a soul. Winter was harsh and hunting could be scarce, even for the animals.

I needed this little one to make it through. I'd found in him a friend the likes of which I'd never find in the human world. He couldn't talk, and there was something about that fact that made him dearer to me than almost anyone else – almost. Our friendship hadn't been built on conversation, on exchanging our ideas and views. It had been built on the utterly basic grounds of me having saved his life as a tiny owlet. It was months ago now that I'd found him lying in the snow, expelled from the nest at too young an age to survive, but with some gentle care and attention, he'd recuperated beautifully. In a very different yet hauntingly similar way, I could relate to him. I, too, had been raised without a mother.

Uxi's round, yellowish eyes watched me like circles of candlelight set against his snow white feathers.

"The sky has turned red again," I said as the meat disappeared down his gullet. "I wonder if you noticed it. I wonder if you know what it means." I crossed my arms against the cold and leaned against the trunk of a fir tree.

He shook out his feathers, round eyes fixed on me.

"Perhaps you do know," I went on. "Perhaps you can sense the danger." Maybe those red lights meant something to the animals, too. Did it set them on edge, make them wary, even if they didn't know why?

His eyes moved away from me, staring off into the forest with that sharp intensity. I turned too, imagining I could see through the endless fir trunks and all the way to the Kall Mountains, away in the far northwest. Even from here I could feel them, feel their frozen forms looming over us, harbouring countless dangers that never crept beyond the ice and stone of the peaks, that let us exist in safety far below. A handful of my people had ventured in their direction over the years, but most got as far as the snowbound foothills before turning back, the menace of the mountains outweighing any curiosity or bravery they'd felt. But some had powered on, and that was the last we saw of them.

A cold breeze hit my face, and I turned away,

shuddering. Perhaps my sister was right. Perhaps this was a fool's errand. Those mountains meant death and everyone knew it. Yet they called to me. They beckoned me in a way I couldn't resist, because some small part of me would never be able to live with itself if I didn't try. I had to go, even if the mountains wcrc haunted. Even if all of the stories were true.

If they were, then may the Goddess rest my soul.

Chapter 10

Following my announcement at the bonfire, one of the villagers offered me their horse, and I gratefully accepted it. When the scouts didn't come back, the Ør would most likely move quickly, attack us at our weakest after the plague hit. For all we knew, they might be waiting offshore, beyond our line of sight.

As I took a last look around my father's cottage, I couldn't help but wonder, if I did lose my life to the Kalls, how would I go? Crushed under the fist of some giant? Torn apart by a mountain wolf? Or slip on ice and fall to my death into a stone chasm? I tried to force such thoughts from my mind. They were selfish, I told myself. This is a journey to save hundreds, not to fret over the safety of my own neck. And yet, when the image of my body lying at the bottom of a frozen, jagged cavern seared my mind, the cold fist of fear began to close around my heart. *No one is without fear,* Ivar had once said. *But without fear, you're without hope.*

I had two packs for the horse to carry, one of which was entirely filled with food. I could hope to hunt along the way, but I couldn't rely upon it. I'd packed as much dried meat and bread as I could fit. The other pack I'd filled mostly with containers of fresh water and partly with extra layers of wraps.

"I'll send you with scrolls," Ivar said, selecting a few from the pack he'd brought with him. "The mountains are ancient, and the Goddess only knows what peoples have been there before you. If you encounter runes like our own, you'll need to read them." He paused, a sort of sorrow pulling at his eyes as the unspoken words, *I won't be there to translate for you*, hung thick in the air around us.

Our gaze met. I couldn't read the expression on his face. His mouth was closed and his eyes were soft, but they also held a sadness that I didn't quite understand. It wasn't fear, and of that I was certain. Just a sort of quiet heaviness that drained the light from his usually brilliant eyes.

I turned away.

He'd been angry since last night and we'd spoken very little. While both of us understood the necessity of his presence here in the village, in case it came under attack, the discovery of the Ør had been something we'd done together. Ivar didn't like me going on this journey alone any more than I did, especially with the possibility of the cursed plague returning while I was away, but there was nothing to be done. I was leaving at a time when everybody in Skane was needed here. *He* was needed here. With me gone, he was the only one who had seen an Ør in person. He knew how they fought, their size, how to engage them. We both understood it, but that didn't stop the pangs of sorrow from weighing us down.

"I could follow you," he said suddenly, catching me off guard. "I could sneak from the village at nightfall, after I've gone to warn the other villages. I'll ride through the night and find you before you leave Išavik. I'll be far away before they realize I'm gone and our fathers can manage the preparations."

"No, Ivar," I said as gently as I could. I laid a hand on his for reassurance. "You know the Ør. You know how to fight. You are needed here and I am needed in the mountains. Our paths diverge here, but we still have the same goal." I didn't tell him that thoughts of the journey felt like a stone on my chest, or that the impending loneliness terrified me after a lifetime in a village with familiar faces. I'd always enjoyed the solitude of the forest, but being wholly alone in foreign territory was something else entirely.

Ivar remained silent, but nodded.

He would ride out with me at midday, and we'd travel the first four miles together before we separated. He was off to one of our neighbouring villages to give them warning that the Ør had arrived, while I would continue towards the mountains. I, too, would spread the warning to the next village I came across. I would spend tonight there, and it would be the last one I'd come to. People may have already seen the bodies of the Ør scouts in the woods, and word could be spreading like wildfire. It was better to control the chaos than to let it roam free, causing panic to set in.

"This book," Ivar said later, placing it carefully into the pack. It was one of very few bound tomes, covered with leather and filled with yellowing pages. "I don't know how helpful it will be, but I think you should have it. It carries information about a little used written language. It's an entirely different way of writing, called Ploughstyle, and we've only seen it once or twice. It was from a culture much older than our own." He tapped the leather gently, fondly. "I suppose it's better to have too much information than too little."

"Thank you, Ivar," I said quietly. The journey would be long and lonely. These bits of literature would offer something to occupy my mind other than my impending arrival at the Kalls. "I know you're angry," I went on, because I felt like someone needed to speak. "I'm angry, too. But it's better that one of us goes than none of us."

I tried to smile to reassure him, but I could tell that it hadn't reached my eyes.

He nodded once, sharply. "I'll never forgive myself if—" He didn't let himself finish. It was better that way. He grabbed the packs and went outside to load the horse.

After a moment, Anneka scuttled from the shadows. She glanced around to make sure we were alone, then moved in closer, her jaw set with a tightness that reminded me of something about to spring. I knew what she'd say. That I was being foolish, pretending to be a hero for the attention. I raised my chin and waited, staring into her cold, grey-green eyes without wavering.

"You killed my mother. You killed Father's wife. If you don't come back with help from the Goddess, do not come back at all."

If she'd taken the knife on the nearby table and stuck it into my heart, she would have caused me less pain. My breath turned ragged, my hands shook, but I forced myself to calm. It was a struggle with Anneka, a constant back and forth in my heart of anger and hurt and defiance. I was meant to love her as my sister, in spite of her cutting words, her cold stares, but one-sided love is always the hardest. When the door opened and we were no longer alone, she smiled softly.

"Don't do anything foolish," she instructed me. "Our father's already lost enough."

"Goodbye, Anneka."

"I'll keep Ivar company while you're away."

I turned slowly to face her, suddenly feeling taller than I ever had before. The words had been intended to make me angry, to hint at something that meant more than just *company*. My lack of response to her earlier mention of Mother had made her resort to going after the one thing she knew meant more to me than my own life: Ivar. And yet, as I stared at her waiting face, her eyes daring me to shoot back some angry reply, the only thing I could do was smile and say nothing. I knew how Ivar felt about Anneka, and I knew that those feelings wouldn't change after I left.

I exited the house.

A knot had formed in my stomach. Everything about life in Skane meant we had to be strong, had to fend for ourselves and stand tall. I was a daughter of Skane and I would face this journey with no fear. I had to.

Móri came forward with his hands raised. In them lay a knife with a carved wooden handle. I took it, placed it with the rest of my packed items, and ran a hand through his messy hair. "If it saves my life," I said, "I'll have you to thank."

"Bring it back with a story," he said, smiling.

"I promise," I replied.

Arvid, the villager with the horse, soon arrived as he had promised.

"Her name's Ri," he said, stroking the horse's muzzle. "I'm not much for naming animals, but I figured you might want something to call her on the way. So there you have it."

She wasn't terribly tall, but she had a sturdy build and a sort of energy about her that I'd need. Her thick coat was a smoky grey colour, her full mane mostly light yellow with layers of darker hair underneath. "Thank you," I said, taking the rope from Arvid. "She's perfect." Ivar mounted his horse and as we began to move off, I let my eyes wander to my father. He stood tall, hands behind his back and chin held high, but despite such a strong stance, I was just shy of certain that his jaw quivered ever so slightly. It seemed to break down something inside me, cracking the wall I'd built and letting droplets of emotion trickle through. He didn't love me. He put my life at risk, and had done so on more than one occasion. But he was still my father. I'd never have a mother, but he was still here. He was a part of me. Leaving him behind, perhaps to die, or to go to my own death, was infinitely harder than I'd thought it would be.

But my resolve soon managed to stop up the trickle and I swallowed the lump in my throat as I turned away.

As we rode out of the village, the forest closed in around us, and ahead there was nothing but tree after tree and smooth, unhindered snow. Soon, I'd be gone, somewhere far away, and there would only be the footprints of the horse to show I'd ever been here. I didn't know what would happen five minutes from now or five days from now, but there was a sort of comfort in this place, in knowing that these trees would remain, quiet and still and waiting.

Waiting for a plague to creep out of the shadows to claim our lives. Waiting for a war that could break out at any moment. And waiting for Skane to either rise up and defend itself, or fall victim to a barbaric invasion that would leave it for ever changed.

Ivar and I didn't speak during the entire ride to our point of separation, where he would strike off to go and warn the other villages. There was so much weight in our ride, so much on our minds that words simply felt useless.

When we reached the place where he would turn left and I would carry on, we stopped. There was a brief moment of silence, and I wished it could go on for ever. It was the last moment in a long while that I'd be in the presence of someone familiar, and I would have given anything for it to carry on longer.

"I feel so small," I said, giving voice to the tumultuous thoughts raging within me. "So small and weak and insignificant in the face of what's coming. Of what I have to do."

His voice was low, his manner much more muted than it was normally, but his eyes were soft. "Even the smallest of movements can start an avalanche, Ósa. And it takes one flurry to start a storm." He paused as his words sank in, then added, "You've always been fiercer than a flurry."

I smiled just a little bit, but enough for him to smile back.

"Read the materials I gave you, yes?" he said. "And be on your guard. Speak to anyone you can in the next village tonight. The more information you have about the mountains, the better."

"I will," I said. My hands trembled where they held the reins. "I hope your preparations go well. I know Móri will keep everyone in line." I tried to laugh, though it got caught in my throat. Then, after a pause, "I'll bring back help, Ivar." But I couldn't promise it.

He nodded, and reached to shake my hand. I didn't want to let go, and on an impulse, I pulled on his hand until he was close enough to wrap my arms around. The horses shuffled closer together, and I shut my eyes, feeling his warmth seeping through the furs. He seemed surprised at first, hesitating slightly before firmly embracing me. I was leaving, and I wanted my last memory with him to be the feeling of his hands around my back and his breath by my ear.

When I pulled away, his eyes were glassy and red.

Suddenly faced with the reality of what I was doing, of where I was going, it took everything I had within me to not turn around and ride back home. To let him go and face my future.

"Good luck, Ósa," he said to me.

"And to you."

For a moment, I thought he'd say something else. His mouth opened and his eyes searched mine, but he stayed silent.

We parted ways.

Chapter 11

More than once, Ivar turned on the horse to stare back into the forest through which he was travelling. Somewhere through those towering fir trees and drifts of snow, Ósa was making her way towards the unknown. Was she, too, looking back the way she'd come? Looking towards home and relative safety? Towards him? Unlikely. If he knew anything about her at all, she'd still be facing forward, her mind firmly on what was to come, the dangers ahead. She was perhaps two hours from Isavik now. There, she'd find food and company and warmth. It wasn't until after she left there that he would allow himself to worry. Not until she struck off on her own.

Goddess knows. The thought of her out there alone, a single girl, no matter how beautiful and courageous she was, was nearly impossible to comprehend.

Beautiful. He flushed a little and looked down at his horse. He'd never allowed himself to think it before. Why now?

Letting out a breath, he looked up again. Bormur was south of Lake Hornsträsk, and southwest of Neska. Four villages – Neska, Bormur, Išavik and the smaller, less-visited one on the coast further south than Neska called Sjørskall – comprised the entirety of the descendants of the Löskan settlers. It was better for them – much better – to stay in larger groups for strength in numbers than to break off into smaller villages dotted around the countryside. At least, that was the thinking back when they'd first settled, and the idea had stuck. The naming of the villages hadn't taken place until a few decades ago, as they'd previously just been *the village* to those who lived there. Travel between them was infrequent at first, as they worked to learn the ways of the storms, how to get through the deep snow, and how to find the other villages without losing their way.

Smoke from a chimney curled into the air in the distance and Ivar hurried the horse on. Despite the unlikeliness of an attack coming in the immediate future – there were no signs of it off the coast, the abandoned boat the only evidence the Ør were close – time felt short and haste required. He entered the village at a trot, but looks of alarm from those in the streets made him slow his pace. Ósa would be more diplomatic. She would find a village leader and give him the news behind a closed door, but that wasn't how Ivar would want to hear it. He'd want to know what they meant directly.

"I bring news from Neska," he said loudly. Heads turned and ears perked up. News rarely travelled between villages, because so few things happened that required anyone outside of their own communities to know. But before he continued, a child standing beside her mother caught his attention on the street. She shouldn't have to hear it like this. Let it be broken to her more gently at a later time. He looked from the girl to her mother, and his face spoke for him.

"Run off to find your brother, Gerda." The mother smiled softly and patted the girl's shoulder.

When she'd disappeared into a house, Ivar continued. "You all saw the lights, no doubt. I'm sure you know what they mean. The plague will soon return." He shut his eyes briefly, the weight of his words making it too difficult to speak. "And in Neska, we have learned something else."

A general collection of whispers passed around those gathered and more villagers emerged from their homes to listen.

"I was returning from the lake with a fellow villager, when we were followed into the woods. We'd seen tracks, but hadn't been able to determine what made them." He paused, the memory of those forms through the trees, their screams piercing the forest, freezing him to silence.

"What were they?" a man shouted.

"Aye, tell us!" another added. Many people pressed closer, anxious for an answer.

"It was the Ør," Ivar said.

The way the faces around him tightened, jaws clenching or mouths falling open, ignited a faint sense of sympathy within him. He wished he didn't have to be the one to break the news, but at least they hadn't found out while face to face with one. Those scars, those sickly eyes of burning white with centres of deepest dark...

"And if perhaps," he added, "you require some sort of proof, let me offer this. But for the faint of heart, let me caution you to avert your eyes." He pulled the Ør necklace of teeth from a pocket in his cloak. "We took it from a body. I trust you've heard the stories."

A woman cried out somewhere in the crowd, and several people turned away.

"Time is important to us now," Ivar said firmly, replacing the necklace. "All of us, in every village, will have much to do to ready ourselves to fight. Only if we stand together can we—"

"You're a damned fool!" someone shouted from the crowd. A small man, his hands wringing before him and his face twisting in a strange mixture of blind fear and anger. "Banding together won't offer us any more of a chance than one of us standing alone. We're better to go quickly and painlessly before they reach us!"

A handful of others shouted their agreement, while

the rest looked on in horror. Ivar's mouth fell open, and for a long moment, no one spoke.

"Surely you can see the folly in that," he said presently. "If we give up before they even arrive, we will have no chance whatsoever. They'll have won before the battle has even started. But if we train, if we learn to fight and ready everything we have, then there's at least a *chance* of our survival."

"Nonsense!" the same small man shouted. "How dare you spread lies and false hope at a time such as this?"

"That is ... not my intention," Ivar replied. "There's another hope, one that I am quite aware we cannot place our full trust in, but one that could mean more than anything else."

Silence spread through the group like fire through straw.

"We're listening," a woman near to him said softly, hopefully.

"One from our village, the same who fought against the Ør scouts with me, has this very day left Neska to pursue hope in the mountains. I'm a rune singer, and upon translating in a cave by the lake, we have reason to believe that the Kalls offer our only chance to speak to the Goddess and beg for Her help. Perhaps She can be persuaded to hold off the plague, to give us a chance to fight at full strength. She may even be able to help us fight the Ør."

"Why alone?" the woman asked. "Why didn't you send a party?"

"I would have gone with her, but her father is a village leader, and it was the decision of the village that our time and energy would be better spent making preparations here." His jaw tightened as he spoke at the memory of Eldór sending his daughter off alone. If being a leader meant having a callous heart, he'd happily forego it.

"A *girl*?" the small man sneered. "You think our only hope lies with a *girl* who is travelling *alone* to the *mountains*? We may as well place our future in the hands of a babe! Such nonsense!"

Fire rose on Ivar's tongue, but he quenched it before speaking. "I know how it sounds," he said evenly, resting a tightened fist on his thigh.

"I don't think you do," the man interjected.

"I understand your concerns," Ivar continued. "But she's not weak and she's not foolish. She knows her mission and she knows the dangers. If there's anyone to be believed in, anyone whom I know could succeed in this task, it is her. She has a bravery that would render any man a child." He stared into the narrow eyes of the small man, willing his words to have a deeper meaning. When he didn't respond, Ivar continued, "You are all, every one of you, allowed to be afraid. We are all afraid. But when that fear becomes a barrier between surviving and succumbing, it has gone too far. If we bend to one knee and offer our heads to be severed, all of our deaths will be certain. If we can unite and work together to put up even a small fight, then we at least leave room for a chance."

Many of the heads around him nodded, though their faces remained tight with fear.

"They will likely attack from the sea, so Neska will be the central point for our preparations. We invite all of you to come and stay with us to train and prepare. We will make room for everyone."

"We will come," the woman near to him said. "As for me and my family, we will come."

Ivar offered her a small smile in gratitude. "Everybody will count," he said, turning his horse to leave. "And tonight, take a quiet moment to turn your eyes to the northwest and spare a thought for the one whose bravery might well mean you get to keep your head on your shoulders and your teeth in your mouth." With another glance at the small man, he rode from the village.

Chapter 12

It was perhaps two hours to Išavik. I spent the ride imagining the imposing shapes of Ør standing between the trees up ahead, hearing their battle-cries echoing in my head, seeing the teeth hanging around their necks. In a way it was my reminder, my motivation to carry on and not turn back. If my journey meant that those frightful faces, those stone blades and scarred heads, wouldn't be the last thing my people would see, then it made every worry and every moment alone worth it.

When they weren't attacking, though, when it was just them on their Goddessforsaken isles, what was their life like? I tried to picture their children, small versions of the scouts we'd seen, yet every bit as brutal as the adults. Did their children kill and pillage as well?

Soon, the sounds of Ri's hooves crunching into the

snow beneath me faded into the background of my thoughts, nearly to the point of disappearing. There was a faint comfort in being so close to another living thing, out here where life seemed all but absent.

I wasn't far from Išavik when a quick movement to my left made me quickly rein in the horse. Something landed on a nearby branch, half hidden in shadows.

Uxi.

"I haven't any food to spare for you right now," I said softly, relief flooding through me. "But you're more than welcome to follow me." When I urged Ri onwards again, Uxi left the branch and disappeared into the trees, but I knew he would continue to shadow us. I could just imagine if Anneka or my father could see me talking to an owl. It would only work to confirm everything they'd ever thought about me: a silly, impractical girl.

But that made me smile. If silly and impractical was the opposite of Anneka, then I welcomed it.

I'd been to this village a handful of times, mostly to help my father in doing fish trades with them, but I hadn't frequented it enough to be recognized. At the outskirts, the villagers stared at me distrustfully, some concerned. I stared back.

"Have you a leader?" I asked of a young woman who stood in the shadow of her door.

"Who are you?" she asked. Her face was soft, the question rising from genuine curiosity. I couldn't blame her. Save for trade, which I clearly wasn't here to do, our villages tended to keep to themselves. Spending our entire lives around the same set of faces meant that newcomers made us wary.

"I'm from the village on the sea," I answered, pointing back behind me. "Neska. I bring news."

Her eyes darted back the way I'd come. "It's Gregor you'll want. I'll take you to him." She moved away from the door and walked off.

I swung down from Ri and walked beside her, past one home after another. In many ways, this village was much like my own. Our houses had been built in the same manner, using the same materials, and smoke curled out of the chimneys on the roofs. The biggest difference was the set of unfamiliar faces I passed. I didn't know these people, didn't know anything about them and their lives, yet here I was, delivering perhaps the darkest news they'd ever hear. It made me sad that I'd never got to know them, and now I might never have the chance to do so.

We finally reached the far side of the village. It was a small house we stopped at, and there was a post outside at which I tied Ri.

"I know where there's some dried grass the village keeps for the animals," the woman said, knocking on the door. "I'll go and find her some once you're inside."

"Thank you," I said, warmed by her kindness.

An aging woman opened the door.

"There's a girl here," my guide said. "She's from the coastal village and says she brings news. I thought Gregor might wish to speak with her."

"Aye, I'm certain he will," the older woman replied. "Come on in, girl, I'll fetch you a drink."

I entered into the warmth of the house. A fire blazed in the centre, and unlike so many of our open, roomy houses, this one was small and filled with furniture and scrolls. Here and there I even saw a handful of leather-bound tomes, generally thought of as a rarity. Leather was valuable and better used for more practical purposes. On a chair that rocked back and forth on the earthen floor sat a man, older than the woman by at least a few years.

"A visitor, Gregor," the woman, whom I presumed was his wife, said.

"So I see," the man replied, lying a scroll which he'd previously been perusing on his lap. "I know you," he said after a pause. "You're that fisherman's daughter."

"I am," I replied. "Eldór."

"That's the one. Tough man, him. I hope that you're a bit gentler."

I shrugged. "We're related by blood. Nothing more."

His wife offered me a cup full of warmed water with dried winter berries. The first sip sent a delightful heat through my body, creating a wave of comfort that chased away the day's cold. I thanked her, and she pulled up a chair close to the fire and motioned for me to take it. I obeyed.

"So you've got news, have you?" Gregor asked. "You're alone, dressed for a long ride, and you're carrying the weight of the world in your eyes."

"It's dark," I said. I would want honesty if someone were relaying this story to me. "You saw the lights, surely. You must know what they mean."

A solemn nod. "Yes, we all saw them. The village is heartbroken, of course, but there is little to be done except wait."

I drew in a breath. "There is more. The Ør are coming."

The fire cracked, my cup steamed in my hand, and no one spoke. As if a cloud had entered the house, a shadow settled on the man's face. His white beard moved a fraction, where his jaw tightened. "You shouldn't say those words lightly," he whispered.

"I'd never."

I relayed the rest of the story, recounting our trip to the cave, our encounter with the Ør scouts, and the things that had been decided in our village. When all those points had been laid out, I included why I was here and where I was going. At the end of the story, both he and his wife were silent for so long that I wondered if they'd understood me. When at last he spoke, his voice was so low it barely reached my ears.

"You must have heard the stories," he said. "About the mountains."

I nodded. "Some." So few people ever went there that few stories ever came back. Mostly, we just knew never to go.

"That girl who brought you here, Stína," he said, his eyes moving to the fire. "Her great-grandfather made a journey to the mountains. He was the only one I know of who ever came back."

"Why did he go?" I leaned forward, interested. Perhaps I wasn't the only one desperate enough to speak to the Goddess that I'd risk everything to get there. If so, perhaps he'd learned something while there. Something that could prove useful to me on my journey.

"Curiosity," Gregor replied, and I sighed a little. "He wanted to see if the stories were true. He left in the night so no one could stop him, leaving a note with his wife. Her cries could be heard all around the village the next morning. Two weeks he was gone, and when he returned, despite everyone's having given up on him, he was skinny and ... battered, like he'd been thrown around against a wall and forced to walk back home. And the stories he brought back with him ... they ensured that none of us would ever venture there again."

I still held the cup, but I couldn't force another sip down my throat. It had constricted, his words strangling me.

"It started with the jōt," Gregor said darkly. His eyes

114

seemed to grow distant, shadowed, recalling memories that weren't quite his. "He was skirting one of their camps when he slipped down an icy rock face and landed in the middle of it. From such a close range, he said his heart nearly stopped from their height alone. The ground was layered with bones, broken and scattered. Some were human, jawbones still lined with fractured teeth. Some were animal, pointed rat skulls and wolf snouts. The jōt were gathered around a large bonfire, the flames themselves twice his height, over which they were roasting an entire wolf. Skinned, surprisingly skilfully, as if it was something they did often and did well. They took him as a prisoner, no doubt with the intent to kill him once they'd finished with the wolf, but before they could do so, they entered into a fight with another clan of jōt passing through, and he escaped during the fray. They were monstrous, he said, nearly naked despite the cold, save for a few scraps of furs or leathers. Their eyes were large, bloodshot, and their skin as hard and thick as the leathers they wore."

Gooseflesh rose on my skin.

"But it wasn't just the jōt that chased him out of the mountains." Gregor raised his eyes to mine as a shiver started at the base of my neck and slithered its way down my spine. "He said there were all manner of strange, sudden occurrences. Rocks would tumble from above, seemingly undisturbed by anything. Sometimes he'd see

115

a shadow, as if from a living being, but it was cast by no one. There were noises, voices, but they belonged to nothing. Sometimes he would spend hours searching for whomever or whatever they belonged to, following the elusive notes on and on through the Kalls, only to wind up lost, all the rock and ice blending together until nothing stood out. More than once, he was certain he'd never again find his way out, or would go mad before he did so. The thing that saved his life was stumbling upon an outcropping that looked down on the country below. From there, he could see east and a way out. The entire length of his time there, he ate nothing more than the remnants of food he'd packed with him and some mountain berries."

I said nothing. Could I afford to let his words deter me? I'd known this going in. Known that there was almost nothing in the mountains but danger.

Almost.

The mountains were also my only hope of speaking to Her. That man had only gone out of morbid curiosity, out of a desire to test the stories and see what truth they held. My reasons were vastly different, and perhaps that would work in my favour. Perhaps the Goddess would bless me in a way she hadn't done him.

I thought of my mother and took in a deep breath.

"The red lights," I said at last. "She's the one who puts them in the sky. She's the only one I can ask for help. If I don't do it, we'll never stand a chance. We'll be overrun like Löska, our people will cease to exist. I'd rather die in the mountains trying to find Her than at home, on the end of an Ør's blade. Our people gave so much, so many died for Skane. Now it's my turn to thank them and to continue the fight they began."

"Your courage is admirable," Gregor said. "Though foolish."

His words cut me, despite my having expected them.

"My mother died last time." The words escaped suddenly. My heart raced and my eyes stung. "She died in the plague a few days after I was born. I lived, somehow, but she didn't. I think about it all the time. I'm reminded of it all the time. I don't remember anything about her and yet I can't escape the memory of her. I don't know what she looked like. I don't know what she sounded like. My older sister hates me for it, and I don't think my father will ever forgive me." My jaw quivered as I worked to keep from crying. "I have to go. I have to do this, Gregor. For her. For them, so they'll forgive me."

"Oh, child," said his wife.

"You have to know it wasn't your fault," Gregor said softly. "You couldn't help being born."

"I made her weaker," I said, my chest heaving with a sob. "She couldn't fight any more, not after I was born." They fell silent. When I'd regained my composure, I said, "I need to speak to Her."

Gregor sighed and closed his eyes. "You think She doesn't know your plight? You think She doesn't know what you're doing? She always knows. Once before..." His voice faded and he looked to the door, as if people might be listening. "Once before, She even helped us. At least, that's what we think."

I waited for him to continue, rapt. Never had words like these reached my ears.

"When my ancestors came to settle this village, they nearly all lost their lives. The whole lot of them. They were new to this land, travelling through the countryside, searching for a place to lay down roots after breaking off from a larger group that were building near the coast."

My village.

"It was slow-going, trying to locate a decent region. Before they'd found one, or any kind of shelter, a violent storm blew in. One of those storms like we just had, that make you fight to see a hand in front of your face. It took only hours for some of them to die, frozen to death or smothered beneath the snow. The others didn't even notice, at first, couldn't tell who was still with them and who had fallen. A third of them had perished before something ... changed." He sat back in his chair and stared into the fire for a long moment before continuing. "There were *things* in the storm, maybe beings, maybe not. No one was ever able to describe them afterwards. They led my ancestors through the snow and wind to the shelter of trees, where the remainder of them managed to survive until it blew over. When it had passed, in the pre-dawn glow, the lós were just disappearing from the sky, giving way to the sun. But they all swore, swore on everything they held dear, that the lights were *gold*."

My breath caught in my lungs.

"They were very near to this exact spot, and this is where they founded the village. They said it felt right, felt like the things had wanted them to live here, so they stayed. They were also the ones who wrote an addition to that song. You know the one."

"About the lights," I said softly. "Of course I know it." Everyone knew it.

He began to hum the song, making his way through the colours. Green. Blue. Red. And then:

> "*Gold, gold, the lights glow gold*
> *Reawakens something old.*"

Chapter 13

Ivar had never been to Sjørskall. Eldór did little trading with them, if at all. They weren't like the other villagers. Quiet, watchful, more superstitious. He knew well enough how to find the village, though, or at least in what direction to travel from Bormur until he ran into it. The ride was a long one, and he kept the horse at a steady pace to fight the setting sun. His ride had taken longer than anticipated, but his family was still expecting him home tonight. If he was delayed much longer, or the weather turned and he was forced to spend the night here, they might fear the worst.

The sun was slipping behind the horizon, the horse slowing down after a day of cantering through the drifted snow, when he saw a curl of smoke in the distance. It was comforting after such a long ride, but it also made him uneasy. This wasn't a village he looked forward to visiting. There were stories about their unwelcoming nature, their mistrust of strangers and their way of keeping to themselves. While the other villages were more open, more widely visited, this one liked its privacy.

For now, he'd get in, share the news, and get out.

Most seemed to be indoors, partaking in the evening meal, though a few souls roamed the streets as he entered the village. A skinny old man, lines criss-crossing his face like an ancient map, frowned from a doorway. A young girl stopped walking to stare, a bucket of water in her hands.

"I have news," Ivar said, to anyone who might listen. "Who may I speak to?"

"What sort of news?" asked a man with an armful of firewood. He was about Ivar's father's age, perhaps a little older.

"Of the lights," Ivar replied, quieter.

The man's eyes flashed with curiosity. "We saw them," he said gruffly. "No need to tell us what we already know."

"I doubt you know this," Ivar told him. "Unless you also know *what* the lights mean."

He swung down from the horse. "Who can I speak to?"

The man glanced around again, then jerked his head towards his own door. "Inside. I'll go and fetch a few other elders. You'd better have something important to say – people round here don't like to be disturbed."

Ivar tied the horse outside and entered the warmth

of the house. It was empty of anyone else and sparsely furnished with an old wooden chair, a bed in one corner, and a few stools and cooking supplies. Against one wall sat a basket of knitting, covered in dust and seemingly having not been touched in years. He pulled up one of the stools closer to the fire and stretched out his hands toward the flames. They were numb from the cold, though he'd been cold for so much of the day that he'd hardly noticed it.

A few minutes later, the man returned with two other men and a woman. He offered no introduction for them, but grunted his own name – "Areld" – before taking a seat across the fire. "Now, what is it you've got to tell us?" he asked.

Ivar met the gazes of the newcomers in turn. They stared at him, distrust burning hot in their eyes. The woman, perhaps the most severe of all, made no attempt to conceal her suspicions about his presence.

"You all saw the lights, I understand," Ivar began, poking at the fire with a stick. "You know of the plague. But shortly after they shone, myself and another villager encountered two Ør in the woods." It was blunt, perhaps too much so, but the sooner he delivered the news, the sooner he could leave.

There were a few sharp intakes of breath, and eyes narrowed even further. Ivar looked away from them and continued to poke the fire, waiting for the news to sink in and the questions to start.

"Impossible," one of the men whispered.

Ivar shook his head. "It's the truth. We believe they were scouts and that more are coming. And I can assure you..." He paused, then shook his head at the memory. "I can assure you that they are every bit as terrible as we always imagined. More so."

"Goddess spare us," the woman breathed, a hand pressed against her mouth.

That reminded him. "But I also bring better news," Ivar continued, laying aside the stick. "Someone from our village departed today for the mountains. We found runes. Runes that told us we might speak to the Goddess there, in the Kalls. It's a dangerous journey, but it offers us hope."

Silence. Eyes bore into his, though he couldn't read their expressions.

"In the meantime," Ivar went on, "we here in the villages are preparing, training, making weapons, for as long as we are able to. We don't know when they will come, but they will likely come from the sea nearer to Neska. That's where we found the scouts' boat. You are all invited to come back to our village and train with us. If the villages unite, we stand a much stronger chance."

"We'll all be slaughtered," the woman said quietly, shaking her head. "No one stands a chance against the Ør. Surely we've all been raised with the same stories."

"We have," Ivar answered. "But the Ør took Löska

without warning. With even a little time to prepare and a strong will, we can at least stand a chance. If we discount ourselves from the beginning then we only welcome our end. Skane is stronger than Löska. We've grown. We've learned. We're ready."

The woman shook her head again, slowly, like she pitied Ivar. "Madness," she whispered. "Utter madness."

Ivar took this as his signal to leave. Standing, he said, "Think it over and discuss it amongst yourselves. Bormur has already agreed to join with us. We hope to have you as well. Just remember that time is short."

He made to move towards the door, but Areld stood in his way. "I think you'd best be staying here tonight," he said in a tone that gave Ivar the distinct impression that he had no choice. The others nodded, glancing at each other. "Here, in fact. You can have my bed."

Ivar stared at each of them in turn. Something had changed in their demeanour, something that he couldn't quite understand, but that flooded his mind with warnings. The others sent knowing looks to one another, seeming to speak a language with their eyes that Ivar couldn't comprehend.

"Make yourself comfortable," Areld said, backing towards the door. The others exited behind him. A moment later, he pulled the door shut, and there was a distinct sound of locking. A moment after that, he heard footsteps as his horse was led away.

Turning quickly, on fire with alarm, he examined each of the walls for an opening of any sort, a second door, but there was none. The chimney overhead was little more than a small hole in the wall with a partial covering to keep out the snow. The only way in or out of this house was the door which had just been locked. He stood in the middle of the room and laced his fingers behind his head, thinking. He had no solid proof that they wished to harm him, only that they were keeping him in Areld's home, perhaps for more questioning. It wouldn't hurt him to spend the night indoors, anyway.

Lowering himself slowly, he sat cross-legged by the fire and thought of Ósa. Hopefully she was in Isavik, warm in someone's home, by a fire much like this one before heading off on her own tomorrow. How had they taken the news? With any luck, far better than Sjørskall had done. Their unnerving and superstitious glances played on his mind, making the hairs rise on his arms. Ósa was sharp, and strong. If she ran into this kind of trouble, she'd find a way out. There was no doubt about it.

A faint tapping came from the door. He stared at it for a moment, unsure if his ears were deceiving him out of a desire to get free, but then it came again. Standing, he slowly crossed the room, tilting his head to listen.

"Are you there?" came a soft voice, almost certainly a child.

"Yes, who is it?" Ivar whispered back, pressing his ears to the frame of the door.

"I live in the village," came the reply. "I know they've locked you up. I wanted to warn you."

"Warn me about what?" Ivar asked.

"They're going to kill you."

Silence. Ivar sank back on his heels, staring at the wooden door. Terror shrieked through him; his heart pounded. "Why?" he whispered.

"They believe it will help. They say the Goddess knows all. That She sees, from Her place above. Her eyes never leave us. They say that we have settled on an island that was never ours, grown too easy, and it has made Her angry. That She uses the lights to bend the island to Her will. She sends storms to keep us on our guard, to remind us of the dangers lurking behind each sunrise and sunset. And when they glow red, She is angry. It means it is time for Her to remove most of us and let us begin again."

A pause.

"They say She is unhappy with us. That we have taken and taken and taken from Her island and given nothing in return. We burn its firewood and hunt its animals and draw fish from its sea, and with little thought. That must change. They believe that the time has come to give the Goddess something, after so many years of taking. And a life is the most valuable thing we can offer, when we have so little."

Life.

"Why are you telling me this?"

"Because I don't believe it."

"Then let me out."

"I can't. They've locked you in. They'll kill me if they see me talking to you." Quickly, as if he'd never been there at all, Ivar heard retreating footsteps as the boy dashed away.

If he didn't get out before they came back, he might not live to see the morning.

Chapter 14

A hand on my arm awoke me well before dawn. They'd made me a bed by the fire, a pile of blankets into which my tired body sank. I'd fallen asleep instantly, but I didn't dream. The night was a wide chasm of darkness.

"You'd best be on your way," Gregor said when I sat up. He was already dressed, a cup of warm water in his hands. "There isn't time to be wasted. Once you leave the forest, there's a large plain between us and the foothills. You have to be off the plain by nightfall or the wind will claim you and your horse. There's shelter in the foothills, caves and trees to offset the weather. If you leave now, you'll reach it by sundown."

"What of the foothills?" I asked. "What should I know of them?" I stood and donned my wraps and boots, my body screaming with aches and pains after so much time on horseback the day before.

Gregor hesitated. "I don't know," he answered. "I've never been there. But remain on your guard. You seem smart enough to know that. Use all of your senses, and most importantly, don't be on the plain at nightfall. Don't think of what awaits you in the foothills. Think of sparing yourself from the slow, aching death of succumbing to the cold where no one can help you. Let that be a fire beneath your feet."

I nodded, swallowing a knot in my throat. "And my horse?" In my hurry to leave my village, I hadn't thought to pack her food.

"I've prepared you a pack of grain. It's a rarity, worth a lot, but you're a good enough cause. We all want to see you succeed." His words were kind, though the way his face fell as he spoke them said, *We don't think you will*.

Outside, the air was biting cold, yet somehow invigorating. It was still, devoid of wind – before dawn was the coldest part of the night, when the sun had been out of the sky for so long that all hints of warmth had been long since chased away. To me, though, it had always felt like a safe time, a time when all the dark things that came out to play at night were retreating to where they'd come from, anticipating the approaching light. The sky was crisp, clear, the stars overhead glistening fiercely. Few sights could be more beautiful than that, I thought. Yet appreciating the beauty of anything right now felt wrong.

Ri was tied to the post, though she'd spent the night in a nearby stable.

"She's been fed and watered," Gregor told me, patting her shoulder fondly. "The grain's in this pack here." He tapped one that hung with the rest of my bags. "Don't give her much in the morning or she'll be full and lazy during the day. Make her bigger meal at night. It'll give her energy in the morning."

"I will." I ran a hand under her mane. Her coat was warm, comforting.

"Don't run her into the ground on the plain, but don't stop for anything. Keep a steady pace and you'll make it to the foothills by nightfall."

I mounted and stretched my stiff neck, ready for a long day of riding. "What else should I know?" I asked, soaking up the last few minutes of another's company.

"Stay out of the jōt's way. Once you reach the mountains, only light a fire if you have cover. You never know what might be attracted to the light. And think of us here once in a while. The Ør are a fierce foe."

"I could never forget," I told him, looking back in the direction of my own village. A shot of fear coursed through me, but I quelled it quickly. "If you go, you know my father already, but find Ivar. He'll help you. He'll answer your questions."

"Ivar," Gregor repeated, nodding. "I'll remember."

"Here, take this," his wife said, emerging from the house. She handed me a leather flask. "It'll warm your insides this morning," she said, and gripped my hand in a farewell gesture.

"Best of luck," Gregor said, patting the horse's rump. She began to walk.

"And luck to you, as well," I said. "Go and speak to the people of my village. Everyone must work together."

"Indeed, I shall!" he shouted back.

I put the village behind me.

The trees lasted for perhaps an hour after our departure from the village. As we passed the last of the trunks, I brought Ri to a brief halt. Before us stretched the most vast expanse of nothingness I'd ever seen in my seventeen years. Even the open sea offered more than this, what with its rolling waves and white crests. Here, white snow spread as far as the eye could see. In the darkness of predawn, the only thing I could make out of the mountains were faint, tiny shards of black silhouetted against the stars. I shivered at the sight. Until this moment, they'd been nothing more than stories and the accompanying pictures created by my mind. Now they were real. They were real, deadly, and my destination.

From here, they seemed impossibly far away, but this was deceptive. As the day went on, they'd grow and grow like the ground itself was pushing them up towards the sky.

I urged Ri on. The snow was deep, nearly up to her chest, and while our progress wasn't fast, I remembered Gregor's words about pushing her too hard, and let her make her own pace. We had the entire day ahead of us to reach the foothills. If we kept up this steady rate, I was sure we'd make it in time.

Here in such a vast space, with no village lights or trees to hinder the view, the stars overhead blossomed. Hundreds of thousands of the tiny points of light seemed to emerge from hiding, like candles to guide my way. There was a comfort in the stars. They were reliable, familiar, and even so far from my village, I felt at home. In the northwest sky, the Horned Horse seemed to watch my steps. They were a creatures of legend, never seen in the real world, but I wanted to believe they might have walked somewhere, once upon a time. People said that horned horses were the mounts of the first peoples to ever walk the earth, fierce immortals who, despite their immortality, had somehow disappeared.

Just to the south of it, as if to challenge the Horse's prowess, sat the Wolf. Another creature no one had ever seen, it was painted in the stories that surrounded it, a predator much, much larger than the smaller wolves that roamed Skane. There was a list we learned as children: The Five Greats. They represented the five biggest constellations in the sky. The Goddess, the Giant, the Horned Horse, the Wolf and the Warrior. The Warrior was just coming into view as the year wore on. His sword became more and more visible on the horizon every day.

I tilted my head a little as we rode on. The sky seemed ... not quite right, but I couldn't place what it was. Something in the heavens had changed, yet it was too subtle for me to detect.

I thought, then, of Gregor's words from last night. Of golden lights shining in this very sky, a meaning I didn't understand. Never, in all my years in this world, had I heard that story before. The red lights always portended some sort of end, some sort of death. But this strange thought – *gold* lights – something old reawakening, sent fear like spiders crawling down my spine.

Dawn broke in an explosion of orange. It was faint at first, not more than a glow in the eastern sky that soon blossomed into a fiery orb that was reflected off the snow. The few clouds were cast in a multitude of colours: red, orange, pink. The higher it rose, the less intense the colours became, until at last morning had finally broken. At one point I turned to look behind me, but the trees were out of sight. There was nothing except pure, flat snow in every direction except forward, where the mountains were slowly rising taller and taller.

Loneliness set in. In the woods, even when there were

no other people for miles, the trees seemed alive. They stood tall, watching and old, and in their shadow, I felt comfort. Out here, a minuscule figure in such an infinite space, isolation seeped into my very bones.

An hour after midday, the sky changed. Dark, brooding clouds crept in from the south, and before long, they'd blotted out the sun. A chill wind picked up, whipping my curls about my head and into my eyes. I grabbed another wrap from my bag and tied it around my face, leaving only my eyes exposed. Perhaps it was no more than passing flurries, here to drop a centimetre or so of snow and move on.

But the angry sky overhead, roiling like the sea, didn't bespeak a day of gentle flurries. I'd seen skies like this too many times before to believe that.

Afraid the storm would slow our progress and we'd be stranded on the plain after sunset, I urged Ri on a little faster. At the rate we were going, it would take us longer to reach the foothills than we had daylight left.

"There's a storm coming," I said aloud, as if perhaps she'd understand. Glancing over my shoulder at the onslaught of clouds, I lightly patted her shoulder, Gregor's words haunting me. "I know you don't want to be out here any more than I do."

Maybe there was something in my tone that encouraged Ri, because her steps quickened ever so slightly. It was small comfort, though, knowing just how much distance we still had to cross. Eventually, I didn't know whether to look at the growing storm behind me or the growing mountains in front. Both of them filled me with dread, and a small part of me wanted to stop and bury myself in the snow and just forget about it all.

Flurries began to fall. They spun and swirled about, taunting me. Now, no matter what direction I looked, the blue sky had vanished.

The storm set in with a vengeance. I held one hand aloft, and could barely make it out through the furious snow, mere centimetres from my face. The sun might as well have slipped behind the horizon again, for it was so dark there was no differentiating day from night. Gregor had warned me about the plain at night, but certainly the plain during a storm such as this was far worse.

I remembered, then, another storm such as this one.

I trudged through the woods behind Father, my short, childlike legs burning with the effort it took to carry myself over the snow. More fell every second, burying us. Yet on we walked, Father determined to see us home. I wanted to stop, wanted to find shelter of some sort and hug my own body until I felt even faintly warm again, but I couldn't break off from his lead. If I lost myself out here, I'd die within the hour. Carry me, I wanted to say, working to stop tears from building behind my burning eyes. But he would never. He hadn't held me since I'd learned to walk.

I tried to move my feet faster and faster, pushing against the snow until they burned with pain, but slowly, slowly, he disappeared from view. The snow swirled around me, surrounding me in every direction. I screamed for him, screamed until my voice gave out and my mouth simply moved, soundlessly. As panic began to set in and I imagined dying out here, never seeing my sister again, never seeing Ivar again, I stopped walking and closed my eyes. I saw a warm house. A fire in the hearth. Food on the table. It wasn't my home, but it felt like it was, more often than not. I could see Ivar seated by the fire, scrolls lying all around him, lost in a world of symbols and markings.

I wanted to be there with him, safe and warm, more than anything else in the world. That longing somehow pulled me back to the present, back to the wind and snow.

We'd been walking east, towards the village. I envisioned the stars in my mind, pictured which ones would be where and which ones I'd need to follow to get back home. For all I knew, I could have been turned around. Could have been heading in the entirely wrong direction. I followed my instincts. I hadn't had many lessons with Ymir yet, but I knew enough to not get lost.

When I opened my eyes again, I pressed onwards, and when at last I reached home, I didn't speak to my father for three days.

Ri's legs kept moving, though I no longer knew in what direction we travelled. Perhaps we'd turned and were heading back towards Išavik. Perhaps soon the shelter of those trees would engulf us and the wind would die down. Curse this wind, this biting, evil wind. My face, my eyes were so cold, my hands long since numb, I couldn't find the energy within myself to stop Ri. Even moving my head was a struggle, my bones giving complaint with the smallest of movements.

I'd left home yesterday and already Skane wanted to claim me.

Snow.

Wind.

Darkness.

It never seemed to end.

If it hadn't before, certainly by now the sun had gone down. Cold as I was, I could feel the temperature dropping. It wouldn't be long until hypothermia set in. If I survived, I'd be one of those poor souls who'd lost limbs to the cold. Then I'd be no use in the mountains. No use in a war against the Ør.

I slumped forward on to Ri's neck, and soon she stopped walking, unwilling or unable to fight through the storm any longer. Better that we sit here together, and perhaps fall asleep from the cold. Then we wouldn't have to be awake, wouldn't have to feel it when death came for us.

A presence.

Something changed in the air around us. I fought to open my eyes, peering through my wraps, and there was *light*. The snow continued to swirl around us, but something shone through the darkness. And it was moving. Coming closer and closer. I couldn't sit up, couldn't move towards it or away from it. If it was danger, my mind was too numb to recognize any instincts. I simply lay there, blinking the snow from my eyes.

And then Ri began to move again, unbidden, her legs carrying us on to the Goddess knows where. Another bit of light joined the first, and then another. I was so, so tired. So close to giving up. I let my eyes close, let myself fall into a beautiful abyss of darkness where there was no more wind and no more cold.

Chapter 15

Ivar felt nearly every bit of the walls again and again. He examined every nook and cranny, and even stood on a chair to have a look at the chimney. As far as he could tell, there was no way out of this house except for through the locked front door.

The only option was to wait until someone came back, and either try to talk his way out of this, or fight. He did still have a knife on hand, and there would likely be other items that could serve as weapons lying around the house, but if they returned armed as well, it would be of no use. He'd be vastly outnumbered. Eventually he just stood in the centre of the room, staring at the door and imagining a hundred different ways their next interaction could go. He'd been told of the things terror made people do, but this seemed far worse than any stories he'd heard.

He tossed another log on to the fire, determined to at least keep warm.

It was the small hours of the morning when they came for him. Ivar must have fallen asleep because he sat up groggily at the sound of shuffling feet and the door being pushed open, bringing with it a whisper of frigid air.

"What's happening?" he asked.

"You'll see," answered a voice, though he wasn't sure if it was Areld or one of the other men dragging him from the house.

The pre-dawn air was biting cold, even more so after his closeness to the fire. The only good it served was to shock his mind into full clarity. Questions rose in Ivar's throat, but he knew before speaking that they would refuse to answer him. Now was his time to watch, listen, and take the first window of opportunity he saw to escape. He tried to walk in a manner that kept his cloak around his knife, in hopes that no one would notice it and remove it from his belt.

The same group he'd spoken to earlier shuffled him out of the village, but more and more joined them as they progressed. After ten or so minutes, there were perhaps fifteen people following them. All wore sombre, stony expressions as they moved along the narrow pathway which began to rise steadily upwards. The trees began to thin, until they stopped atop a small, snowy knoll that offered a view of the surrounding forest. But it wasn't the view that held Ivar's attention. It was the wooden post that had been dug into the ground, and the kindling piled around it.

"No," Ivar said quickly, shaking his head. "You don't want to do this."

"But we do," said Areld, pushing him against the post. "It's the darkest part of the night. We can see Her clearly" – he swept a hand up to the constellation of the Goddess – "and She can see us. By sacrificing you, we don't have to lose one of our own. It was as though She delivered you to us for this exact purpose."

There were murmurings of agreement throughout the group.

"Why do this now?" Ivar shouted as he struggled against his hands being tied around the post. "I've told you we have someone on her way to speak to the Goddess. She could be there within days. You could keep me until then. Just wait long enough to give her a chance!"

"The plague may be back within days," said a man a few paces away. "Or the Ør, if your story was true. We don't have days to lose."

"What if you're wrong?" Ivar tried again. "What if sacrificing me angers Her? You could bring something down upon Skane far worse than whatever was already coming."

The hands tying him faltered, but then continued.

"People survived last time," Ivar said, as one of the

men removed the knife from his belt. He gritted his teeth in fear and frustration, his voice rising. "People have always survived. You can survive again."

Areld motioned for a woman with a torch to come forward. The flames illuminated her face in a sickly yellow glow.

Ivar shook his head over and over, panic rising. "No. Don't do this. Don't do this. You won't solve anything."

"That's for us to find out," Areld told him. "Your lot can wait for days and pretend to train with weapons, but we have studied the Goddess and chosen the right path. It is time for Skane to give back, and you should be honoured that it's your life we offer."

"If it's such an honour then why don't you sacrifice yourself?" Ivar hissed through his teeth, kindling crunching beneath his feet.

Areld took the torch from the woman and bent to light the kindling.

Ivar tried to shrink away, but the post remained strong. "Please don't," he whispered, as the first few sticks caught fire. Fear shook his body. Tearing his eyes away from the flames, he forced his eyes to the sky, where the stars shone like sparkling snow in the sunshine. There was such darkness behind them, but each one blazed with a power that spoke of hope and defiance. They spoke of the kind of strength Ósa carried within her, the kind she had been born with, and the kind he had always admired. Even without him, that hope would live on. She wouldn't let it die. She would fight for Skane until her lungs could no longer draw breath. He closed his eyes as the first flames curled around his feet.

There was a snapping noise that made all those who were gathered jump. An arrow pierced the rope tying Ivar's hands to the post and seconds later, another followed, freeing his feet. Confused faces turned to stare into the darkness. Areld and his men pulled knives from their belts and held them at the ready.

Two figures on horseback rose up the hill. One was short, with a mess of blond curls that could only be Móri. The other Ivar recognized in an instant: his father. Móri rode close to Areld and held a strung bow to his face.

"Get on," Sigvard ordered his son, who snatched his knife from where it lay beside the post, and then jumped on to the horse behind his father. The crowd shrank back, their faces fearful.

"Another minute and there wouldn't have been much to save," Ivar said, eyeing the flames engulfing the post.

"We knew something was wrong when you didn't come back," Sigvard replied, a long knife held tightly in one hand. Then, to the others, "You are forbidden from entering our village or any of the villages who will come to join us. May the Goddess have mercy on your wretched souls."

"You don't understand," Areld spat, swatting away Móri's bow. "We're trying to help you, not hurt you."

"If you hurt my son, you hurt us all," Sigvard said.

"Even if killing him could save everyone else?" Areld moved closer, anger and desperation rampant on his face.

"It's not too late," Ivar offered, gesturing to the fire. "If you're so sure it will work, you have a perfectly good fire all ready to go."

Areld looked around, then grabbed hold of a boy standing a few metres away, whose eyes were wide with fear. "Very well," Areld said through his teeth. "You'll do."

"No!" the boy shouted, trying to wriggle free. "I never wanted to kill anyone!"

"Let him go," Sigvard warned, sliding down from the horse. The menace in his voice made even Areld's men take a step back.

"It's the only way," Areld said, shoving the boy towards the blaze. When Sigvard moved to stop him, Areld only moved faster. Screams split the night as the edges of the boy's clothing caught on fire.

In a blur, Ivar leaped down from the horse and sped across the distance to the fire. With a firm kick, he pushed the boy off the flames and rolled him into the snow, his clothing sizzling. When he turned around, Sigvard and Areld were locked in a knife fight, metal clanging and clashing.

144

"You'll ruin everything!" Areld shouted, his breath ragged from the exertion. "This is the only way!"

"Fear and desperation is no reason to take an innocent life," Sigvard answered in between blows. "Especially not my son's."

"Then you're all going to die," Areld hissed back. "Every single one of you. And it will be your own fault." He stopped fighting Sigvard and took a step back, a strange sort of calmness seeming to come over him. "But not me," he said, quieter. "That, at least, is something I can control."

He dropped his knife and turned towards the flaming post. Then, closing his eyes, he entered the fire.

His screams erupted into the night, ceasing only when the flames had silenced them.

Chapter 16

Smoke permeated my nostrils. I opened my eyes, blinked, then sat up quickly.

A cave.

Stone walls surrounded me, a roof stretched over me and beneath my body was a pile of the wraps I'd brought from home. A few metres away was a fire, slowly smouldering. Just inside the entrance, where daylight shone in, stood Ri, one foot cocked as she rested, her eyes closed.

The very last thing I remembered was the plain, a storm blowing around us, beating down, and then falling asleep. We'd still been so far from the foothills, and with the state we'd both been in, there was no way we could have reached them. Not without any sense of direction. Not before freezing to death. *Don't be on the plain at nightfall*, Gregor had said. Yet we'd done exactly that.

I stood, my body aching. It was dark, the light not reaching very far from the entrance, but it was relatively warm and safe. I grabbed a handful of the grain from the pack and offered it to Ri; she ate it lazily. The rest of the packs were piled inexplicably on the floor.

"How did we get here?" I asked, patting her shoulder and gazing out of the mouth of the cave. The sky was overcast, but the snow had stopped falling. Some of it had blown into the entrance, piled a few centimetres deep in miniature drifts. I wracked my brain for a memory, a fleeting hint that would shake free some thought of what had happened the night before, but there was nothing. I'd simply come from the plain, to waking up just a moment ago, like a book with pages missing.

Back in the part of the cave where I'd been sleeping, I tied my cloak around my shoulders. We were out of the direct elements here, but the air grew chillier the longer I stood still, especially away from the fire. Had I made that fire? None of the materials to do so were anywhere in sight.

It was while I was taking a long drink of water that I noticed the writing.

The walls around me were covered in runes. For a moment I stared dumbly, spooked to silence. Then I dropped my flask and grabbed a candle from my bag, lighting it on the still smouldering fire, and holding it aloft. Shapes and scrawls spread out before me, so many that some seemed to run into one another. It was as if the writer was running out of room and began to write in overlap. I would never have the time to translate it all, to read every inscription, but perhaps I could grab snatches, small bits that may or may not prove useful.

Thank the stars Ivar had thought to pack me the scrolls. If only he was here. He could start reading it right away, making sense of the madness before me without having to refer to the papers.

Taking some of the scrolls from my shoulder pack, I flipped through them, searching for a handful of the runes before me. It was slow-going at first, the pages filled with rune after rune, and the walls teeming with marks that I couldn't seem to find a definition for. How the hell did Ivar do this so quickly? Once I'd established the pattern in the scrolls, the order in which they'd been written, it became easier.

The first word that stood out to me made me hesitate. Jōt.

I kept going, scouring the scrolls and studying the walls until my eyes burned.

The jōt walk near.

It was almost certainly not an exact translation, but I didn't have to dig any deeper to know what it meant. Giants roamed these hills, as I'd both expected and feared. But this was their land, I reminded myself. Here, I was an intruder.

I skimmed ahead, looking for other single words that might jump out at me.

Tall.

Voices.

Hunt.

I forced my eyes away from the wall. If I continued reading, I might be encouraged to turn around and go home. That couldn't happen. I'd come too far. Returning the scrolls to their bag, I gathered my belongings and tied the packs to Ri in preparation for another day of travelling. If my body ached this much, I couldn't imagine how she felt.

It was just as we were about to depart from the cave that something else caught my attention. There was writing on the wall that wasn't runes. It was our own writing, the kind we wrote and spoke today. It was Agric.

I became caught in a storm on the plain. Forced to stop. Lights. They just disappeared.

My breath all but left me. The words were written in my own hand.

Chapter 17

Feelings of intense panic and of warmth spreading throughout the kindling under his feet plagued Ivar's mind. He couldn't escape the memory of such a blind terror. And then there was the memory of Areld's screams as his body was consumed by fire. It echoed in his sleep and haunted his quiet thoughts when no one else was around.

Early in the morning, Ivar and a small handful of other villagers left to trek north and south to find the ship on which the two Ør scouts had arrived. Ivar was in the southern party with Sigvard, his father, and Eldór was in the northern party with Leiv and a hunter named Torald. He and Eldór brought in the vast majority of Neska's meat, as well as that of the surrounding villages.

Ivar opted for the southern party, partly because, after

Eldór's doubt of his daughter's eyesight on the boat, he was afraid of what he'd say to him when they found it; biting his tongue would be a struggle. The other reason was because, judging by where the Ør had found them in the woods, his instinct told him they'd find it in the south.

They first made for the familiar bits of coast just outside the village, filled with well-trodden pathways and the occasional wandering soul, out looking for berries or collecting firewood. Their approaching footsteps frightened the wanderers, white faces and round eyes staring at him and his father, before recognition dawned. Ivar couldn't blame them. At a time like this, everyone feared their own shadows.

When they left those paths behind, the terrain was much less accessible. They had to walk single file in many places, where the only ground on which they could get a foothold was so narrow that they risked plunging into the crashing waves on their left. Ivar walked behind Sigvard, glancing into the trees now and then, as if the hulking form of an Ør might emerge at any moment. He was on edge, tightly strung, like a bow about to be released.

Somewhere between one and two kilometres to the south, they found it. The land jutted sharply inland, forming a sort of icy cove that was nearly impossible to get to without careful consideration of every step. The waves were far less rough here, as they'd lost much of their power upon entering the inlet. A wooden boat, affixed with a black sail that had been torn ragged in the wind, lay almost on its side, washed ashore.

"There she is," Sigvard said under his breath, shaking his head like he almost couldn't believe it. "Let's have a look at what's on board, shall we?"

Ivar's stomach twisted as they made their way painstakingly down, imagining Ósa having seen that wretched sail out at sea. Imagining her father not believing her.

Every few steps, his feet tried to slip from underneath him, but he held on to any rock and root in sight, until at last, they were firmly on the beach. The boat loomed larger now, not so large that the two Ør alone couldn't manage it – if indeed there were only two – but big enough to set Ivar on edge. They approached it slowly, and he half-expected to see scarred heads and ragged hair poking over the railing, though there was nothing.

Ivar was first to climb aboard, as his father walked as far around it as he could without entering into the water. The boards beneath his feet sent shivers up his legs, all the way to his neck. Monsters had built this boat. It was evidenced in almost all the aspects of its creation, from the dark, rough wood – foreign to Skane – and the black sail, to the oars that lay idly by, made from the same unusual wood as the boat. Tall points, spikes, of sorts, were positioned every few metres around the railing.

Whether they were for tying ropes or hanging heads, he couldn't tell, but they were unsettling, like jagged teeth surrounding the mouth in which he now stood.

This very boat had sailed all the way from the Ør Isles, all the way through the White Water, and to this spot, carrying with it two monsters who had planned to take back information about them. To kill them.

Ivar shut his eyes and breathed in the cold, salty air. *Your scouts are never coming back*, he thought, and a small bit of satisfaction tickled his mind.

"They didn't leave much here, it seems," Sigvard said after climbing aboard. "And I don't see any shelter."

"Perhaps they don't need it," Ivar told him, staring out of the inlet to the open sea. "Perhaps they're built to weather anything." Judging by their strange, leathery skin, it seemed true.

"What's that?" he asked, pointing to a partially open wooden box tied to the mast.

Ivar made his way over, fighting the sharp angle of the boat, and opened the lid. He pulled out a tattered bit of white leather, on which was a series of lines and markings.

"It's a map," he said, turning it over. "At least, I think it is. I don't understand the writing."

"Just keep it," Sigvard said. "Hell knows why, but it's not worth losing."

Ivar rolled it up like a scroll and deposited it into his pocket.

"Well," Sigvard said with a sigh, "it won't do us any good to keep the boat, and using the wood just doesn't seem right."

Doesn't seem right felt like a gross understatement. The Ør had killed many of their ancestors, chased them from their homes and torn apart their families. The very thought of introducing this dark, foreign wood to Skane felt like defiling something sacred. No, there was only thing to be done with it.

After Eldór and the others had a thorough inspection of it, they burned the boat.

Back at the village, a small group of men had retrieved the bodies of the Ør on sleds. By the time they were brought in, wild animals had got to them, as evidenced by the torn skin and missing limbs. They'd left the bulk of them, though; perhaps the animals could taste the evil in their blood.

They were burned in the centre of the village. Only a few came to watch. Others hung well back, covering their mouths and turning away every few seconds, like the sight of the Ør was too much to bear. Ivar stared at their bodies, stared until the flames had engulfed them and reduced them to nothing more than a pile of smouldering ash in the village, and the memory of what had happened in the woods.

Ivar let another knife fly, and with a satisfying thud, it joined five more that were already stuck into the trunk of the tree. He'd just finished a lesson with a handful of villagers on how to throw them, and now he poured his energy into doing it on his own. There was a war in his mind, one that had started when they'd encountered the Ør scouts. No, perhaps it had been earlier than that. Perhaps it had started with the intense feeling of defeat when the red lós had shone in the sky. On the one hand, it felt like none of this mattered. Teaching children and elderly folk to throw knives wouldn't defeat the Ør. It was foolish. But there was still that tiny flame of hope that was fighting to stay alive somewhere within him. The one that reminded him how much he believed in Ósa and her ability to see this through.

"I'll bet you my snowshoes you can't do it," he said to her. They stood under the shadow of a towering fir tree that was starkly green against the vibrant blue of the sky. It was in the warmer months and the air no longer bore that biting cold which lashed at one's skin and throat. They wore their lighter wraps, leather boots instead of fur.

Ósa's neck was craned and she stared towards the very top of the tree, hidden by branches and needles. She had more blonde curls than several children combined, and the breeze kept blowing them into her eyes.

"You promise I'll get the snowshoes at the end?" she asked, reaching out a hand for Ivar to shake.

"You'll never make it, so that's an easy promise." He shook her hand.

155

Removing her outermost layer, Ósa hoisted herself up on to the lowest hanging branch of the tree, making sure to send a smug glance his way before the needles of the tree swallowed her. Soon, all he could see was vague movement and shuffling, hear twigs cracking and snapping and an occasional grunt of effort. But within a few minutes, he couldn't see or hear anything at all. Small amounts of worry pulled at his mind as he watched and waited.

"Are you all right?" he called up, but there was no answer.

A few more minutes went by before he heard a light thump thump thump. A series of large pine cones came dropping down from above, bouncing off the branches and the trunk and a few of them hitting the top of his head.

"All right, I get it!" he shouted, stepping back and shielding himself from the onslaught. "You can have my snowshoes."

The memory made him smile – when Ósa set her mind to something, she usually achieved it.

There were footsteps in the trees, and he froze.

"You should teach me," said a familiar, high voice. He closed his eyes and turned to face her.

Anneka smiled and tilted her head. "You never miss your mark." Her arms were folded across her chest and her cloak was far too thin for the time of year. Underneath, her dress clung to her body, her pale skin visible in places. Her hair, usually pulled back and tucked neatly away, was now braided down the right side of her head and hung over her chest and folded arms.

Ivar kept his eyes on her face.

"I practise."

"I'll practise."

"No."

It was about three years ago, shortly after he'd turned seventeen, that he'd started to notice how she acted around him. Why it had started, he didn't know. Perhaps it was due to the amount of time he'd spent at their home. Time he'd been spending with Ósa.

Her smile faded, but returned a moment later. "What wretched news, no? How terrible. How utterly terrible." She moved a hand to her mouth in a dramatic display of worry. "After all these years, the Ør..." She shook her head, as if she couldn't allow herself to continue. "And I'm so sorry about what happened to you. My father told me."

"What do you want?" She hesitated at the shortness of his words. He sighed and turned back to the tree, hurling another knife into the trunk. "I'm sorry. I'm worried about your sister."

He could feel her prickle behind him. "Ósa will be fine. Leaving was her choice." The way she said it, as though she didn't care what became of Ósa, sent fire roaring through his veins.

He turned to face her again, and something in his face must have given his feelings away.

"Of course, I worry too."

"Do you?"

She fell silent. Then, "Good to see you, Ivar." She smiled, a forced, small smile, and left him.

She'd only been gone moments before hooves crunched through the snow. He peered into the forest around him. Three men on horses were approaching from the northwest.

"Who goes there?" Ivar said, loud enough to carry through the trees.

They didn't answer until they'd stopped beside him. One was an older man, his short beard white. The other two were younger, perhaps the age of his father. Ivar didn't miss the way their eyes quickly travelled over him, no doubt looking for signs of illness. He couldn't blame them. Everyone was keeping a watchful eye. No one knew when the plague would strike.

"The name's Gregor," the man with the beard said. "We're from Isavik, back that way." He pointed over his shoulder. "Ósa sent us to you."

Ivar breathed in so deeply, he thought his lungs would burst. "She reached you?"

"Came and went," Gregor replied. "She brought us the news. Left our village this morning, off to cross the plain to the foothills. Brave one, her."

Rubbing both hands across his face, Ivar nodded. "So she told you."

"Indeed she did. Said we should come and speak to

her father about preparations, and someone named Ivar. Know where I can find him?"

"I'm Ivar," he replied, relieved and complimented that she had given his name. "I'll take you to her father." He yanked the knives from the tree trunk and stuck them in his belt. The men followed him through the woods to the village. Groups of people filled the streets, all lost in their work. A whittling station had been set up, where arrow after arrow was being carved from wood. At another, stone was being pounded and hammered to form any sort of blade they could make. At yet another, large shells that had washed up on the shore were being sharpened into small throwing knives.

Ivar pounded on the door to Ósa's home. Her father answered. "This is Gregor," Ivar said, sweeping an arm behind him. "They're from Isavik. Ósa passed through there last night and brought them the news."

"Ah, come in," Eldór replied. "We have much to discuss."

Ivar joined them. He'd heard the same speech a hundred times now, but if Ósa was off on such a desperate mission for help, the least he could do was help with the preparations. Even if that meant listening to the same story and telling his own a hundred times more.

Anneka sat knitting in the corner. She glanced at Ivar briefly before her eyes returned to her work. Ivar crossed his arms and leaned against a wall.

"So our plan is to fight back?" Gregor asked when Eldór had finished explaining about the Ør scouts.

"With everything we have," Ivar answered for him.

"Futile, perhaps, yet our only hope," Eldór said gravely.

Not our only hope, Ivar wanted to reply, though he didn't.

"We could run and hide, but they would find us. They won't leave Skane without destroying us all."

Gregor and the others nodded. "I'm afraid you're right," he said. "We can hope for salvation, like Ósa, but our only real chance is to put up one hell of a fight."

Ivar looked to Eldór, and despite his usual stern appearance, lines pulled at his eyes at the mention of his daughter. He was worried about her, perhaps more than anyone, but he'd never say it. And why shouldn't he worry? He was, after all, the one who'd sent her to the mountains alone.

"We need to band together," Gregor said. "You're the easternmost village. This will be our strongest point, if they attack from the sea. Our only hope is to meet them on arrival. If you have room to host us, we'll all gather here."

"We will make room," Eldór said.

"What of the bodies?" one of the other men asked. "May we see them?" There was a slight undertone of incredulity to his voice.

"We burned them," Eldór replied. "But we kept these."

He moved to a wooden box at the far side of the room. From them, he withdrew a stone blade and a rope necklace hung with bones and teeth. "This," he said, holding up the necklace, "was likely one of his last victims." He tossed it across the room and the man caught it, pinching it gingerly between two fingers.

"So if we'd like to avoid being the next piece of jewellery," Eldór continued, "I say we get on with the preparations."

There was a cave down by the water, a short walk from the village. At high tide it filled halfway, but at low tide it was empty. It bore runes, a handful of them, but to avoid the water, they'd been written on the ceiling. It was the first cave Ivar had been taught to translate in, and a favourite of his. Even at low tide, the cave still echoed the nearby crashing waves, reminding him of low thunder.

Today, it also echoed the voices of women and children, collecting shells and stones from the beach, despite the bitter cold. Ivar sat on a large rock and stared upward. The runes were hard to see without direct light, but a few of them could just be made out. It wasn't terribly interesting, just his ancestors recording how they'd made the first boat to use to fish. Many skills, like boat making, had been brought over from Löska, but they'd had to be refined and changed. Different trees. Different tools. Even the way they fished had to be adjusted. Skane's waters were cold, rougher than Löska's.

The voices from outside echoing around him suddenly changed to screams. He leaped to his feet and bolted out of the cave, searching the beach for the cause. The women and children were gathered around a boat that lay on its side, washed up in the waves. Ivar ran, half-slipping down the rocks to where they stood. As he approached, his stomach turned. One woman faced away, retching on to the ground.

Inside, tied to the wooden bench at the front of the boat, were the heads of Albrekt and another fisherman. They had gone out to sea that morning – the people still needed feeding, they had to catch fish. Their faces had been mauled almost beyond recognition.

Their bodies were nowhere to be found, and blood ran from their mouths. He knew why.

Something out there had a new necklace.

Chapter 18

I stared and stared at the writing on the wall. When had I done it? I didn't remember making it to the cave. But these words meant that I must have been awake. So how could I not remember?

And what had made me forget?

To my astonishment and delight, Uxi was sitting on a branch outside the cave. Unable to keep from smiling, I offered him a bite of food, an idea forming. I'd left the village days ago. Perhaps Gregor had given word to my father, to Ivar, that he'd seen me, and that I was still alive, but even if he had, they might well presume me dead after that storm. And what if the invasion had already begun? Perhaps a word of hope would help to see them through, at least for a little while longer.

I tore off a small, empty piece of scroll and wrote a message with a bit of charred stick.

I have reached the mountains.

It wasn't much, but it was the best I could offer. Wrapping it into a tiny band, I cut a bit of string from one of my wraps and tied it to Uxi's ankle.

"Home, Uxi," I said, praying he'd understand. I pointed the way we'd come. "Fly back to the village. Please, please find Ivar." He didn't move. And why would he? He was faithful, even a little bit tame, but he didn't understand words. Why did I ever think he would?

I'd leave it there, though. Just in case.

The light seemed excessively bright despite the sun hiding behind the clouds. Everywhere was white, blinding and brilliant. I shielded my eyes for the first few minutes as we rode in the direction of the mountains, trying to make out our location. Mist clung to the ground, swirling about Ri's hooves. Here in the foothills, the land rose and fell, gentle slopes interspersed with jagged cliffs and rocky outcroppings. In some places, ravines cut through the ground like the aftermath of some giant knife, and occasionally we'd splash through a mostly frozen river or stream. They were shallow, running from mountain springs somewhere high above us.

When I tilted my head to look up, defying the brightness of the clouds, the looming mountains stared back. The top half of them was shrouded in fog, but I could still see the snowy, rocky cliffs and black holes where caves cut deep into the sides of the mountains. Down here far below, I felt so open, so exposed, as though anything that lived up there could see my every move.

I had to hope that nothing was watching.

I couldn't see which of the peaks was the tallest. With any luck, the clouds would burn off later in the day and I'd be able to determine which one was my destination, or else risk wandering the mountains until I became so lost there would be no finding my way back out again. I contented myself with winding carefully through the foothills, the ground unmistakably rising up, up, up. The air would grow colder the higher we went.

A rabbit ran from one shrub to another, a flash of furry white that vanished in seconds. It feared me, yet that thought seemed so absurd. I was the last thing to be feared in these mountains.

As I nibbled on dry, stale bread, a poor breakfast in an attempt to save the dried meat, I spotted something not far to our right. Disturbed snow, imprints that beckoned me to investigate. Reining Ri in, I swung down and made my way towards it. They were tracks, though of what, I couldn't tell. They were large, but the snow was so deep, the top layer frozen, that they were hardly more than holes with little to no shape. They led onwards, in a similar direction to where we were heading, though veering off to the right. There was no one and nothing in sight, but no snow had filled them in, so they'd been left recently.

I returned to Ri, who didn't seem at all nervous. Whatever it was wasn't anywhere in sight, and I was just passing by. If I didn't disturb them, perhaps they wouldn't disturb me. In the story Gregor had told me, Stína's great-grandfather had come to be imprisoned by the giants when he'd fallen into their camp. Maybe if he hadn't done so, nothing would have happened. Maybe that was true for everything in the mountains. If you kept to yourself, they let you be.

We pressed on, climbing one side of a hill and descending carefully down the other. At times, Ri seemed to struggle to keep her footing on the ice and rock and snow, making our progress slow. There were more trees here, more cover to help shield us from prying eyes, which offered at least a little comfort. I tried to keep us to the shadows as much as possible, moving from tree to tree and rock to rock. With any luck, foolish though the thought may be, perhaps I could slip in and out of the mountains without ever being noticed.

A growl floated on the mist to my ears. I didn't have to ask Ri to stop, she immediately pulled up short, her neck raised, her ears standing alert. That wasn't the growl of a content, full animal. It was one of something who'd spotted prey, signalling a hunt. Something knew we were here. I pulled the reins to the left, urging Ri to the shadow of a large fir tree. Running away would be difficult. There was too much ice and uneven ground.

Seeing nothing, I swung down to the ground again and turned slowly in a circle, taking in the whole of the surrounding forest. The breeze taunted me by lifting the branches of trees and fir needles. Every time I saw movement, it turned out to be harmless. I had almost completed my turn when something caught my attention perhaps twenty paces away. I strained my eyes, confused. The snow seemed to be ... moving? Something white was rising over a nearby hilltop, and—

When it reached the top, I nearly stopped breathing. A bear, whiter than I'd ever seen, was staring at us, piercing black eyes standing out against its fur. It tilted its head and growled, its open mouth the size of my head.

We'd seen bears before, back in the village, but they weren't common. They would pick off a human who was far from anyone else, who was caught alone in the woods, especially in winter. But entire villages made them nervous. The noise, the scent of fire, it pushed them away, keeping us safe. I remembered one thing my father had taught me: never run. Running meant fear, and fear was something they preyed on. Fear meant you were something they could overpower. Also, no one had ever outrun a bear. Their legs were too long, too powerful. If I could establish myself as a threat, he might move on.

Standing as tall as I could, I took a step forward.

If I was lucky, such an aggressive move would show intimidation and he'd wander off. The mountains were full of smaller prey, rabbits and foxes and all manner of life that would no doubt prove an easy meal for such a beast. A girl and a horse might be more trouble than we were worth.

The bear didn't back down. Instead, it moved towards me, letting out another long, reverberating growl that shook my soul. Ri started, her ears pinned to her head. I didn't know whether the bear wanted me or the horse, but I couldn't spare either of us. I pulled my knife from its place at my waist, ready to throw if it came any closer. I didn't want to kill it. Wouldn't, unless I absolutely had to. A knife would do little more than slow it down, make it bleed, and hopefully establish myself as a force to be feared.

It lumbered forward, those giant paws sinking into the snow with a kind of weight that warned me to run. It was suddenly all I could think about, wanting to turn away and flee through the trees, run until I couldn't take another step, until I was so far away that the bear and this fear felt like nothing more than a distant, fading memory.

Never run.

Ri backed away slowly, her breath ragged and terrified. The bear, however, seemed more concerned with me, perhaps for my small size. As the distance between us began to disappear, a heavy growl emanating again from deep within its chest, I remembered a time many, many years ago when I'd climbed a tree on a dare to win Ivar's snowshoes. I'd climbed nearly the whole way to the top, until the branches were too thin to support my weight. I glanced at the tree behind me. It wouldn't be easy, but if I was fast, I might be able to make it work.

After a quick look at the bear, I shoved the knife into my belt and jumped, latching my arms around the lowest branch and hauling myself upward. I hadn't anticipated how heavy I'd be, weighed down by warm cloaks and furs, but I fought against my shaking muscles and pulled myself on to the branch. Just as I was reaching for the next branch, a scraping sound below me forced my gaze downward. The bear, seeming to have caught on to my escape, had latched on to the tree in a sort of brutal embrace, the sickeningly large claws protruding from its paws finding easy purchase on the bark.

Could bears climbs trees?

I couldn't wait to find out. If it could, it almost certainly couldn't climb as fast as I could, and that needed to be my focus. I needed to reach the higher points of the tree that it wouldn't be able to get to, where the branches would be too thin. Sooner or later, it would have to give up.

My heart beat so loudly it seemed to overwhelm all other noises as I made my way steadily upward. Small twigs and branches lashed at my face, and I felt a warm trickle on my left cheek, but there wasn't time to stop and wipe it away. My arms shook, my legs throbbed, and each new branch I reached was a miracle. *Pull. Stand. Reach.* I worked to find a rhythm, a comforting repetition that would ease the pain, but it only worsened.

Over the pounding of my heart and the rustle of my clothing against the bark of the tree, I heard a loud thud. Cautiously allowing myself to look down, dizzy from the height, I saw the bear had dropped to the ground. Surely it hadn't yet reached its limit. What had urged it away?

It lifted its head into the air, sniffing, and then turned and *ran*. As it retreated, it paused once to look behind it, as though it were running from ... something.

What would scare a bear? Something much, much bigger than me, I realized with a sense of mounting dread, as thundering footsteps reached my ears.

Chapter 19

The silence of the cave was both suffocating and beautiful. It was an hour-long trek south of Neska, and Ivar was supposed to be hunting to add to the food stores the village was building up so that there wouldn't be cause to leave. So that all of the focus could be poured into preparing for the Ør's invasion. But his feet had led him here, because the quiet familiarity of the cave welcomed him in a way he couldn't deny. There was little to be gleaned from the sparse scratchings on these walls, and yet he'd somehow formed a strange attachment to the person who'd written it. Perhaps, he thought, as his eyes fell on the marks, it was because the writer had left their signature. Isól. It could have been a man or a woman, but knowing their name seemed to break down the years and years of separation between them, as though, if he said the name out loud, they might hear him. Perhaps part of them still haunted this cave, the cave that had at one time been their refuge. Their place of peace.

Ósa didn't know about this cave, or if she did, she'd never said. Close as they were, there seemed to be some level of importance in having a place of one's own, of having somewhere to go to be dead to the world and to allow oneself to become lost in the windings of one's own thoughts. There was a beauty in isolation, but also renewal.

He dug his palms into his eyes, the realization of just how tired he truly was settling into his bones. During the day, while helping others train and throwing knife after knife in demonstration, he could keep up the appearance of strength, even while others wailed, panicked when in close proximity to anyone else in the village. He could try to be the voice of reason when others acted irrationally, but when he was alone, those walls began to crumble, and pure, unhindered exhaustion crept into the very core of his being. He slept at night, at least for a few hours, but his dreams were dark and frightening, his sleep often fitful. The light of dawn was a welcome sight, even if it was the start of another wretched day of waiting. It meant that at least he didn't have to sleep again for hours.

Footsteps crunched in the snow outside the cave. He leaped to his feet as quietly as he could, knives in hand. He crept to the mouth of the cave, keeping to the shadows as he peered outside. A trail of people were moving by, headed north with boxes and carts and piled with belongings. With a sinking of his stomach, he recognized a few faces. When he emerged from the cave, a familiar boy stopped and stared at him. They were from Sjørskall. It looked like most of the village was trekking north, towards Neska, no doubt.

"What brings you to the north?" he asked, sheathing one knife but still gripping the other.

The boy gestured to those around him, many of whom continued their journey with nervous glances in his direction. "We've come to join you," he said, his voice full of hope. "With Areld gone, many of us are happy to get away. We wanted to apologise for what happened in our village by bringing you our added numbers and whatever weapons we could gather." He pointed to a cart rumbling by, carrying old knives and crudely-carved arrows. "Please accept our help."

Ivar watched the cart roll by, remembering the heat of the flames beneath him, the certainty he'd felt that those were his last few moments. No one in the village had helped him, and without the sudden arrival of his father, he might not be alive today.

And yet.

How could he deny them safety? Their very presence here was an apology. Their willingness to join a fight such as this said something, and he could not turn them away to certain death. "You will have to speak to my father and our leaders," he told them. "I cannot guarantee that they will have you after what happened, but I will do my best to convince them."

It took the better part of an hour for the villagers to plead their case, but at long last, with the promise of new hands and weapons, Sigvard and Eldór agreed to let the newcomers stay.

The next morning, the sky was just beginning to hint at an approaching dawn. The stars overhead began to fade, losing their vibrancy as the sky eased from black to grey. Ivar stood just outside the village, his hands buried inside pockets within his cloak, his breath creating bursts of white fog. Sleep had refused to come to him, and the walls of his home had never felt so close. So confined. Some small part of him felt pangs of guilt. *If Ósa can't have the comfort of home, neither should I.*

Where was she now? Safe? Warm? *Alive?*

He'd known it would take time, but as days slipped away, day giving way to night giving way to day, the Ør were coming ever closer. While his hope in Ósa remained, the more logical part of Ivar's mind began to take over. Even if she did make it, even if she did survive, she would almost certainly be too late. And that understanding sat in the pit of his stomach like a rock.

A bird departed a nearby branch and snow fell to the

ground with a gentle patter. The forest was just beginning to come alive, awakening to start a new day. Colours began to bloom, chasing away the dull grey of the night as the sun fought to regain control of the sky. There was something sacred in this hour, when night began to die and day was born again. New snow had fallen, stretching almost entirely unbroken around him in hills and valleys of white.

It was at times like these that Ivar struggled the most. The village was still asleep. He could slip into a stable and steal a horse before anyone else knew. He could be a few kilometres away before anyone woke up, riding north to find her. If he rode night and day, eventually he would catch up to her. A small smile pulled at his lips as he imagined that reunion, so far from home and so unexpected.

He could do it. He could do it right now.

But then he saw smoke rising from a few chimneys, and in the village voices carried to him on the breeze. Gregor and the other leaders would soon meet again to continue their discussions and preparations. One figure, shorter than the others, emerged from a house and looked about, his eyes finally settling on Ivar.

Móri.

Ivar wanted to be alone, but it was too late now to avoid being seen. The boy made his way to him through the snow, pulling his cloak tighter around his slight form.

He was still thin, not quite tall enough to be a man, but not that far off, either. Ivar couldn't remember his exact age, but reckoned it had to be somewhere around thirteen.

"Hunting?" his cousin asked when he was close enough.

"No, just standing here. It was quiet."

"I'm sorry." Móri looked down, clearly disappointed with himself.

"Don't be. I was just about to come back. I couldn't sleep." Ivar sighed and turned to face the woods once more.

"My father is going hunting later and I'm going with him. He said it will be good practice with my bow. I get to shoot whatever we find." Móri gently patted the bow strung across his back. "I've practised almost every—" He stopped short and sniffed. "Do you smell that?"

Ivar lifted his head and breathed deeply, facing into the breeze. Sure enough, it carried with it a subtle but distinct smell.

Smoke, thick and pungent.

Without stopping to think, Ivar bolted back into the village, where he hammered on the door of his home. "Father! Get out here!" Without waiting for an answer, he ran to Arvid's house. Aside from the horse he'd given to Ósa, Ivar knew there were three more in his stables. He pounded on the man's door and kept pounding until it opened.

"What has got into you?" Arvid hissed, his eyes still glassy with sleep.

"We need to borrow your horses. Something's happened in the north, something's on fire." Ivar turned and flung open the doors to the stables, Móri following close behind him. Behind them, Sigvard hurried in, pulling on his cloak, his eyebrows knitted together in confusion.

"What is the meaning of this?" he asked, grabbing his son by the shoulder until he stopped to face him.

"There's smoke coming from the north," Ivar said. "Ask Móri. You can smell it in the trees."

Sigvard glanced at the younger boy, who nodded solemnly.

"We need to hurry," Ivar said, untying one of the horses and leading him from the stable.

"Grab a knife and a horse. We'll explain on the way," Ivar shouted to Eldór, who had emerged from his home to investigate the commotion. When he turned to ride into the trees, Móri stood in his path.

"I discovered the smoke," he said, chin held high. "I deserve to come with you."

"We don't know what it is, Móri. I don't want you to—"

"I'm coming with you, Ivar. You would wish the same if you were me."

Ivar stared at the boy for a moment. Yes, he was young, but it was that sort of fire and fearlessness that Skane needed. He was old enough to choose for himself.

So, without answer, he reached out a hand and swung the boy up on to the horse behind him. Moments later, they left the village with Sigvard and Eldór.

It was difficult to make good time in the trees, both from the varying depth of snow to the tall trunks constantly having to be avoided. Whenever there was a clearing, they urged the horses forward as fast as they could go, then reined them in again to circle the trees. The further they travelled, the more intense the smell of the smoke became. It began to sicken Ivar's stomach, hanging thicker and thicker in the air. Even the horse's pace began to slow, his ears darting around as he sniffed nervously.

Sigvard moved to ride beside them. "Whatever we find up here, it won't be good," he said.

Minutes later, the ruins of Išavik lay before them. The houses had been burned from the inside out, the snow still hissing and melting away. Anything that would burn lay charred and blackened, smoking and crumbling to ash. Blood sat red against the snow, bodies fallen haphazardly around the village. No one moved. No one breathed.

"Devils," Sigvard breathed. Eldór remained silent, staring.

"How did they get here?" Móri asked.

Ivar jumped from the horse and walked slowly to the nearest body, which was not yet cold. Motionless. Eyes glazed over with death. Teeth missing. "They might have come in the boat with the others," he said quietly. "Or on one we haven't found." Then, after examining the body more closely, he said, "This is new. Look for tracks."

"You think four of us can hunt down an unknown number of Ør?" Eldór asked.

"If they don't know we're coming we'll have an advantage," Ivar said, remounting the horse. "We have to stop them before they reach another village. This must be their plan. They're going to try to eradicate our people village by village, before we can all stand together, working their way down from the north. Take us out without needing a fight." He didn't wait for a reply, only steered the horse away and began searching the snow for tracks.

He swiftly found some, leading out of the village and into the forest headed south, on a different route than Ivar and the others had taken to reach Išavik. They must have passed each other with too much distance to notice. The tracks were large and messy, difficult to read, but after a few moments, they all seemed to agree on five. Five Ør. That's all it had taken to destroy an entire village.

"All right," said Eldór, finally finding his voice and speaking with his usual air of authority. "We track them down, but when we're close, we abandon the horses and go on foot. Sigvard and Móri carry bows. That will give us two surprise shots to take two of them down before they realize we're following them. Do not miss." He stared into their faces in turn, intimidation causing Móri to nod, but Sigvard only to stare back. "Once they know we're there, we'll rush them as fast as we can. Ivar, how many knives do you have?"

He felt at his waist, and answered, "Two."

"Throw one and don't miss. Use the other for fighting."

"Ivar never misses," Móri said defiantly, then looked quickly to the ground after a silencing look from Eldór.

"Are we all clear?" he asked a moment later. No one replied, but he seemed to take their silence as consent. "Once we find them, Sigvard and Móri will circle ahead for a clear shot. Ivar and I will attack from the rear."

Ivar rested a hand on the hilt of one knife for comfort, though he found none. They had not come prepared for a fight, Móri least of all. He shouldn't have to face this, but their group couldn't afford to lose one man. There was no way around it, they had to find the Ør and stop them before they reached another village.

Eldór remounted his horse. "Keep the horses reined in. We don't want to to give away our presence."

With the two other men riding in front, they set out following the tracks. Ivar sat ahead of his cousin Móri, eyes staring into the woods, searching for any sign of the monsters. There was nothing except tree after tree, and a blanket of snow that was broken by the large footprints – and, here and there, droplets of blood, probably from the new teeth they'd stolen. Ivar hoped Móri hadn't noticed, though judging by the utter lack of colour in his face, he almost certainly had.

No one spoke, and when the sound of the horses' hooves gently pushing into the snow faded away into the background, silence set in. Ivar wondered how Ósa had dealt with it, with the loneliness and quiet of having no one else around. That sense of isolation, mixed with the knowledge that the burden of salvation rested upon her shoulders, would be enough to drive anyone mad.

Time dragged by. The tracks led on and on, never ending and never arriving.

Until, after perhaps an hour, a new sound reached their ears.

Water.

Of course. They must have been nearing the Horn by now, the river that led down from the north and passed close to the lake. It wasn't deep by any means, but it would have to be crossed, and if they had to cross it ... then so did the Ør ahead of them.

"Stop," Ivar whispered, but the two men before him seemed to have already caught on. Everyone reined in the horses and swung quietly to the ground, then tied them to a few low-hanging branches. The sound of the river grew louder as Ivar trailed the others through the trees. It didn't take long for their footsteps to falter and stop altogether, as five large forms became visible in the distance. They stood on the bank of the river, seeming to be wrapped in some sort of conversation about which way to go. Now and then, one would point across the river, and another would point downriver, as if to follow it.

Ivar and the others hung back, peering out from behind the trees. Móri's mouth was open in horror, but there was also an unmistakably determined knit to his brows. Lines of surprise pulled at Sigvard's and Eldór's faces, though they visibly worked to remain calm.

"The wind is from the north," Sigvard whispered. "Móri and I will trail downriver and try to get ahead of them."

"Eldór and I will stay in sight of them and wait for your arrows. That will be our sign to attack. Móri, would you rather I go in your stead?"

"No," Sigvard replied for him. "Bows are safer than knives. He can keep his distance."

Ivar nodded and rested a hand on the boy's shoulder. "Just think," he said, as lightheartedly as he could manage, "you'll have stories of your own arrows to tell Ósa when she gets back."

Móri smiled a little, and nodded.

"Let's be off," Sigvard said. "It should not take us long to get around them, with the sound of the river masking our movements. If we haven't fired in half an hour, the plan is off."

Everyone nodded, and after a final pat on the back from Ivar to his cousin, they moved away through the trees.

When the sound of their departing footsteps vanished, only the rushing of the river remained. The Ør were still conversing amongst themselves, and every few seconds, Ivar's gaze moved to Eldór's face. He'd known him since childhood – or rather, he'd been aware of him. Despite being the father of the one person he'd spent more time with than anyone else, he knew so little about him. They rarely spoke, Eldór almost never acknowledged his presence, and right now, when it was just the two of them with nothing to do except wait, a million questions he'd always wanted to ask him flooded to mind.

He contented himself with studying the man's face when he wasn't looking, searching for similarities to Ósa. He had her nose, straight and balanced, but that was all. Everything else she must have got from her mother.

Minutes ticked by. Ivar's attention gradually moved back to the present and his current situation. They both stared at the Ør, waiting, watching, until—

Seeming to have come to some sort of agreement, they turned right and began walking downriver. Eldór tensed beside him.

"They'll run into our men," Ivar whispered, hand moving instinctively to a knife.

Eldór nodded. "Follow them."

They moved from behind the trees, but slipped from trunk to trunk and shadow to shadow as they trailed the monsters. If Sigvard and Móri weren't already in position, the Ør would be headed straight for them. They couldn't afford to lose the element of surprise. It was their only advantage.

Slowly and quietly, Ivar and Eldór narrowed the distance between themselves and the monsters, working to keep to the right of them and out of the direct breeze. Ahead, the Ør spoke now and then, and though their voices were muffled, the sound made Ivar cringe. It wasn't a growl, but it wasn't speech either. It was a strange mixture of harsh sounds and grunts, and at one point, one of them seemed to laugh. The stilted, guttural noise made the hairs on the back of his neck stand on end.

There were about fifteen metres between them when an arrow shot out of the trees in front of the Ør and sank into the neck of the forerunner. He crumpled to the ground with a garbled cry. A second or two later, another arrow followed, but missed. Bad. That was bad. It left four Ør still standing, and that was too many to take down.

"We have to go now," Eldór hissed, taking a deep breath and holding up his long knife.

"Go for their heads and necks," Ivar said quickly. "The armour on their chest is too thick."

The man nodded, and together they ran forward. The Ør, still shouting in their twisted, broken language and staring in the direction from where the arrows had flown, didn't notice their advance until the last moment. Ivar picked the one to the left and charged with as much speed as he could gather in the snow. Just before he pummelled into the monster, it let out that now-familiar scream and drew a knife. Ivar ignored the advice he'd given to Eldór and tried to slash through the Ór's wrist so it would drop the knife, but the leather gauntlet was too tough. It raised its long arm, those ghastly pale eyes locked on his own.

Ivar ran a few steps backwards, slipping on the rocks that lined the riverbank, trying to put as much distance between himself and the beast as possible. It ran towards him and closed the distance quickly. As Ivar's own knife clashed with the Ør's, he tried to clear his mind of all other thoughts, including what was becoming of his companions. Thinking of them in this moment could only lead to his own death, and that could not happen. He would fight with every bit of strength he had. Turning his mind instead to images of the destroyed village, of bodies and blood littering the streets, he pressed forward with a renewed strength.

A scream, so blood-curdling and shrill that Ivar couldn't tell if it came from one of the Ør or one of his companions rang out. He wanted to look, to see who had done it, but distractions were deadly and his opponent was losing patience. His attacks were heavier, fuelled by frustration and agitation. As the seconds wore on, Ivar fought back less and less, out of breath, just trying to evade blows and duck a swinging arm. When he was beginning to fear he might collapse, or that the next blow would bring him down, an arrow whispered through the air and landed in the Ør's neck. Ivar took the brief opportunity to glance at who had shot it.

Móri. But the boy was turned towards him, bow still held aloft without another arrow strung, and one of the monsters was rushing towards him. Ivar's own opponent yanked the arrow from his neck – it hadn't gone in far enough to cause true damage. Any moment he'd be after him again. Móri had only seconds left, if he didn't turn around.

"Móri!" Ivar shouted, and started to run towards him as fast as his legs could move. His cousin turned and saw the approaching Ør, but in the seconds it took for him to reach back and grab another arrow, it was too late. Ivar took quick aim and hurled his knife cleanly through the air and into the side of the monster's head, but not before the tip of its knife slashed down Móri's front, chest to belly. When Ivar's knife sank in, the beast fell forward, trapping Móri underneath.

All sound seemed to melt away, leaving only the silent beat of Ivar's heart beneath his furs. He fell to his knees and tried to pull the Ør away from his cousin's body, but it wouldn't move.

"Ivar! Get your knife!" He didn't know who shouted the words, but he stood slowly, unsteady and shaking. Warmth spread from his fingertips to his heart, then through the rest of his body.

Móri. They'd killed Móri. Móri was gone.

His teeth clenched together and his breath came quicker and quicker until a scream of rage rose from his throat, and he yanked his knife from the skull of the Ør. Holding it with both hands, he turned back to the fight, where two of the monsters remained standing. Sigvard bled from a shallow wound to his cheek and Eldór was limping, but those seemed to be the only injuries. With another shout that boiled up from the rage in his core, Ivar ran into the fight, a new strength behind every sweep of his arms.

It didn't take long. With the three men against the two Ør, and Ivar's renewed fury, they brought the beasts down within minutes. When the final one had collapsed, injured but not dead, Ivar kneeled beside it. Blood ran from its face and neck, those white eyes starkly clean against the mess. It watched him, face contorted with pain and anger, and hissed something at him in that ugly language he would never understand.

It walked like him. It spoke. It had skin and eyes and a mouth and probably a heart. But this thing wasn't human. And this thing's companion had killed Móri.

"Step aside," Sigvard said breathlessly. "I'll finish it." He strung his bow and held it up, but Ivar raised a hand.

"No. I'll do it."

He took the bow from his father and strung the arrow,

then pointed it at the monster's head. It hissed again, and said something incomprehensible.

"For Móri," Ivar whispered, before he let the arrow fly.

Chapter 20

I took Ri's lead and we sank further into the cover of the trees. The footsteps pounded on, bouncing off the tree trunks, but they weren't coming towards us. When I was satisfied that we couldn't be seen, I peered out from behind my tree and watched. Waited.

Then they came. There were four of them, walking on the same path I'd been traversing in a gangly, awkward manner, their arms swinging around as if to balance them. Thick, leathery legs carried them forward, and set into their foreheads was one large, round eye. A single eye. I'd never seen that before. Never even heard of that. But it was their size I couldn't comprehend. Despite having heard time and time again about how tall they were, seeing it with my own eyes left me at a loss for words. Even if I stacked three of myself on top of each other, I still wouldn't be able to look them in the eye. In my own mind, even knowing they were so strong and deadly, I'd always painted a rather comical picture of them, lumbering around mindlessly. But these were not comical. Nothing about them was. They were large, brutal creatures, ones who could pop my head right off its neck as if they were plucking a flower. There was nothing humorous in that.

The very thought made me raise a hand to my neck, as if to ensure my head was still attached.

They thundered on, leaving my line of sight. A few moments later, I heard a tussle in the distance, then a roaring growl, and then silence.

Sweat had gathered on my palms despite the cold, and my head swam from my shallow breathing. *Jōt. I'd just seen the jōt.* Darkness clouded the edges of my vision and I kneeled in the snow to collect myself. All of the childhood stories and whispers of the giants that roamed the mountains couldn't have prepared me for the sight of them.

I waited another few minutes before leading Ri back through the trees. This time, I stayed off the path and walked parallel to it from afar. Their footsteps were so large, three or four times the size of mine. As I walked, contemplating their size, their origin, where they lived, I dared to entertain perhaps one of my more foolish ideas. As if, after travelling all the way from the coast to mountains, alone, with almost no defined plan, anything could be more foolish.

But after seeing that bear run, dreading the approaching jōt, part of me wondered if I kept close to them – though still far enough away to not be seen – would all other life in the mountains let me be. The danger of this plan backfiring was far from lost on me, but the more I thought about it, the more sense it made. The mountains feared the jōt. I feared the jōt. But that fear, if I kept a safe distance, might work in my favour.

My hands shook, though not from the cold. An all-consuming terror had found its way into my veins and surged throughout my body. I fought to think rationally, to keep my head free from panic, but with every footfall into the snow beneath me, my dam of resolve cracked a little more.

Up ahead, I could hear their footsteps again, travelling onwards to the Goddess knows where. Their camp, probably, wherever that might be. Once they reached it, I'd have to make off on my own again, but for this brief time, hints of safety began to peek through the fear. Ri didn't feel the same way. Her ears kept twitching forward and backwards, listening, anxious.

A new sound wafted through the forest, just barely reaching my ears. I struggled to understand it at first, tilting my head to take in as much of the sound as possible. A full minute later, I realized it was notes. Song.

Gregor's words replayed in my mind, about the man who'd ventured into the mountains and heard singing that came from nowhere.

The notes stopped and started again, ebbing and flowing like the tide. I continued through the trees, listening as hard as I could over the sound of our footsteps. All other noises in the forest had vanished. No birds sang, no small animals chattered, but whether that was from the jōt passing through or the voices on the breeze, I couldn't tell.

When we crested a forested hill, I could see them below. They were still carrying on, nearing the mountains themselves, but they had a new addition. Hanging on a large stick that was carried by two of the giants hung the bear. That must have been the growl I'd heard.

The bear was so *big*. It would take a handful of grown men to lift it. *These aren't men*, I reminded myself, taking in their enormity again even from such a great distance. *Far from it*.

When they'd rounded an outcropping of rock, hiding all but the tops of their leathery heads, I dared to descend the hill. I still walked beside Ri rather than ride her. Being on my feet left me more nimble. More ready for what might come.

The notes grew louder, then faded away. Then grew louder again. I peered through trees, over rocks and into shadows, but all I found was snow. White, still snow.

Perhaps the snow itself is singing, I thought to myself. Such a lighthearted thought felt out of place here, but it cheered me a little. The only other time I'd felt cheered since leaving home was when I found Uxi outside the cave.

Which reminded me that I hadn't seen him again.

I prayed to the Goddess that he was returning home, somewhere high over the plain making for my village. Let whatever had guided me to that cave in the storm guide him to Ivar. I tried to imagine what Ivar would do, say, feel when he received it. Would it send him relief or would he still worry? Worry that perhaps I'd been killed since sending it. Worry that Uxi had been lost in the storm and the words were just echoes of my ghost.

I'm still here, I thought, squeezing my eyes shut, as if I could send the thought on the wind, across the plain, through the trees, and to Ivar's ears. If only.

When I opened my eyes, I stopped.

Set into a large indentation in a cliff face – not quite a cave, for it had no roof – was exactly what I'd imagined. Broken bones made up the floor, and at the centre was a large fire, larger than any bonfire I'd ever seen. Beside it, one giant was working to skin the bear, though it looked small in its hands. Others were erecting a spit over the fire, and others sat by doing nothing.

And between me and them, there wasn't a single tree. If one of them turned their head even the tiniest bit, surely they would see us, standing here in the open like we were waiting to be caught and skinned. I began to back away slowly, willing my feet not to crunch into the snow. Ri's head hung low, her ears back – well aware of the danger mere metres ahead.

The singing had stopped.

Ever so slowly, I encouraged Ri to walk backwards, until we'd gone around the corner and out of sight. Then I moved us both well into the trees, far enough away that they'd have to truly be looking to find us. After tying her securely to the low-hanging branch of a tree, I slipped through the trees towards the jōt camp again. I didn't need to get too close, but I'd heard so many stories, so many rumours passed from one generation to the next, that I owed it to my people to see for myself. Any knowledge I could bring back – assuming I made it back – would be new and useful.

Ahead, the outcropping where their camp was set up loomed, but I had an idea. Crossing the pathway, I moved quietly to the opposite side, where the ground sloped upwards to form the wall of the jōt's den. It was a sheer cliff face, and with Gregor's words about that man slipping into the camp playing over and over again in my mind, I made sure to stay well away from the edge. Snowy shrubs clung to the corner when the rock ended in a sheer drop, giving me just enough cover to peer down if I kept low to the ground.

They had almost finished skinning the bear, and

the spit was being removed from the fire to roast it. I couldn't help but be at least a little surprised at the sight of them. Somehow, I'd always imagined them as base, crude, lacking any manner of skill or refinement. Yet they knew how to make fires, how to use spits, how to skin an animal and preserve the meat. They were civilized in their own strange way.

On the edge of the camp, another giant, smaller than the others, used a large, rough stone to sharpen a long stick to a point. Shivering, I returned my eyes to the fire – and met the gaze of the giant skinning the bear.

She sat perfectly still, her head turned up and her eye locked on mine. She made no movement to come for me, showed no visible signs of having seen me, but I could feel her eye staring into mine so clearly. Her nose twitched a bit, and I realized with a little burst of hope that she perhaps had sensed me instead. I was surrounded by shrubs and high enough that she would have to strain to see me.

Then, slowly and deliberately, she laid aside her work and stood, eye still locked on me. One giant, heavy arm lifted into the air, a finger extended.

She was pointing at me.

I shouldn't have moved. I should have stayed motionless and waited to see if she had, but I didn't. I let out a small gasp before covering my mouth with a hand. The noise, though soft, only confirmed their suspicions. Within seconds, the camp was swarming. The bear lay forgotten on the ground, skinned and still, while the giants scrambled towards me in a frenzy. Forced to sacrifice cover for speed, I stood and turned, ready to bolt in the opposite direction as fast as my shaking legs could carry me. I tried to run, tried to force my body away, but instead I lost my footing on the slick rocks around me and plunged to the earth.

My head swiped against a stone on the way down, and before I knew it, there was only darkness.

Chapter 21

Crackling fire. Heavy grunts. The clatter of what sounded like. . .

Bones.

Long, thick bones surrounded me, tied together to form a sort of makeshift cage. They were just close enough together that I couldn't fit through the cracks, but far enough apart that I could see the rest of the camp. The bear roasted over the fire, turned every now and then by the smallest of the jōt. The high walls of the rocky den bore down, glistening in places where falling water had frozen. Sunset was fast approaching. The sky, or what little I could see of it, glowed a dark orange, offering only minimal light here on the floor of the den.

I shifted my weight, causing a raucous crunch of bones beneath me. A handful of eyes turned sharply in my direction – each one the same slate grey of the stone. One of the giants, the female who had first spotted me, stood and lumbered over, reaching out a hand to shake the cage. I froze, terrified into silence as the bones rattled in warning. Her sheer height looming over me, so close and monstrous, brought tears to my eyes. When she was satisfied that I would make no more noise, she returned to the others.

I sat perfectly still, terror prickling my skin.

This was it. I was living one of the worst possible scenarios I'd imagined, one of the many ways to die here in the mountains. This was just like what had happened to Stína's grandfather, although I wouldn't likely end up so well. He'd got free in a stroke of luck, whereas I... Well, there wasn't much hope of that.

My throat tightened and my eyes burned. I stared into the flames, imagining I was back in the village at one of the bonfires, listening to a story about a dragon made of ice or invisible house elves who would come in with snowstorms to keep the fires going. I might tell one, too, about the stars, or an adventure finding a cave with Ivar.

Ivar.

His face filled my vision, disorderly tawny hair and eyes that could smile even when his mouth didn't. I stared at him in my mind, holding the gaze of those sea-storm-blue eyes for as long as I could until the vision began to fade. The thought of never seeing that face again, never

198

again seeing the way he looked at me, like he truly saw me and everything that I was and wanted to be, was a kind of pain I wasn't built to bear.

I'd tried, and at least I could die with that certainty. I'd left the village to get help, knowing the risks. Knowing what could happen. Perhaps, though hope was small, someone else from the village would try. Perhaps Ivar would follow me to the mountains and finish what I wasn't able to. Perhaps someone else would save Skane. This treacherous and wonderful island would mean enough to someone to risk everything they had to save it.

The evening grew ever darker. I strained to look up and see my stars, but they were blotted out by the walls of the den and the smoke from the fire. Even without being able to see them, I kept staring. They were up there, somewhere, and somehow just knowing that helped to instil a peace in my heart that made thoughts of my forthcoming death a little easier to deal with.

In the distance, a wolf let out a long, lonely howl. The sound and the ensuing echoes made my skin prickle, but the giants didn't seem to take notice. Their lack of interest in such a frightening sound only worked to remind me that they were the ones to be feared, here in the mountains. I was a captive of the highest in command, of the creatures at the pinnacle of the predator chain.

At length, one of the giants deemed the bear to be finished, and they removed it from the spit. Their eating of it did not seem to be governed by any sort of order. They pulled and tore and argued until there was nothing left but bloodied bones. I forced my eyes away, nauseated by the carnage that to them was no more than a standard meal. Even without looking, the sounds were inescapable as they picked away at every last bit of meat. It took them only minutes to finish the thing, and afterwards, it was obvious that the bear hadn't been enough. They poked around at the pile of bones, grunted every now and then, and one even made a show of rubbing its belly.

If the jōt were still hungry, and the bear was gone...

I swallowed, almost forgetting how to breathe.

One of the giants turned to stare at me, a knowing gleam in its large eye. *No. Not me.* It stood and moved towards me, grunting to the others who nodded enthusiastically, rising and tripping over the bear's carcass as they made their way towards my cage. I shrank away as far from them as I could go, my back pressed against the bony confines made from the skeleton of the Goddess knows what.

"No," I said aloud, shaking my head as though it would make any difference to them. "No, no, no."

One of the giants licked their lips, and in one far too easy motion, broke apart my cage. It splintered into a hundred pieces, shards raining down on to the ground. On an impulse, I leaped up and made to run under their legs. Perhaps if I was small enough and fast enough I could outsmart and outrun them, then disappear into the night and hide in a tree until morning. I saw all of it in a flash, all of the possibilities of surviving tonight, of making it out of this damned den alive.

But a large, roughened hand closed around me before I'd made it more than a few metres. I fought against it, kicking and pushing and screaming to get free, but it was far too strong and I was far too small. I shrank into a ball and shut my eyes as the world spun around me, the fire coming ever closer.

This was how it would end. After seventeen years of daily reminders of my failures, of scorn and aversion for having inadvertently ended the life of my mother, I would die failing to save my village. Sobs shook my body and I covered my face with my arms. I didn't want to see the flames. Didn't want to see my death. If this was how it would come, let it come while I closed my eyes and thought of those I'd left behind.

Something cold brushed against my arm on the way up to my face. I sat upright in the giant's hand, as they seemed to be deliberating over something through the use of grunts and hand motions. My knife. They'd forgotten to remove my knife: it offered just enough of a distraction for me to escape.

In a swift motion, I pulled the knife from my belt and plunged it into the giant's hand. It roared in surprise and pain, and dropped me. The world blurred and spun as I fell, and when I hit the ground, all the air burst from my lungs. I fought to take in a breath, but it was as if my body had forgotten how to work. Odd gasping sounds came from my throat as I forced small bits of air back into my desperate lungs.

Overhead, silhouetted against the glow of the large bonfire, the giant whom I'd injured raised a great fist that would, any second now, come crashing down. I couldn't yet breathe enough to even roll away, so I closed my eyes so I wouldn't see the motion that would end my life. In the midst of my panic, I again thought of Ivar's face, let it hang in my mind so it would be the last thing I'd remember. The last thing I'd see. Something about seeing his face this time – the last time – awoke in me an emotion I'd never felt. A feeling I didn't recognize. Unfamiliar as it was, it flooded me with a warmth that made these last few seconds just a bit more bearable.

Silence.

All sound in the den had ceased. I opened my eyes to find the giant still standing there, fist raised to crush me, but it was looking away into the night. I could feel it listening, ears straining.

Song notes rose in the darkness, frightening and enchanting all at once.

I'd heard those notes before, while walking through the forest with Ri. It was much closer this time, hovering somewhere just outside the den. Although . . . I realized all at once that it wasn't just one voice. There were several joining together, surrounding the den. The giants began to draw nearer to one another, almost as if they were...

Frightened.

What would frighten the jōt?

Something white shot out of the dark and wrapped itself around the giant's fist. It roared in anger and clawed at the stuff, but it wouldn't move. The others began to run around frantically, covering their heads and howling so deeply it shook the earth. For a moment, I was stunned into quiet stillness. None of the events going on around me seemed to make sense, and yet, in the background of my shock, I knew I didn't have the time to understand it. I leaped to my feet and searched for the exit to the den.

The notes had stopped, but without waiting to see if the giants were collecting themselves, I bolted for the opening. Thundering footsteps followed me, but I didn't turn to look. I willed my legs to move faster than they'd ever moved before. I ran and ran and ran, yet the footsteps behind me only grew closer and louder. If I could just get into those trees and surround myself with darkness, I could disappear.

So close. So close.

Something yanked my arm, pulling me sideways into a snowbank.

Then all was silent.

Chapter 22

It was Ivar's turn on the watch. They'd established it after the heads came back in the boat, for it undoubtedly meant the Ør were out there, waiting somewhere offshore. Waiting for what, though? Other ships to arrive? Weapons to finish being made? The wives' cries could still be heard when Ivar passed by their houses. Albrekt's wife had been one of the women on the beach when the boat had washed ashore. What she must be feeling, after seeing her husband's severed head tied to a boat, Ivar couldn't begin to imagine. Trying to understand such a pain that wasn't his felt as though it were bordering on disrespectful.

And then there was Móri. Sigvard had offered to be the one to tell his mother and father, but Ivar had done it, instead. Perhaps out of a sense of duty, perhaps out of guilt. It was difficult to tell. Ever since they'd returned from the fight, his heart felt so heavy it might stop working altogether. His throat constricted every time he saw the boy's face in his mind. At night he had nightmares where he saw it happen all over again. He tried to sleep as little as possible, but had to succumb eventually.

Fresh snow lay on the rocks around him, and though he tried to keep from thinking of it, it was everywhere he looked. When the storm swept in, Ósa would have still been on the plain, about halfway across, if she'd been making good time. There was no cover out there, Gregor had said. Nowhere to seek shelter. Though he'd worked to fight through all manner of hopelessness and disapproval about her choice to go, since the storm, even he'd lost hope. In a way, giving up felt like sentencing her, like condemning her to die out there alone, frozen. But perhaps it had already happened. Perhaps this very moment, Ósa no longer drew breath.

That meant so much. It meant he'd lost his closest friend, his companion since childhood. The only person in Skane whom he could picture as a companion for the rest of his life. He could keep up his appearance, look hopeful for those around him, but his heart had given up. Hoping felt foolish. Soon, these waves would continue to crash, this sun would continue to rise, and his people would no longer be here. What would it look like when they'd gone? How changed would this landscape be? The Ør would set up their kind here, build whatever homes they lived in, hunt whatever food they ate, and spread their brutal existence around the whole of this cursed island.

The sun was about to set. The ocean was cast in a dull, deep blue colour, and far in the distance, the first star sparked into view. After the first, more and more seemed to follow its example, springing to life in the growing darkness. No sails, yet. Just sea and sky and stars. Right now, it was still beautiful, still as he'd always known it.

"That star," Ósa would say of the first one. *"That belongs to the knife of the Warrior."* She was always talking about the stars, ever since she was a child. He'd asked her why, asked her many times where her fascination with them came from, and she always had a different answer.

"Because I don't know what they are."

"Because they tell a story, and one we can never know the beginning or the end of."

"Because they symbolize that, even when the world is shrouded in darkness, there can still be light."

He picked up a handful of snow and let it fall back on to the rock. *There can still be light.*

It felt almost cruel to think the words, cruel to think of continuing this fight without her, after everything she'd given for it. Everything she'd sacrificed. But it would be wrong and unfair to give up on it now. To make her death be in vain. Even without Ósa, there could still be light in Skane. They could follow her example, stand up and give their all.

He stood and threw a fistful of the snow out into the water. "You won't have died for nothing," he whispered, and the wind carried his words away. It blew to the northwest, and he turned to stare in that direction, wishing the wind could carry his words all the way to wherever her body lay and whisper them in her ear.

Something overhead, a shadow, made him look up. A bird was circling down, down, down, towards him.

Uxi.

It was that owl she'd loved so dearly. She'd mothered it for ages, feeding it and mending its wounds just because it was in her nature. He'd told her it was foolish, that the poor thing would die anyway, but that was the thing about Ósa, as her journey was evidence of: she did things others thought were irrational or reckless. She did them, and most often, she succeeded, managing to somehow still retain her gentleness and grace. The owl had survived, and now it followed her around like a shadow. Surely it had followed her on her journey. So why was it here?

It landed on a dead shrub stuck between two rocks, something tied to its ankle. His heart pounded as he slowly reached for it, afraid to chase it away. The owl didn't move, only stared at him with wide, round eyes. He carefully untied the string and unfolded the scrap of paper.

I have reached the mountains.

He fell backwards on to the rock, tears welling in his eyes. Blind happiness soon gave way to a million different thoughts. She'd made it. Against all odds, she'd reached those damned mountains on her own. And with her, she'd carried the hope and future of Skane, all the way across the plain. She'd proved the villagers wrong. Proved that she could do what others thought was impossible. And despite the dark events of the past few days, despite the red lights and the Ør and Ósa's father sending her off alone, Ivar smiled. There was something about her, a fire, a will to survive that could not easily be quenched. Eldór was cold, harsh, always preparing her for survival. And now, at last, seventeen years as his daughter had paid off.

He folded the paper and tucked it gently into his pocket, but when he returned his eyes to the horizon, his movements froze.

Set against the darkening sky was the sight they'd all be waiting for, all been dreading and anticipating and imagining since learning about what was to come.

Sails. So many sails, spreading from left to right, as far as the eye could see. More sails than there were villagers in the whole of Skane. With Ósa rested hope, life, a chance at a future. And with those sails came torture, death, and the beginning of the end.

Chapter 23

I counted in my mind, buried with no way to tell up from down.

One, two, three, four, five.

All was silent.

Nothing was coming for us.

Six, seven, eight, nine, ten.

Stillness.

When I'd reached twenty, I dared to move. Pulling myself in the direction I could best guess was upward, my head emerged from the snowbank. Someone sat beside me, their head cocked unnaturally, staring at me.

Dressed entirely in snug white clothing, a mask of white wraps covering their face that thinned around the eyes but still made them only faintly visible, they almost completely blended into the snow.

They didn't move. I couldn't even detect their chest rising and falling with breath.

My first instinct was to move, to run, but there were giants nearby, and this ... person, this creature, had pulled me to safety. Shouldn't that be a sign of friendliness? My heart wanted to say yes, but my mind whispered no. The creature sat there, so unmoving and seemingly not alive. I noticed Ri, then, standing untied a little way away.

"Who are you?" I whispered the words, terrified to let the jōt hear me yet too curious not to.

The figure didn't answer, but tilted its head even more. I couldn't see eyes, yet I could feel their stare. In all the stories of the mountains, I'd never heard of *people* residing here. Never heard stories of life beyond the jōt and the bears and wolves and predators. But this thing in white was distinctly human-shaped, with arms and legs and a head like my own.

I repeated my question. "Who are you?"

A sound came from the figure's face, then, one that both curdled my blood and triggered familiarity. It was singing, the same singing I'd heard through the trees. I couldn't see a mouth, and its head didn't move, but the sound came from it, I was certain. Slowly, it stood, rising above me. Movement around us caught my attention. I turned to look, and my mouth fell open.

There were more of them, at least ten, all singing and

210

rising out of the snow, undaunted by the near presence of the jōt.

In a way, I'd been right, I thought. The snow had been singing.

I stood as well, almost entirely surrounded. For a moment, we all stood silently, staring at one another. Save for slight variations in height and a difference in the chest where I could differentiate men and the women, they were all identical. White wraps from head to toe, slender bodies, tilted heads. In a way, they reminded me of curious children, trying to understand something they'd never seen.

"Who are you?" I asked again, on edge.

"Who are you?" the one before me asked, voice low, accent thick in a way I'd never heard before.

I swallowed and looked around at all of the faceless people staring at me, awaiting my reply. "Ósa," I whispered, though my name would mean nothing to them. "I've come from the south, by the sea."

They looked at one another in silence for a moment, then the one closest to me asked, "Why have you come?"

I brushed hair from my face, shivering and pulsing with an anxiety I'd never felt before. "I've come in search of the Goddess," I said finally. "I know I can speak to Her in the mountains."

"You seek our Goddess's council," said another, to my left.

"I do," I said, sparking with hope. They knew of Her. They understood why I was here. That had to be a good start. "Could you set me in the right direction?"

There was a long, silent pause, all gazes still trained on me. I shifted uncomfortably, crumbling under those invisible stares. A breeze whispered through the nearby trees, but all wildlife had ceased its noise. The forest felt dead. Silenced.

"You will walk with us," said the person closest to me. Perhaps it was a gesture of help, but the command, leaving no room for a decision on my part, added to my growing discomfort.

"Will you lead me there?" I asked, without making an effort to move. It could prove helpful, following people who knew the mountains, knew what trails to avoid and perhaps even knew how to reach the peak. I'd already managed to get tangled up with a bear and a den of giants. These people could lead me, and I couldn't take their lack of friendliness as a sign of danger. They had, after all, pulled me to safety.

They ignored my question and began to close in tighter around me, shuffling as a group towards the mountain peaks.

I reached for Ri, who stood up to her shoulders in snow, but the person leaped between us. He held his hand out, fingers stretched towards the sky. *Stop.*

"That's my horse," I whispered, motioning to her. "I must bring her."

He repeated the movement with his hand, repeating the same notes to me. Then he turned to Ri and began removing her packs and reins.

"No!" I said as loudly as I dared. "Those are my things!"

Again, a hand told me to stop. Fighting back felt futile. There were too many of them, and if I simply turned around and left, I'd risk another run-in with the jōt. I watched helplessly as they took my packs, slinging them over their shoulders, and tossed the reins aside. They sank into the snow, disappearing.

"I need her," I said softly, feeling my eyes burning.

Ignoring my pleas, the creature laid a palm on Ri's forehead and began to sing. The notes were soft, calming, and her eyes were alert. I'd have sworn on my life that she was listening. Then, without looking back at me, she turned and left me, down the mountain in the direction we'd come.

I reached a shaking hand out to her as if it would make her stop, but I couldn't bring myself to speak. Ri was my familiarity here, my life rope, my only way home. I'd known in the back of my mind that I couldn't bring her all the way into the mountains, but I'd hoped I could stash her in a cave somewhere, with enough food and water to last until I could return. Without her, I'd never make it back across the plain. I'd never make it home, even if I survived. Out of all the ways I'd imagined this journey failing, this had never been one of them.

"No," I whispered, as a sob escaped my throat. If she defied the odds and made the journey home, that would destroy my village. Destroy Ivar. She would turn up without me, without any of my things, and they'd give up hope. Hope was all they had left. My father, though. He would tighten his jaw and shake his head. *It was foolish from the very start*, he would say. I wanted to slap him, slap that imaginary face that hung before me. *She knew what she was getting herself into*, my sister would say. I gritted my teeth.

I turned back, and through tearful eyes, found a hand outstretched to me. It didn't matter any more. I wouldn't get far on my own, not without a horse. I had no choice but to go with them and stay alive in the mountains long enough to reach the peak, even if I never made it back. Taking the hand offered to me, we moved forward towards the Goddess and possible salvation.

As the hours passed I began to grow accustomed to my new companions. A few kilometres beyond where Ri had abandoned us, one of them impatiently stopped me in my stride. She was much shorter than the one who had first taken me by the hand and seemed to be gesturing quite intently at my legs. I had been walking along a ridge of exposed rock, and it had certainly been making the walk easier to be on hard ground rather than snow. She had gently wrapped her gloved hands around my ankle, and by tugging at my leg repositioned my feet into the snow. I'd glared at her and started to climb back on to the rock, but before I could do so she had leaned over and tapped lightly with her fist on the rock, echoing out some high-pitched notes to accompany it. She then tapped on the snow, singing lower notes.

She repeated this a few times until understanding dawned across my face. The crunching of the snow was louder than footfalls on the rock, but my footsteps had a sharper tone when not muffled by snow. As I saw the rest of the group fanning across the hillside I noticed how I could only hear the very nearest members; the sound of snow didn't echo in the same way a tap on a rock might. This must have been how I'd heard the singing, but never the footsteps. Near our villages, where trees rustled, birds sang and rivers ran, you'd never notice. But up here where the wind alone prevailed, a very different set of priorities took hold. You can't be eaten if they can't find you; you can't be found if they can't hear you.

From then on, I worked to make my footsteps mimic theirs, stepping lightly into the snow, keeping my knees ever so slightly bent to allow for softer steps. They clung to shadows, to rock faces and what few tree trunks we passed the higher we climbed. There was a strange sort of release in my going with them, in walking with strangers in a foreign land, no other defined destination save for somewhere in the mountain peaks.

One of the snow people, as I'd decided to call them in the safety of my own mind, who'd been walking at the front of the group stopped suddenly and let out a single, low note. The others froze, absolute silence following. Then a rumble. Then a thud. One I recognized. Approaching jōt!

As if it had been rehearsed a hundred times before without fault, they all vanished. Some folded into crevices in the rock face, others lost themselves in snowdrifts, and still others seem to disappear over the ravine, perhaps holding on to the edge. The drop couldn't be less than a couple of hundred metres down to darkness shrouded in mist. The short one who'd been instructing my steps motioned me to a snowbank where others had hidden themselves. She pushed me in first, gently but firmly, and used the white of her clothing to cover me.

We'd just barely disappeared from sight when, through the hole we'd made in the snow, the enormous form of a giant came into view. In one hand it bore a large stick and in the other a string of small animals: rabbits, foxes, unfamiliar birds. An addition to the roasted bear, no doubt. His single eye roved, searching. Could he sense us? Smell us? The way he moved, the way he looked about, said he was on alert, that he knew something lurked nearby. But on he walked, rattling the very ground around us, and we didn't move until his footsteps had vanished somewhere further down the mountain.

Strange to think, I realized, as everyone crept out of their hiding places, how many of these snow people I might have passed before encountering them directly. They were so agile, so adept at hiding, I could have stepped over one and never been the wiser.

When all the others had gathered, climbed back over the edge of the ravine and out of the crevices in the rock, we pressed onwards. Occasionally, they sang to one another as they went and I worked to differentiate the sounds. Always, they spoke in song. Never a single, lonely word left their mouths.

Night fell swiftly in the mountains, where there were already so many shadows and dark places that the light never reached anyway. The last of the clouds left over from last night's storm were swept away and my beloved stars were visible overhead. Sometimes it was only in snatches, between the high rock faces and trees that clung precariously to the sides of the mountains, but each one I saw warmed my heart, a tiny bit of warmth in the cold.

Finally, there, silhouetted against the sky, I saw what I'd come in search of. The boldest, highest peak of the Kalls looming over us, so close, yet still so far. It made the others look weak, small, and here in the shadow of it, I felt almost non-existent. I couldn't see an access point, couldn't see any way to reach it on foot, but night hid many things. Perhaps when dawn broke, it would reveal something new. Seeing it, tall and powerful and watching, my lungs filled with a breath of relief. Despite what happened from now on, I'd made it this far. I'd reached it.

My companions also paused in their steps, some eyeing me as I stood staring, and some turning to look up to the peak as well.

A few moved in closer, and again the feeling of being surrounded pressed against me.

My legs ached beyond reason. I longed to stop for a rest, even if only for a few moments, but my companions were so uninhibited by the journey that I was afraid to look so fragile.

We'd been on this seemingly carved-out pathway clinging to the side of this mountain for what felt like hours. The waxing moon climbed ever higher in the sky and I was just contemplating giving up, letting my legs give out and falling to the inviting ground beneath me, when I saw more of the snow people up ahead. The group I'd travelled with sang out notes to them, and one raised an arm in my direction, as if alerting them to my presence.

We approached the newcomers, the two groups singing to one other, carrying on the most absurd, enchanting conversation I'd ever witnessed. I wanted to add my voice, wanted to know what those captivating words meant, but it was wholly unintelligible. Unlike any language I knew of that had ever existed in Skane.

How Ivar would love to hear them.

As if the two new folk were satisfied with the answers they'd received, they pushed the large stone to the side, opening up a sort of narrow tunnel lit by sconces hanging every metre or so, until it twisted away and I couldn't see any further. A breeze blew out of it, caressing my face, both inviting me in and pushing me away. When one of my guides held out an arm, beckoning for me to follow, I glanced about me, taking in the mountains and the stars again. I didn't know what was inside or what would happen once I entered, but running would get me nowhere. I was so vastly outnumbered, so far from my own element up here that I'd fail this mission before I rounded the next corner.

Swallowing all hints of fear and uncertainty, I entered the tunnel.

Chapter 24

Some time before midnight, Ivar made the trek from the coast to the village to take a small break from his watch. The sails hadn't moved after appearing, hadn't changed. No smaller boats had been seen, sending forward an onslaught of the Ør, but word of their arrival had spread quickly. It wouldn't be long now. Any moment they could come ashore, and there was no further sign of hope coming from Ósa, after Uxi had delivered her note. It had been a long shot, but in such a dark time, he'd wanted to hold on to it.

In the village, there was movement. Surprised, as he'd expected everyone to be locked indoors, on their knees praying to the Goddess for salvation, he quickened his step. There was a man he only vaguely recognized and a woman who must have been his wife, pushing a wooden cart piled with goods through the snow. They started at seeing him, then whispered amongst themselves.

"Where are you off to?" Ivar asked, prickling.

They paused before answering. "You're not a leader," the man said at last. "You can't stop us."

He didn't have to explain any more. There was another family with another cart, approaching not far off. They were leaving. They were running away, now that the sails were here. All of these preparations, these words, this talk of the impending attack were easy enough, so long as they remained only that. So long as they stayed in a strange limbo where they never actually came to be. But now that it was here, now that it was time to stand up and fight, they couldn't face it.

"You can't leave," Ivar said, as unthreateningly as he could. He managed to keep his voice deadly calm. "We need everybody we can find."

"You're young and alone. You don't have a family, a wife, a baby." The man pointed to the bundle in the woman's arms. "If you did, you wouldn't sit by and wait to be slaughtered."

"But you don't understand," Ivar pleaded. "Leaving the village won't save you. They will track you. They will hunt you into the ground and kill you so far from our safety in numbers. We must remain together."

The man shook his head. "We'd rather take our chances on the road than wait. I can't look at those damned sails for another minute. I'm doing what I think is best for my family."

"As am I," said the second man.

"But I've had word from Ósa," Ivar said, pulling the note from his pocket. "She sent a message saying she's reached the mountains. She's there. She's there getting us help."

"She may have reached the mountains," the first man said, "but that doesn't mean she's still alive and you know it. Don't be such a fool. Moreover, some can't help but wonder if this . . . scheme of hers was a way to run, much as we are about to now. Disguise her as our saving grace all you want, but we're here and she's far away. Now we are leaving. May the Goddess have mercy on your souls."

Ivar could do nothing as his pulse thundered in his ears, his veins. He just stood helplessly as they continued on down the road and disappeared into the night.

A few metres from his house, he passed a door from which familiar voices wafted. His father and Leiv, their village's oldest rune singer. Leiv had taught Sigvard, and Sigvard had taught Ivar.

Ivar rapped softly on the door, then pushed it open at a call from within. Smoke and drying fish engulfed his senses as he closed the door behind him. The two men sat at a table, cups and half-eaten food before them. Despite the late hour, sleep wasn't likely for most of the village. Not after what had appeared on the horizon.

"Come on over, boy," Leiv said, waving an arm towards their table. "We're all desperate for friendly faces at this hour, no?"

Ivar nodded and spun a chair around to straddle it, resting his chin on the back. "No changes out there, yet," he reported, staring at the table. "Villagers are leaving."

The men leaned forward, suddenly tense. "What do you mean *leaving*?" Leiv asked.

"A handful of them, they're on their way to who knows where. Said they can't wait around for their deaths."

Leiv and Sigvard made to jump up, but Ivar raised a hand to stop them. "There is no use," he said. "I tried to convince them to stay. They will have none of it. We can't keep them prisoner here."

Sigvard rubbed his eyes. "We don't need cowards on the battlefield, anyway."

A moment of silence.

"No change in the sails, you say?" Leiv said. "No doubt they want to give us time to raise chaos and fear amongst our people. Then we'll be at our weakest."

"That's the truth," Sigvard put in, shaking his head. "We've just been speaking about what can be done once the ... once the invasion starts." He cleared his throat and tapped his fist lightly on the table. "Going over what we know from the runes."

"Aye," Leiv said, pulling a scroll from the end of the table. It held more curl than most Ivar had seen; it was rarely opened. "We've been working to make heads or tails of this one. This was one of the oldest rune findings thus far," Leiv said. "If not the oldest. It was written just after the Löskans' arrival on these shores. They were smart, almost desperate to document their story, so they picked a medium that would last the longest. Cave writing. I translated it with my father some twenty years ago now, but the ill-written runes were so hasty and scattered that we never found it to be particularly relevant to our day to daily lives. So we set it aside, and here it is now."

Ivar stared at it, the words jumping out to him even from upside down. Seeming to notice his attempt to read it, Leiv picked it up.

"You won't be liking what you find here," he said softly. "Not with what's coming."

"Never mind that, Leiv," Sigvard said with a dismissive wave of his hand. "He's a grown man now, not my little boy any more. If he's man enough to face a fight with the Ør, he's man enough to know what it says."

"Just tell me what I need to know," Ivar said, swallowing a lump in his throat.

Leiv laid the document on the table and glanced over it, perhaps skimming for the more suitable bits. This time, Ivar didn't try to read it. He kept his eyes on the man's face, bracing himself. After his run-in with the Ør scouts in the woods, he was almost certain that nothing about them could surprise him. Their appearance, their actions, those damned screams during the fight, none of those details had been written about.

Leiv scratched his head and looked away. "There were thousands of people in Löska when it was overrun. No one saw it coming." He shook his head. "But you already know that. What you might not know was what the unfortunate ones who didn't escape went through. Sometimes people got lucky; the Ør's barbarous nature meant many died swiftly, by a blade or a broken neck. But ... but not all were dead when the fighting was over, when the brutes came to collect their teeth, their skin. And they didn't bother killing them before they started."

Ivar shut his eyes, violent images dancing in his mind. Unthinkable. All of it was unthinkable. What would the villagers do, think, if they heard this? Many of them knew bits and pieces of it, knew about the skins and teeth and the fall of Löska, but no one, to his knowledge, knew of the victims being alive. That was different.

Goddess go with you, Ósa, Ivar thought, silently praying for her to return.

A cry from outside made everyone jump. Ivar flew to his feet, his chair knocking loudly against the table before him, and ran to the door. Only one thought prevailed in his mind: the Ør were coming ashore. The time had at last come.

As the three of them hurried outside, their eyes to the coast, Ivar became immediately aware that the cries were coming from the trees on the edge of the village. Turning, he ran through the streets, following the sounds of the voices as others emerged nervously from their homes.

Two or three people were gathered around a tree, their hands shakily covering their faces as they cried out.

A man dangled from a branch, a rope around his neck. His head tilted unnaturally to the right, broken. He still swung gently, like he'd still been breathing mere minutes ago. Tied to his boot was a note, which Ivar unfolded.

Take your own life before they take it for you.

Chapter 25

I followed my companions along the tunnel, watching as they passed in and out of the shadows of the candles, sometimes glowing, sometimes disappearing. On and on we went, and as pressure seemed to build in my ears, as my sense of direction all but left me, I could *feel* us travelling deep into the mountain. How ancient was this place? How old was this stone? Surely it had seen the very dawn of time itself, had watched Skane transform into the land it was now.

And surely it would watch us fall, watch us die one by one, if I failed.

It was a constant battle in my mind, of trying to focus on the present and my circumstances in the moment while thoughts of the plague and the Ør and the red lights forced their way in.

On and on. Around corners, sometimes up, sometimes down, but always forward. The others seemed undaunted by the walk, as though they'd done this so many times before.

My hope died a little more with each step, until, at long last, light appeared ahead that wasn't cast by a sconce. I willed my feet quicker, willed my body out of this wretched, never-ending tunnel, and finally, out I stepped.

A chorus of voices met me as I emerged from the darkness and into a vast, stone atrium. Walls stood all around us, so tall I could barely see the roof. It sloped inwards, upwards, a cathedral carved from stone. Up the walls, levels appeared to have been carved out, with balconies and rooms and terraces occupied by more people – all like my companions – than I'd ever seen in one place at one time. They all wore white, all looked identical to one another, and they all sang. Hundreds of voices melded together to create one large, enthralling voice that filled the giant room. Hundreds of lanterns made of stone hung from the balconies and walls, illuminating the room as if it were daytime. To the left, there seemed to be a sort of makeshift market, tables laid with an array of goods – meat, skins, leathers, baskets of winter berries, *bones* – and those gathered around appeared to be trading. It was a whole world in the centre of the mountain, a life, a culture I'd never known existed.

Against the wall opposite the tunnel from where we'd

come, sat a throne, made from the largest bones I've ever seen. On it was another individual, on whose head sat two horns, carved from what looked like the same bone as the throne. Tied around his shoulders was a cloak of the purest, whitest fur I'd ever seen.

One of my companions motioned me forward, towards the throne, and I followed. Those nearby stopped their work to watch me pass. Everything about me, my manner of dress, of walking, my exposed face, was new. They stared, turning slowly to keep watching until I'd passed. Had they ever seen anyone like me before?

When we were before the throne, those who'd brought me kneeled in front of the man seated there. I looked around, unsure of whether or not to do the same. This was no king of mine, no ruler, and kneeling before him had implications, had meaning.

Submission.

Slowly, those who'd kneeled turned their heads to look at me, waiting.

I fought against it, delayed as long as I could. And yet, standing here in the heart of a mountain, on ground I didn't know, with seemingly only one way in and out, which was guarded, I had little choice. Drawing in a breath, I turned my eyes to the ground, and I kneeled before the strange king on the throne of bones. In the edges of my vision, I saw the others look away from me, satisfied with my action, and I saw the king rise.

The voices in the large chamber died, trickling away into nothingness until silence reigned. I raised my eyes to the figure before me. I couldn't see his eyes, or any other features on his face, but I knew he was staring at me.

Notes came from his mouth, and they were unlike the others. Deep and resonating and profoundly beautiful. They continued on for a minute or so, and when he stopped, there was silence again, as though he were waiting for me to respond.

"I ... I only speak Agric."

My heartbeats were all I could hear. He turned his head, turned that mysterious white face crowned with horns, and looked to my companions. The one closest to my right sang out a handful of notes, something I couldn't understand, before he returned his attention to me.

"You have come from the south," he said, his voice deep and strong.

I nodded.

"What do you seek from us?"

I made to rise, but the others were still on their knees. "I seek the Goddess," I explained, stone digging into my knees. "My people are desperate. I've come to seek Her council."

He lifted his head, as if understanding had dawned on him, and made a hand motion for us to rise. I stood quickly, my legs giving complaint. I didn't know what to expect once we stood, but when he reached out a hand for me to take, I hesitated. He was a king, of sorts, that much was certain. We didn't have kings in our villages. That sort of power led to corruption and misery, so I didn't know how they behaved, or how I was meant to behave around them. Taking his hand felt wrong, unbalanced, in some way. Yet I took it, because I didn't know what else to do.

There was a power in his touch. Like the lightning that came with storms in the warmer months, his touch was electric.

Turning, my hand still in his, we walked towards a long, carved staircase I hadn't noticed until now, but one that seemed to wind up the entire length of the atrium and disappear somewhere high overhead. There was no railing on this stair, and the higher we climbed, up, up, up this strange room, the more my head began to swim. Still he held my hand, strong and steady and unrelenting. The voices below seemed to come alive again, a chorus of notes that bounced off the walls, echoed through the room and reached my ears multiple times, each more beautiful than the last. Would that I could sing like them, that I could add my voice to theirs, and hear it bounce back to me like it came from the mouth of the Goddess Herself.

As we reached the top stair, an open doorway met us, through which the cool night air blew in. It was rounded, detailed stone art carved around the edge. And when we passed through it, I found myself on a sort of balcony, overlooking the mountains below. Wind met my face, and at such a height, I was certain I could reach out and touch the stars.

As if reading my thoughts, he swept a hand up to the sky, singing a soft note. "The Goddess," he said a moment later. "The queen of the island, the protector of our mountains. It is to Her that we have dedicated our life, our very existence. We draw breath in the mornings for Her, and at night, it is to Her that we sing our final prayers."

I shifted from one foot to the other, moving my gaze from the king to the sky.

"She gives us life, breath, and She has power over the sky."

"When you see the red lights, does something happen here, too?" The question leaped out, my curiosity eager to be satisfied.

He nodded. "Last time, there was an illness. We lost a hundred."

It made sense. The curse of the red lights didn't just hurt our villages, it hurt the whole island.

"She could stop it, perhaps, but She sees fit not to. We've asked, more than once, but She only speaks to those with whom She wishes to speak."

Disappointment tore through me. The writing in the cave hadn't promised that I could speak to Her, but I'd somehow let myself believe that it was a certainty. That somehow, despite my insignificance in Skane, she'd take pity on me and hear my cries. That my voice would matter.

"I must speak to Her," I whispered, staring up at the constellation. "I've come all this way. I have to." *Help us,* I would say, would pour all of my energy into. *Help us fight. Help us know what to do. Don't let them die.*

She shone on, seemingly unaware of my thoughts. But I couldn't help imagining the stars that formed Her mouth curving into a comforting, gentle smile. *All will be well,* it would say. If only. I couldn't remember what it was like to feel comforted as I stood there, barely able to communicate with those around me, racing against time to save my people, but helpless to speed up my return.

The king stared at me. "No one speaks to Her," he said after a moment, and any traces of warmth had vanished from his voice.

"I found writing, near my home. Someone has spoken to Her before. I have to. We cannot lose so many people again. It will destroy us."

A moment of silence. "No one speaks to Her."

I turned slowly to face him, and though unable to see his eyes, stared into his face for a long moment. "Why not?"

"It has long been our duty to protect Her from prying eyes, to shield Her from the many voices who seek Her council. We are charged with guarding Her temple, and honest as your intentions may be, we must also protect

Her from you."

I all but forgot how to breathe. "No," I said. I tried to shake my head but it wouldn't budge. "I will reach Her."

What sounded like a gentle laugh came from his face. "Generation after generation has sought Her council," he said, shaking his head. "Most don't make it this far, but those who have were stopped. To our knowledge, none have reached Her temple, and none ever shall. You will not be an exception."

I clenched my fists so hard the bones could have shattered. "You will not stop me reaching her," I whispered, and then found my voice. "I've faced creatures far bigger than you on this journey and I'm still on my feet."

"Courage is only admirable to the point that it collides with foolishness," he said. "This is simply foolishness. We have guarded Her temple for hundreds of years, and if we do not want someone to reach Her, they will never reach Her."

All traces of warmth and feelings of safety fled my body on the cold breeze. We stood still, me stunned to silence and he awaiting my response. I tried to form words, but my mind was a cauldron of boiling anger and denial. A broken word escaped my throat in a stutter, crumbling away the moment it touched the air. This was it: the end of the road that started all the way back in Neska, that started with Ivar and Father and Anneka and everything and everyone I loved. All that cold and horror and seemingly certain death to be turned away at Her doorstep.

Through the bubbling and simmering in my mind, words finally began to take shape. Words born of anger, passion and an unwillingness to let this be the end of the road. To let this be the answer. One after another, words surged up from my core, riding a wave of fury and fire so that it was all that I could do to keep it under control. *I did battle with an Ør and came out alive. I survived the stormy plain after dark. I'm a child of the snow and wind, daughter of an island where the sky speaks, where red lights portend the end but we are forced into obedient silence. I had sea legs before I could fully walk and learned to love the stars when love at home was foreign. I am nothing if not a survivor and I will reach the Goddess if I do so with my dying breath.*

But.

There were other words, quieter ones from another part of me that whispered, *You are at their mercy. You are deep in the mountains, beside a king whose throne is carved from bones. You are vastly outnumbered. You will bend to their will.*

I gave one slow nod, shaking from anger and frustration, but he didn't move. Didn't reply. He stood there, still staring at me through his wraps.

"I can see the fire in you," he said presently, and while his voice was heavy with power, it was also tinged with admiration. "Something within you burns bright, but here in my kingdom, that will get you nowhere. We will not treat you as a prisoner if you do not give us a reason to do so."

I couldn't tell if it was an honest proposition or a subtle threat, but either way, I nodded again. I understood their might and power and my smallness in comparison. There was little I could do here, at their mercy in the mountains – little, but not nothing, and I planned to find out just what that little something might be, as soon as all eyes were no longer trained on me.

After our meeting, they took one more opportunity to show me just how far their power went.

A small part of me hoped I wasn't being taken to a cell as I followed them across the large room and to the marketplace I'd noticed earlier. We crossed the large room and exited through a doorway, which opened on to a narrow staircase. It led deeper into the mountain and was barely lit, save for a candle that one of the guides carried before us. I stayed close behind, straining to see the steps in the near darkness, until at long last we reached the bottom, and another doorway. This one was closed, and the guide in the front knocked on it a handful of times, singing a few low notes. The one nearest to me turned and touched a finger to his mouth, again bidding me to be silent.

The door gently opened, a guard on the other side

beckoning us through. She started at the sight of me, but the others quickly put her at ease through a brief, gentle song. When she was satisfied, she motioned for me to come through. As soon as I was, I shrank against the wall, wishing to be back out again.

A series of narrow tunnels that ran from somewhere outside the mountain opened up overhead, covered with a crosshatching of wooden bars that were far enough apart to let in the moonlight. In addition, there were a few lanterns placed here and there along the walls, but the large room was generally quite dim. Running along the centre were giant wooden structures, raised off the ground – enough for a person to pass under freely – forming rounded wooden shapes overhead. On the rounded structures were what could only be spider webs, and I looked in horror at the large, fox-sized spiders that rested in the corners of each one. They went on for ever, disappearing out of sight somewhere further down the room. One of the spiders moved, changing its position slightly, a disturbing, sticky noise coming from where its feet moved about on the web.

I could hardly breathe, hardly force my lungs to fill with air.

Three guards emerged from another door, singing softly to each other. They stopped and stared at me for a moment, then continued on towards the webs. Each of them carried a large wooden bucket filled with something that *moved*. They took them to the left side of the room and dumped the contents out in unison. Large bugs with a hundred legs that all writhed and crawled and tried to escape.

But not before the spiders caught sight of them. Slowly, with that sickening sound of stickiness, they made their way from their webs and towards their prey the floor, their too-large legs spreading out across the floor. Bile rose in my throat as I tried to push my body into the wall. Further down the room, other guards were also depositing buckets of crawling creatures, and more and more spiders were leaving their webs to congregate at the new feeding ground. Once they'd left, the guards moved to the wooden structures and began cutting down the webs with knives. Somehow, the strings didn't stick to their gloves. They just passed over it like it was any other kind of rope, like the kind my father used on his ship.

A soft note pulled my attention away and I was beckoned back to the doorway. I hurried through it, thankful when it closed behind me.

Why? I was desperate to ask. *Why are you farming spider webs?*

The shadowed image of their large, bulky bodies and the sound of their feet sticking to the webs haunted me on the long walk out of the belly of the mountain.

Chapter 26

I was given a small stone room to rest in, though the guard waiting outside gave it the distinct feeling of a cell. I paced for the first hour or so, alive with frustration but my mind slow with exhaustion. Eventually I must have found my way to the mat in the corner, because I awoke with a headache and a heavy heart.

My village, I thought, as soon as my eyes opened. *What's happening in my village?* The question had been haunting me, no matter how hard I tried to push it aside. Worrying would get me nowhere, yet it always managed to spring back, often stronger than before.

Had the Ør come from the sea and bore down on my people yet? Were any of them still alive, still breathing? Had the fever swept through them yet? The last time, it had taken days for the plague to arrive. Mere days.

I moved to the doorway and peered out. The guard shifted uncomfortably, perhaps worried that I'd try to leave and he'd have to stop me. I'd been brought here with little to no explanation other than that the king would summon me when he was ready. Ready to what? To execute me? To set me free? Were we friends or enemies? I didn't understand these people and they did not seem keen on remedying that fact.

"Are they going to kill me?" I asked suddenly. The guard turned his head my way.

"I don't know," he answered, and something in the way he said it told me it was honest. The king seemed to only keep certain guards in his immediate confidence, so this one likely knew very little. But if he couldn't tell me that, perhaps I could at least glean some other information from him.

"The Goddess," I said softly, in case my voice bounced off the stone. "You worship Her and guard Her peak, but why? Why not let anyone reach Her?" I sat on the cold floor and hugged my knees, back against the wall.

The guard was silent, and at first I thought he wouldn't respond, but his soft voice reached me a few moments later.

"We were some of the first to reach these shores," he said, his voice just barely audible over the hum of sound below us. "This land was nearly empty, untouched." He fell quiet.

"Nearly," I repeated, seeking an explanation.

"The jōt were here, and the animals. My ancestors, they saw Her stars, saw the way they never moved in the sky, even when all the other stars did, and they knew it meant something. The mountain, Her temple, all of that was already here, whether forged by Her own hand or peoples far more ancient than us. But we found it, and we protected it, even if ... even if it meant killing those who sought entrance."

My head spun at his words, at the thought of their being here long before my people had crossed over from Löska. All these years, all these generations, we thought we'd been alone. We'd imagined ourselves as the only humans on this island, staking out an existence in a land that was never truly our own.

"But She was here long before you," I said, resting my head against the wall. "She's been in existence far longer than any of us. Why" – I chose my words very carefully – "why did you start to guard Her temple? What gave you..." *The right.* "What gave you that responsibility?"

Another pause, during which I both awaited and feared his reply. I heard him shuffle around, feet sliding against stone. "I don't know," he said finally. "I wasn't there." His voice sounded off in a way I couldn't quite place. I thought our conversation would die down. I was out of questions that would get me anywhere and he did not strike me as the chatty type, but he surprised me by asking, "Why do you wish to speak to Her?" He said it much more quietly than he'd said anything else.

I closed my eyes and considered my reply. I was here for my people, but why did *I* wish to speak to Her? There were many reasons, certainly, but which one was he after? "My world is about to be shrouded in darkness," I told him. "A plague will soon wind its way through our veins, killing some, weakening others. Monsters will come from the sea and try to sever our heads, pull out our teeth." I hugged myself, and I heard him draw in a long breath. "We never know when it will happen, but every few decades since we arrived, my people have suffered great pain and death and I want it to end. I want to ask Her why. If it can't be stopped, I want to know. I want to know that, in a few weeks' time, if many whom I knew were dead, there wasn't something I could have done to save them. I want answers."

The guard never replied.

I peered down to the large room below. The king stood before the throne, seemingly lost in conversation with a group of others. They would come for me shortly. Perhaps once they thought I had escaped, I could somehow double back and try to reach the peak and the Goddess on my own.

"May I go down to the market?" I asked the guard in the gentlest voice I could muster. My insides were all worry and rage, but neither of those would get me help.

It had to be before dawn, but perhaps this far north the sun rose late, because I heard voices and the gentle clinking of goods below.

He shifted from one foot to the other, face turning towards the king. "I... He didn't tell me to keep you here, only to stay with you."

"Then that's settled," I said, without giving him time to change his mind. I exited the room and headed for the stairs. "You can stay with me down there."

I heard a shuffling behind me as he moved to keep up. It was interesting, conversing with someone whose face was covered. Their voice and stature helped to paint a picture in my mind, but I couldn't know how accurate it was. I couldn't know the details, like the shape of their nose or the colour of their eyes. It made our conversations feel strangely one-sided, like I was vulnerable and exposed while they remained wary, hidden.

At the bottom of the stairs, I paused to glance at the king. He hadn't yet noticed me and carried on in his conversation with his guards.

"Do not try to lose me," the guard said from behind. This time, there was a sharpness to his voice. He didn't want to get into trouble any more than I did.

I wound around the tables, glancing now and then at the king, and eyeing the goods on display. No money seemed to change hands. Instead, their business appeared to be conducted by trading. If there was something an individual or family required, they would gather up what things of theirs they could spare and lay them out on a table, waiting for someone with the required goods to come by. Sometimes there was haggling, which I didn't need to translate to understand. The gesticulating arms and shaking heads spoke clearly enough for me.

At the end of one long, wooden table, a woman beckoned me over. "Come, come," she said. Her movements and slightly hunched back told me she was old, older than my father. What business did she intend to conduct with me?

In a basket before her was a pile of bones. They were small, when compared to the giant bones of the throne, but I couldn't tell what they'd come from. An animal, I hoped, praying that the basket before me wasn't filled with the remains of a human.

She mimicked picking up the basket and tossing the bones on to the table, then pointed to me. It was an old ritual done by those who thought they could read your future and your past. Our villages had forbidden us from doing it long ago, saying it invited in things to our world that didn't belong there. But this woman was out in the open, amongst many others just like her, so perhaps here it was allowed.

Having nothing to lose, and too curious to walk away, I sat in the chair opposite her. Eyeing me for a moment, she drew in a long breath. "You wish for me to read the bones," she said. It should have been a question, but it wasn't.

"I do."

"They may not say good things."

I stayed silent. She regarded me for another long moment. I wasn't here to be fed lies and shiny falsehoods. If bones could speak, let it be in honesty.

I laid my arm on the table. She removed her left glove and took my hand. Her skin was covered in wrinkles and lines, and very pale. At her touch, I was reminded of Ymir, reminded of just how old she was, and wondered what sort of things she'd seen. How long had she walked this earth? I burned for an answer, but the question felt out of place in the moment.

"Are you prepared?" she asked.

I nodded. I wasn't entirely sure how high a stake I was putting into this ordeal, but my stomach twisted with nerves. I shook it off, all ears for whatever she might tell me.

She took the basket of bones, seemed to draw into herself, breathing in deeply, and then scattered them across the table. Broken hand bones, jaws, toes. These were once inside a living thing, I thought, fascinated and repulsed. They were the structure of something that was once alive, just like the bones beneath my own skin. Would they, too, someday end up in the basket of a bone caster? I felt aware of each of them now, the bones

245

running along my arms, my legs, the ribcage protecting my lungs. Each one felt alive, individual.

Though some bones reached the very edge of the table, none fell to the floor. The woman was skilled in this, practised. The moment the last bone stopped moving, she seemed to tense. I stared into her wrapped face, imagining what sort of things she saw as she ran a hand over the fallen bones. Where was I? What was I doing? My hand started to shake, but I couldn't tell if it was from her or my apprehension at knowing what was to become of me. *Will I live?* I wanted to know, wanted to scream. *Will my family live? Will . . . will Ivar live?*

Somewhere in the back of my mind, I counted while I stared at her, counted the seconds until at last she let go of me.

Thirty. How much of my future could she see in thirty seconds?

I realized, as she sat perfectly still, perhaps recovering, that the voices near us had fallen silent. Everyone was watching her, watching me. Everyone wanted to know what the bones told her. *Has the king noticed?*

She sang a beautiful note. It was gentle, light, and made me think of the very stars themselves. Then she seemed to soften and turn to me, whatever visions she'd seen passing away.

"I see the sky," she said, still holding my hand. "I see the stars, but they are fading. Fading until the sky is coloured in darkness, until there's nothing left but one single, solitary star hanging alone in the sky. I see it moving, still alone, still burning. One star travelling across the sky, travelling through darkness."

I stared at her, wide-eyed.

"And I see a skull," she said, softer. "I see a bone-white, unbroken skull resting in darkness." She raised a finger to me and sang a dark note, one that raised gooseflesh on my arms. "I see death," she continued in a whisper. "I see death."

Mine?

"You wished for me to speak the truth."

As panic rose, I wished she hadn't. I got up quickly, my chair falling backwards.

The king stood behind me. Jarring my thoughts from the bone casting, I faced him, my head spinning. He nodded to the guards, who moved away, and then held out a hand for me to take. He led me up the stairs and out on to the balcony that overlooked the mountains. Fresh snow had fallen, lying undisturbed at our feet.

Dawn would soon break over the distant horizon. I stared, a gentle pang tugging at my heart. I used to love dawn, to cherish the quiet newness of it, as though all of the heartbreak and exhaustion of the previous day had been wiped away. As though every morning, we could begin again. But what was this dawn bringing to Neska? To the other villages so far away? My mind flooded with images of plague-ridden children, of the fever caves filling with bodies, and of dark sails haunting the horizon, until my eyes stung with tears.

I didn't know what he wanted to say, but I spoke first. "The red lights," I said, clearing my throat, "they don't bring only the sickness this time. There is something else coming too."

He tilted his head to the side, curious.

"Monsters from the distant isles," I told him, turning away from the view to face him. "The Ør. They chased my people away from our homeland, and now their greed is bringing them here, to our sanctuary."

"The Ør," he said, and while I'd thought he wouldn't know the name, it seemed to mean something to him. "How do you know this?"

"I encountered two of them in the woods, near my home. Scouts. More are coming." I rubbed my palms against my eyes, exhausted beyond reason despite my rest. "This is why I need to speak to Her."

He stiffened, a king once more. "The Ør are a fierce foe," he said, "but I have faith in you. You may overcome them with your will alone."

I looked up to his face, heart sinking.

"We will send you back to your village, unharmed. Three of my guards will escort you to the foothills, where you must set off on your own. We are being gentle with you, but I will leave you with a warning to never again return to the mountains. Her mountains."

"But—"

He held up a hand. "Others like you have come this way before and made the perfect sacrifice for our beloved Goddess. I could easily do the same with you."

I shrank away, limbs turning to ice.

"So you will return to your people and fight your own battles, or we will drain you of your blood and present it to Her on an altar. You have perhaps noticed from the sky, she has a taste for red."

My back hit a stone wall and I was forced to stop retreating. The king slowly closed the distance between us until he towered over me, horned crown making him seem even more of a giant than he was. This was it, this was my choice: leave the mountains alive and return home a failure, or stay and die at the hands of this king.

I wanted to scream, I wanted to beat my fists against his chest and see the bruises that formed. I wanted to sever the wraps around his head and make him face me the way I faced him.

Time was heavily against me, though perhaps I could part with his guards in the foothills and sneak back a different way. It would cost me more time than I likely had, but it was better than nothing. It was better than returning empty-handed, worn out and with nothing to offer. It was something.

"Gather whatever things you brought to my mountain," the king said finally. "You will leave immediately."

The guard who had followed me earlier was sent to retrieve me. He found me crouched in a corner, crying. *She's my Goddess too,* I spat in my mind. She would hear me out, somehow I knew it. She would hear me before she would hear a crazed mountain cult who worshipped Her to the point of delirium.

"We must go," said the guard, his voice gentle. Even with a soft voice, he was just as guilty as the rest of them.

I stood and wiped my eyes, muscles aching from the cold.

From the mountains below us, a roar burst into the quiet dawn air. In unison, we ran to the edge of the balcony and peered through the darkness. In the distance, I could just make out the form of a giant, writhing and spinning around as if trying to shake something from his body. Below him were a handful of white forms, deftly avoiding his thundering body and shooting what looked like silk from large bows. The spiders I'd seen. The webs. That's what it was used for.

They continued to shoot it at him, over and over again until he crashed to the ground, unable to fight back any longer. Even from so far, the force of his body hitting the ground rumbled the stone beneath my feet.

"What's happening?" I asked. "Why are they doing that?"

The guard looked at me for a moment, then returned his gaze to the fight. "We have borders, lands we call our own. When they cross the line, we kill them, just as they would do with us."

The jōt were forbidden from entering their mountain. The one in the distance was small, by giant standards, so maybe he was foolish or didn't know the rules. I stood and watched as a handful of other jōt came to stand by, watching as two of the snow people readied a large blade. Something in my mind snapped at the sight of it. They could pluck my dream like a weed and burn it to ash, but I wouldn't watch them be so cruel to something else.

"Stop!" I shouted, then, frustrated, flexed my fists. "Don't let them kill him," I said pleadingly. "There are monsters coming, and when they arrive, these mountains will need to defend themselves. You will need all of the strength you can muster."

He stared at me for a moment, no doubt alive with questions, and then jumped into action, cupping his hands around his mouth and singing out a series of powerful, emphatic notes that carried all the way across the distance between us. When he'd finished, he paused, and those we watched seemed to hesitate, looking around as if to find out where the song came from. The snow people realized it first. Their tiny forms turned in our direction, and as they did so, the guard repeated the same notes.

The blade was placed on the ground in a show of

consent, and a moment later, the giant rose and stumbled backwards. As soon as he was far enough away, he turned and disappeared down the mountain. The other jōt who had gathered, to my immense surprise, bowed low to the snow people who'd just released him. It was fascinating, I thought as I watched, how while we feared the jōt for their enormity, the jōt feared the snow people for their power. There was a hierarchy in the mountains and not one that was easily defined.

"Thank you," I said to the guard, touching my hands together in a show of gratitude.

He said nothing, merely eyed me for a long moment. In the silence, something seemed to change. The air around us became softer, and in a way too subtle to be clearly understood, I had the impression that I was no longer standing on the balcony with an enemy, but with a friend.

Chapter 27

Three guards walked with me across the large room, heading for the tunnel by which we'd entered. I hesitated once to turn and take in this strange and beautiful place, this home to a people I'd never known existed until now. The king was watching me from his throne. I met his gaze for a long moment, the distance between us seeming to melt away. Nothing else existed but that wretched king, leaning back comfortably on a throne made from bones. That spark of anger evolved into a flame, but I fought to control it. Rage would do me no good here.

Perhaps I should have bowed, or offered some graceful nod in parting, but I simply turned away. This man deserved no respect, so no respect he would receive.

The tunnel closed around us. My guard – I'd heard

him called Sejer – walked behind me, while the other two walked in front. I let my steps slow, fighting the urge to turn and run back, to demand access to the Goddess. My slow steps made Sejer walk closer to me, so close I could hear his breathing.

No, that wasn't breathing. Was he whispering?

I tilted my head just enough to hear better.

"Stay close."

My eyebrows furrowed, but I nodded. Where else did I have to go? There were three guards and me in a tunnel barely wide enough for me to extend my arms. My options were slim.

"Follow my lead."

This time my steps faltered as I turned to look at him, which caught the attention of the other guards.

"Keep walking," Sejer hissed loudly, pushing me forward. I got the sense it was only a display of power. One of the other guards tugged on my shoulder until I was walking forward again.

What was Sejer trying to do? And, more importantly, had I just messed it up?

I continued at my same slow pace as before, thoughts racing. Did he have some sort of plan, about which I knew nothing? The uncertainty gnawed at me, made worse with each step.

The path wound up and down. The air around us felt thick with unease and worry, and the voice telling me to hurry home with help was no longer a whisper in the back of my mind, but a roaring in my ears. It was too much, almost: the rush to get home, the disappointment of being turned away from the Goddess and the not knowing how to reach Her. Time was my greatest enemy, more so than the king or the giants, yet it was not one that I could outsmart or face in a fight.

When at last we left the tunnel, cold air lashed at my skin. A handful of other snow people stood outside, all holding those strange crossbows hung with spider thread. I took a step back at the sight of them, alarmed, and bumped into Sejer. He didn't move away.

And neither did we. I expected us all to turn and head down the mountain, but for a long moment, no one budged. The two others who had escorted me out looked around, seemingly just as confused as I was.

Then, in a flash of movement that was over before I'd fully registered it, two crossbows shot white thread at the guards, ensnaring their hands and arms. They fell to the ground and writhed about, but the thread held fast. Their shouts fell on the deaf ears of the mountains.

"Hurry," Sejer said, and I rushed to follow him, despite my blind confusion. Was he helping me escape? Why?

We ran up the pathway, past the tunnel entrance to a part of the mountain I'd never seen. The path grew narrower and narrower, until there couldn't have been more than a metre or so between the face of rock and the chasm on the other side. It was a struggle to breathe, to keep my eyes forward and avoid the temptation to look at the death that waited below, but I fought against the urge. Looking down might mean losing my balance, and losing my balance would make the bone caster's prediction about my death come to be.

And that just couldn't happen.

I tailed Sejer up the path, until so long had passed that I couldn't wait any longer. "Where are we going?" I asked breathlessly. His own breathing was calm, even, as though he'd been standing still for the past hour.

He paused and tilted his head, listening. When he seemed satisfied that we were alone, he said, "There's another way to Her temple. It's dangerous, filled with ancient guards put in place lifetimes ago to protect Her. I can't tell how to get past most of them, because I've never done it, but I *can* tell you that in the first room there must be no light. I'm sending you with a candle, but you cannot use it until you leave that room."

My head spun. Dizziness gripped me so intensely I vaguely feared falling over the edge of the ravine. *Rooms? Lights? Ancient guards?* What was down there? "I don't understand," I said, shaking my head.

"You will," he promised. As he spoke, he stopped walking and moved perilously close to the edge of the pathway. Peering over the edge, he pointed. "There. You'll have to jump, but it's the only way. The jōt can't access it and nothing else knows it's there."

Jump.

I backed away until my body hit the rock wall. He turned to face me.

"It's the only way," he assured me. "Either you jump, or you go home, and even that might be difficult if the king finds out about those guards."

"Why did they have to be tied?" I asked, eager to speak of anything but jumping over the edge of the cliff.

"Things are changing here," he said. "There's a divide happening that the king seems unaware of. He's led us for so long and he is loyal to the Goddess to a fault, but many are straying. Many don't want to stay or don't agree with his ways. It's spreading through our numbers like fire. I found a few who would help get you away, but those other two are still loyal to the king."

"What will happen to you when they tell the king?"

He stayed silent.

"If I reach Her," I said, then corrected, "*when* I reach Her, come with me. Come back to the coast and fight with us. Stand up to more than just your king."

He looked around us, at the mountains that made me feel small, and the stars that made me feel smaller. He took in a long breath of the night air before turning back to me. "If you reach Her, Ósa," he said, "and if my king spares me, then I will fight with you."

A surge of happiness and spark of rebellion awoke within me, and I smiled. Somehow, it made the thought of jumping over the cliff seem just a little bit less frightening. I approached the edge slowly and peered over, finding, to my relief, that it wasn't as bad as I'd expected. There was a small ledge a few metres down that led into another tunnel. If I missed the ledge, I'd fall into the oblivion beyond, but if I was careful...

"I've done it before," Sejer offered brightly. "It's not as terrible as it looks."

"It looks terrible," I said, adjusting my clothing and brushing hair out of my face.

Holding Sejer's hand for support, I gently lowered myself until I was sitting on the ledge, my feet dangling in empty space. The cold air in my lungs helped at least a little to counteract the nausea rising in my stomach.

"Take this," Sejer said, tucking a candle into the pocket of my cloak, along with a flint and a knife – the one Móri had sent with me. "Remember what I said."

"Don't light it until I leave the first room," I repeated.

Sounds of shouting echoed up the mountain. Sejer stiffened. "Go now," he said, gently patting my shoulder. "Hurry. If they catch you a second time, the only way you'll enter Her temple will be dead."

My muscles tensed at the thought. "Thank you, for everything," I said quickly, looking into his wrapped face.

The movement made me dizzy, sitting so close to the edge, but I wanted him to see my sincerity.

"You are welcome," he said, and it sounded like he was smiling. "Now. Jump."

I took in a long breath and stared at the ledge. It was now or never. For a brief second, just as I'd done in the giants' den, I let Ivar's face hang in my vision, his dark blue eyes and tawny hair comforting my terrified mind. It was almost as if he were here, readying to jump with me. With him, nothing seemed quite so awful. With him, the sun seemed to shine a little bit brighter.

I'd never thought it before, never really opened up my heart and mind to the idea, but suddenly, sitting there on the edge of the cliff in the frozen mountain air, a surge of yearning and want hit me like the tide. *I want him to kiss me,* I thought, a sob just barely hidden beneath my surface. *Kiss me like the world is ablaze around us and we're all that's left.* It was a foolish thought to have at such a time, but at long last, it was a relief to entertain it. If we still drew breath when all this was over, I'd make sure that he knew.

"Hurry," Sejer whispered behind me.

Breathing in once more to steady myself, I pushed off from the ledge.

I'd jumped out of trees before or off low cliffs into the snow, but that was nothing compared to this. My stomach seemed to come loose from my body, racking me with a sort of intense but fleeting sickness as I plunged through darkness – and then my feet hit the rock below. I landed hard, stumbling forward as my arms pinwheeled through the air. I was perilously close to the edge, to the abyss of nothing, but I fought to anchor my feet to the ground, to find my balance just like I'd had to do a hundred times before on my father's boat.

When all of the movement and dizziness stopped, I caught my breath and turned to look up. Sejer was watching me from above.

"Well done!" came the sharp whisper.

"Thank you!" I clasped my hands together in a show of gratitude.

He nodded and turned to leave, then whirled back. "Ósa!" he said quickly. "In the second room, silence."

"I don't understand," I said, but he had gone.

Silence.

It didn't make sense right now, but perhaps in the moment it would. I made a mental note of it and entered the darkness of the tunnel.

Very quickly, it became so complete that I might as well have had my eyes closed at midnight. He'd warned me to use no light in the room, but he hadn't said anything about the tunnel. Was this the room? I suspected not, as it was open to the air where I'd entered, which could invite natural light during the day.

Carefully, I struck the flint and lit the candle, keeping my hand cupped around the flame. The tunnel was very narrow, the stone walls close around me, but a few metres ahead, it changed. The pathway gave way to stairs that descended into darkness. It was the only way to go, so I took them.

Down, down, down. Hundreds upon hundreds of stairs led me down into the mountain, so far I wondered how I could breathe. Every time I thought I could see the end, they continued onwards. I slipped once, my heel just missing the edge of the step where it had crumbled off, and I fell backwards until I was sitting. My back and thighs stung where they'd struck the rock, but I didn't cry out. I didn't know what might hear me in the depths of the mountain, and the silence all around me was enough to choke out any sounds I might have released.

I rose, gingerly finding my footing again, and pressed on. At the bottom of the staircase was a wooden door. It was so old, layered with dust and cobwebs and clearly never used – or rarely. It also bore a crude locking system similar to the one we used back home: two curved holders on either side of the door, in which rested a sturdy board. Someone attempting to open it from the other side would have to push against the board, and by the looks of it, they'd have to be stronger than the average person. Certainly stronger than I was.

Jōt, I suspected. The door was too short for them

to get through, but something told me that this was the line between territories.

I lifted the board and laid it quietly to one side of the door, then cracked it open. Just as I was about to go through, I suddenly remember Sejer's words – and blew out the candle. Sudden panic claimed me as the realization struck that I was far underground, in foreign tunnels that harboured something a locked door kept out, in absolute darkness. I reached forward, utterly blind and shaking, but it met with only empty air.

I moved into the cavernous, frigid room. Room didn't feel like the right word, though it was so dark that it must have been enclosed. I could feel the size sprawling out around me, and I kept my steps slow and steady, my blindness making it difficult to proceed. I lifted my free hand to my face and was met with only more darkness. Here, there was absolutely no light. It wasn't like those nights with no moon or stars when somehow the snow still seemed to glow. The complete blackness seemed to affect my other senses, even the tiniest of sounds reaching my ears like a roar. My footfalls bounced around me, making it sound like I wasn't the only one in the room. They multiplied and grew fainter and fainter until they disappeared, and others took their place.

Hair rose on my arms beneath my layers as I hurried to whatever lay ahead.

Coldness.

An intense chill caressed my right arm and I stopped. If there was no light in here, there were no windows or pathways leading outside, which meant that there shouldn't be any sort of air movement. Yet this kind of cold was unmistakable. Frightened, I opened my mouth to say something, but stopped myself. If there *was* something in here, the last thing I wanted was to alert it to my presence. What kind of thing lives in darkness, in the belly of a mountain?

I began to count the steps as I walked, entirely blind to space and direction. At twenty steps since I started counting, another coldness brushed the back of my neck. A faint gasp lodged in my throat, and my hand tightened around the extinguished candle. Everything in my body was telling me to scream. Something was in here, something frozen and dark and *old*.

A faint sound reached my ears. It was vague, weak, as if it had come from far away. It wasn't a whisper, and it wasn't a laugh. I didn't seem to have the words to describe it, like it simply didn't exist in my language. The longer I focused on it, as it faded in and out of my senses, I almost managed to convince myself that I was hearing *thoughts*. Hearing the mind of someone I couldn't see. And while they weren't defined words, they seemed to leave an impression.

Darkness.

Death.

Cold.

A distinct sense of doom settled into my very being, and in that moment, I would have given anything to simply curl up on the floor and close my eyes, waiting for it to be over. I pulled away from the coldness, but the sensation was unrelenting. Terror sparked to life within me, soon transforming itself into a blazing inferno of blind fear and trepidation. Breathing was a struggle, my steps were painful. Loneliness so heavy, so real and crushing, seemed to course through my veins. I wanted to run. Wanted to scream and cry to release the pain in my heart, but I was forced to carry on. One foot in front of the other. I continued counting the steps, breathing in and out to ignore another wave of chill that passed over my whole body.

At one hundred and seventy-eight, I reached a wall, bumping into it gently. Running a hand along the stone, I walked back and forth until I came to another door. This one also had a board, though on the inside. I lifted it quietly, moved it to one side, and slipped through. I collapsed to the ground, panting as if I'd spent the past ten minutes suffocating. I couldn't understand what I'd just been through, what sort of cold things had been brushing against my skin, tormenting my mind. I could only lie there, catching my breath and shaking, until I was calm enough to light the candle once more.

The flame offered little comfort.

I wound through a shadowed labyrinth. I moved as quickly as I dared through such unfamiliar territory, urged on by my desire to be out of the bowels of the mountains, but too afraid to run into the arms of another unseen terror. Now and then I convinced myself I heard sounds, but I saw nothing. In the dim light, shadows rolled across stalagmites and dank archways. The water – for it wasn't frozen – and the warm air didn't sit right with me. My body had already adjusted for the winter, having left the warmer months long behind me. Such an atmosphere felt out of place, unsettling.

Before me sprawled a cavernous tunnel, or perhaps it was another room, unevenly formed, but so long I could only see a metre or so in front of me at a time. The light from my candle barely penetrated such utter darkness. I made to walk forward, to continue this bizarre and frightful journey to the Goddess, but the sound of my footsteps made me stop.

Silence.

Sejer's words came back to me. I was alone in the room, or at least so it seemed from the emptiness haunting the limited visibility I had. Yet there had been a sort of desperation in his words for me to be quiet. He'd meant it, with everything he had.

I walked forward, but slowly. My footsteps were achingly careful, but wholly silent. My ears couldn't pick up even the slightest patter on the ground, and each successful step was a relief. *Quiet.* I repeated the word to myself over and over again, careful to make each step as silent as the last one. If Sejer's words and my experience in that first dark room were any indication, I was certainly not alone in this room.

Chapter 28

It was only a few steps later that I saw what it was, and my feet stopped moving. I wanted to gasp, to scream or to run as the dim candlelight fell on their forms, but that terrified part of my mind forced my body to remain still and silent. Along the tunnel on either side of the pathway were figures that stood like sentinels, tall and oddly shaped. Horns jutted from their heads, jagged teeth protruded from their mouths, arched backs gave way to the angled legs of an animal. Thick, grotesque arms ended in talons identical to those of a bird, only larger. They were like nothing I'd ever seen, and yet somehow everything. A horrid amalgamation of human and animal, blended into a single creature that could spawn the worst of nightmares.

A sense of time and urgency beckoned me on, but I remained stationary, staring.

They weren't moving.

The longer I gazed at them, the more I noticed: they were all cast in the same ashy grey colour and stood still as statues. They *were* statues, I realized a moment later, all carved from stone. Nothing more than harmless figurines like the carved animal toys that children played with. Stone couldn't harm me.

I let out a sigh of relief.

There was a soft whooshing sound and I slapped a hand over my mouth.

All of the stone creatures were now looking at me.

My heart thundered like it never had before, as terror in its purest form ripped through me. They had *moved*. The stone had moved. And their eyes, grey and empty, could see me. I was sure of that. With a sickening wave of understanding that crashed over me like a frozen wind, I realized my mistake: I had made the smallest of sounds. I'd known that, but I'd broken the rule. These monsters responded to sound, and now that I had their attention, one more mistake could be my last.

Ever so slowly, I removed my hand from my mouth. *Silence*, I thought as strongly as I could, forcing it to become lodged in my brain, letting it consume all other thoughts.

I drew in a quiet breath, and I took a step forward, recalling everything I could about how the snow people had taught me to walk on our journey through the mountains.

I placed each foot gingerly on the ground, small bits of relief teasing my mind every time I did so without making a sound. It was frightfully slow-going, every footstep a test of my patience, but I knew I was on the right track when my steps took me out of their line of vision. Their heads remained still, looking back where I'd been standing. Not having those vacant grey eyes locked on me gave my body warmth and energy once again.

Onwards. One step at a time. The ground was uneven, mounds of rock and loose boulders dotted at random throughout the room. All of the smaller, broken bits littering the floor meant that each step had to be carefully considered. It felt like hours before I could at last see the end of the tunnel and a small doorway. I'd have to drop to my knees and crawl through it. My legs aching from the exertion of moving my body so slowly, I passed the last of the stone sentinels, taking a final look at their horrifying forms – the sharpest, most dangerous parts of wolves, rams and birds of prey.

I shuddered.

Only a few more metres remained between me and the doorway when my foot kicked a small stone I hadn't seen – I'd been staring at the beasts – and the sound cut through the silence and bounced on the walls. I stopped moving, frozen in place as a strange sort of shuffling sound whispered behind me. I was too afraid to turn around and see what had happened, but too afraid to move forward.

They must have heard the sound, and all eyes would be turned to me once more. The thought was repulsive, the image of those stony eyes watching me.

I felt a strange sort of light breeze on my neck, like the breath of something close at hand, and I could be still no longer. I turned slowly, my heart in my throat, to find every single one of the stone sentinels standing directly behind me, grey eyes now gleaming.

A scream erupted from my throat. I tore my eyes from them and bolted for the door, running as fast as I could force my legs to move. Thundering footsteps followed, along with shrieking howls like predators on the hunt, about to dive on an innocent animal. I was the prey, but if I could just reach that doorway in time...

They couldn't fit through it, I realized as I grew closer. I just needed to get through before they caught up to me. There wasn't far to go.

I kneeled swiftly and began to crawl through the opening. I was so close, so close, but something grabbed hold of my leg, claws sinking through my clothing and into my skin. A scream caught in my throat as I used every bit of my strength to pull away. I kicked and thrashed, bracing myself with a firm grasp on the wall beyond the doorway, and in a sudden snapping movement that sent me hurtling through the door, the creature lost its hold. I collapsed on to my back, their shrieking fainter now that we were separated by a wall.

I lay there, panting, tears wetting my cheeks. My body trembled, my leg stung. I breathed in and out, but it quickly became too fast, and I was consumed by the sensation of not being able to breathe.

In. Out. In. Out. In. Out.

It was a few moments before I could stand, my whole body still shaking. As I finally hauled myself to my feet, I ducked to look back into the tunnel I'd just left. It was dark, without our candlelight, but the creatures were nowhere in sight.

My legs felt foreign beneath me. Weak. Unsteady.

Despite my shaking, I was reignited with a relief so strong it replenished my rapidly depleting stores of energy. I traversed a low stone room slowly, and it soon gave way to a narrow tunnel leading upward. I could feel the straining in my tired legs as I climbed higher and higher.

I longed to be able to speak. To ask someone what those creatures were. What that cold, dreadful sense of doom I'd felt earlier was. I knew reaching the Goddess wouldn't be easy, but I hadn't been prepared for just how difficult it would be. The memory of those chilling eyes haunted me. I hoped, with every bit of strength my body had left, that those stone creatures were the last hurdle before I finally reached the Goddess.

But as the uphill walk ended, and through an archway I caught sight of a vast room partially open to the night and lit by the moon, I knew I was wrong.

The floor of the room was dotted with hundreds of what looked like torches that stood on the stone, unlit, ready. There was nothing around to light them with, save for my candle – who had placed them there, and why?

A groaning filled the room, and something moved across the expansive stone before me. I froze, eyes wide, as a creature white and glistening slowly rose to its feet with yawning movements, as though it had been sleeping for centuries. Somewhere, in the corners of my heart that harboured a love for storytelling, excitement and disbelief sparked to life. The beast's head rose up, up, up, until it nearly rested against the partial roof high overhead. Thin, crystalline wings fanned out beside it, and a long silvery tail uncoiled behind it.

A dragon. A dragon made of ice.

I stood for a long moment, facing off with a creature that, until now, had only existed in tales told at bonfires and in runes on cave walls. But here, in this room, in these mountains where nothing made sense, it was real. It was as real as I was. As real as the stone beneath my feet. And that meant something to me. I had always been the storyteller, the one who knew the stories of the stars better than those of her own people. This creature justified all of those frozen nights studying the constellations with Ymir, all of those hours spent spinning tales to wide-eyed children around fires, all that time I'd spent studying rune stories with Ivar. It symbolized so much: that, despite everything I'd heard from my father, my sister, the other villagers, there was a place in this world for the daydreamers and the souls who dared to believe in the things they couldn't see. For those who believed that stories were more than just words that froze in the air.

These thoughts felt so simple, so out of place in this strange room filled with torches, before a dragon whose jaws could bring death in mere seconds. Yet, after everything I'd been through, they were the thoughts that gave me just enough strength to keep going.

I took a few steps towards the torches, ready to cross this room and find a way past the dragon. It heaved in a breath so large it sucked all the air from the room for a head-spinning moment, and then let it back out in a blazing eruption. White-hot fire engulfed the space, so intense it forced me back as far as I could go. A brutal heat seared my face, my body. Sweat broke out on my back, my neck, and I was forced to shut my eyes as I pressed against the stone wall.

In a few seconds, it was over. Slowly, I opened my eyes. All of the torches were now lit. Hundreds and hundreds of them flaming across the room. That immediate, inescapable heat was gone, but a distinct warmth remained.

I took a step forward to pass between two of the torches, but their flames suddenly flared up so large and hot that I was forced to run backwards. I tried again, moving to walk between a different set of torches, but with the same result. My heart sank as I stared at the wide distance separating me from the other side of the room – and the dragon, who now stood silently, watching.

A few paces to my left, I again attempted to pass between two of the torches, but was forced away. I let out a gasp of frustration as I fled from the heat and again returned to the wall.

"How do I get through?" I said to myself. The dragon didn't move, only continued to stare with its glistening eyes.

I glanced up at the roof, where it gave way to the sky. It was a clear night, the stars bright overhead in their silently watchful way. *Help me*, I said to the sky, because it was the only familiar thing around me. Ivar, my family, everyone I knew was far away. Ri was gone. Everything here was new, different, frightening, but not the stars. The stars I knew. The stars I loved. The stars I could understand. Only part of the Goddess was visible from here, but I wanted to scream at Her, so close to Her and yet so terribly far.

Something sparked inside me as I looked back to the flaming torches. It was probably nothing, but an idea found its way into my mind, and I couldn't silence it. I turned to take in the rest of the room.

I needed to get higher.

There were a few stalagmites here and there, and part of a naturally-formed pillar that looked like it had broken centuries ago. I didn't want to imagine what sort of thing had done that, but it would serve my purpose. Pushing my cloak back over my shoulders, I fought against the aching and exhaustion to hike myself up on to the broken pillar. It took a few tries before I was gently teetering on the uneven surface, pulling myself to balance on my feet.

From my perch, I saw the floor of the room in an entirely new light. The torches weren't random, nor were they placed in neat and even rows. They all had a place amongst the others, a reason for their positioning – and exactly what they symbolized hit me with a sudden force. They were shapes, pictures. Each torch symbolized a star in the night sky, part of The Five Greats that hung above us around the Goddess. As such, I suspected that all I needed to do was walk between the right torches, take the correct path to Her.

I smiled in near-delirious relief as I slid down from the pillar, alight with new excitement. I ensured the dragon was still calm and quiet across the room before I walked a few paces to my right and gingerly stepped between two blazing torches.

Nothing happened.

No blazing inferno turned me away. I was right. Follow the path between the stars. Do not disrupt the constellations, and I'd make it through. I passed one torch after another, sometimes pausing to look around and remember which star was where, and which course to take.

I was nearly halfway across the room when I paused for longer than usual, staring at two different sets of torches. Both looked just as right – and wrong – as the other, and try as I might, I couldn't quite recall which star sat where. I chewed on a fingernail and gazed as them, trying to paint the night sky in my mind. There were so many stars, so many tiny points of light to remember that the harder I tried, the more confused I became. When I looked up to see if the answer was visible overhead, it wasn't. We were traversing our way between the Horned Horse and the Giant, neither of which I could see from the room.

The movement and flickering of the torches grated on my nerves the longer I stood there.

I thought for several minutes. Time pressed against me and I was keenly aware of every second I delayed to the point where, at long last, I chose at random and moved between them.

I felt a rush as the dragon drew in a breath, and turned to run just as it let out an inferno of heat and pain. Just like that, all of that time and concentration was undone in seconds. I was back at the wall where I'd started from, and as the flames from its breath died down, the torches had moved. That meant, I realized with a groan of frustration, that the constellations had shifted and I'd have to approach the Goddess through a new path.

That frustration gave way to anger, and I flung off my cloak and shoved hair from my eyes. I'd crossed the plain, escaped the jōt and survived the mountains this far. I was going to survive this, as well. I knew the stars. This was my one skill and I'd be damned if I let it get the best of me.

Again, I climbed on to the stone pillar with shaking limbs and had a good, long look around. This time, it was the Warrior and the Wolf nearest at hand. I stared at the torches, replacing them in my mind with spots of light in the night sky. I knew these constellations, and I knew them well. I could get through this.

Taking a sharp piece of stone that lay near to the broken pillar, I used it to draw on the floor in scratches. I made a map of tiny spots all around me, drawing the constellations as precisely as I could remember, occasionally stopping to close my eyes and envision the sky. I imagined being back on my favourite rock by the sea, where I'd lie out late at night and watch the sky. I could see it, see everything familiar. Then I returned to drawing furiously on the floor. When I had included every single star I could remember, I traced out a line between them, the pathway to the Goddess. That was my course.

I stared at it for a handful of minutes, counting the stars to the left and right of each twist and turn.

Then I nodded to myself.

With a renewed spirit, I turned back to the torches and walked between the first set.

Chapter 29

I wound through the torches more slowly this time, contemplating each step and often closing my eyes to refer back to the map I'd drawn on the ground. I'd tried to stamp it into my brain, and so far, it was serving me well. Every step was careful, methodical, and though it was a struggle to keep my eyes from the enormous dragon, I kept my head down and my mind focused.

Halfway through. The dragon remained still, watching, waiting. Two-thirds. No missteps. The torches remained lit, quiet, allowing us to pass through, so long as my steps were correct. Almost there. Metres remained between me and the last of the flames.

And I hit a wall in my mind. A large handful of torches remained to pass, yet try as I might, I couldn't recall the pathway for my final steps. I turned in a circle, taking in all of the lights around me, yet no answer presented itself. My skin grew hot with anger, anger at myself for forgetting, at the dragon for barring my way, at the Goddess for making this journey so difficult.

I gripped my hair with both hands and shut my eyes, imagining I was outside in the wide open night, staring up at the stars. I could see the stars spread above me, but the focus and confusion of the night left some of them blurred, made my mind second guess itself when it was once sure. No matter how long I thought or how hard I concentrated, I couldn't recall the answer. I couldn't remember which of the torches to pass through. I hissed a breath of air out through my teeth and opened my eyes. I'd just have to pick. There were two pathways that, in my mind, stood an equal chance of being right. With no obvious answer, I'd have to make the best educated guess I could. If I was wrong, flames would send me running again – or worse, burn me alive – and the whole maze would reset. Time was against me. Anything could be happening back home. They could all have perished for all I knew. I couldn't afford to have to start again.

And yet, guessing was my only option.

With a quick glance at the dragon, who sat with its head still near the roof, gleaming eyes watching my every move, I drew in a steadying breath and stepped between the final set of torches to my left.

Nothing happened.

The torches remained as they had been, I fell to my knees and breathed deeply, the relief so sweet it nearly brought tears to my eyes. Finally, something had gone right. I'd accomplished something, and after all of the fear and exhaustion and heartbreak I'd been through, I allowed myself a quiet moment of relief. I wasn't cut out for these things – at least, I didn't think I was. I could fish and help in sailing a boat, I could feed sheep and help shear them, I could read the stars and tell stories, but I hadn't been born to fight. I hadn't been born to face creatures from myth and fable, to do battle with monsters and outsmart living stone. It was all so much – too much – but this one success offered the sweetest sense of joy I'd ever known.

When I stood up, the dragon hadn't moved. I looked around for a door, turning slowly, but if there was one, it was blocking the way. Why hadn't it moved? I took a step closer, terrified and exhilarated, but it remained in place – and rose to a menacing height until its head touched the ceiling.

A deep, rumbling growl rose from its throat. Shining, translucent wings fanned out from its arched back and consumed the room around it. I stared, barely able to breathe, as it challenged me to pass by. The shaking relief and exhaustion of mere moments before melted away in the blistering heat of my anger. If my suspicions were right, the Goddess's peak lay just beyond this dragon. It was the final few steps before I reached Her, before I succeeded in a mission that could mean the difference between life and death for so many.

This dragon would not stop me. I had a will wrought of stone and ice, and as strong as the sea. I'd been raised by the cold, shaped by an island that traded in death and disaster. This wasn't the first monster I'd faced and it likely wouldn't be the last – but let my soul be damned to whatever hell awaited it if I let this creature stop me from reaching that temple.

It was likely of no use against such a beast, but I withdrew the small knife Sejer had given me from my belt and held it firmly in one hand.

"I am getting to that temple," I said aloud, my voice reverberating through my body. "I am reaching that temple with you dead or alive."

Slowly, the dragon tilted its head to one side, as though pondering my words. If I hadn't known better, I could have sworn it was smiling. I didn't have a plan, not even a hint of one, but I took three bold steps closer to the dragon before stopping. Claws unfurled from its wings, long, narrow claws that reminded me of the icicles that would hang from roofs and doorways. It would be far too easy for them to slip into my skin, to rip my body to shreds and leave me drowning in blood. If nothing else, I *had* to avoid those claws.

This time, it wasn't a deep, low growl that rose from

its throat, it was a thunderous roar that erupted from its core, shaking the room until loose stones rattled on the ground. The terror the sound gave off ignited my spirit and I let out a scream of my own. It sounded small compared to the dragon's, but it was loud in my ears and energizing in some unexplainable way. When we'd both died down, it took a handful of heavy, rumbling steps towards me. I danced to the side, hyper aware that it would take one breath to incinerate me, and one swipe of those claws to eviscerate me. A creature like that didn't have to struggle to kill a girl like me.

There was a *whoosh* as its tail came sweeping towards me. I flattened myself to the ground in an instant as it whirled by overhead, just grazing my outermost layers. Without waiting for it to try again, I rolled away and leaped to my feet. Another violent whisper cut through the air, and I looked up to see a wing – and a set of shining claws – descending on me. I ran as far and as fast as I could, despite the closeness of the room. There weren't many places to go. I saw a glimpse of an ornate, arched doorway behind the bulk of the dragon's body, but it made sure to stay just enough in place that I couldn't get by it. I'd either have to be larger, smarter, or wait for a miracle.

I backed up close to the torches to take in the creature, to see if any opportunities presented themselves, but there was nothing. It filled up most of the space in this part of the room, making any thoughts of sneaking around it impossible. My hands fell to my sides as defeat wound its way around my heart and mind. *There has to be a way. There has to be a way.* I tried once more, summoning all of the courage I had left and gripping my little knife as tightly as I could, and then charged forward with a shout that carried all of my strength behind it.

At my approach, the dragon lowered its head and roared, flattening its wings and tail to the ground until there was no way around it. I stopped my advance, knife still raised, but my will downtrodden. Unless there was another way to Her temple, I'd never get around this dragon. I could keep trying until I passed out from exhaustion or I could give up now.

The dragon blinked its eyes and seemed to tilt its head, watching something behind me. Slowly, it raised its head, eyes still fixed on something I couldn't see. I was afraid to look away, to let those claws and teeth out of my sight, but something held its attention, and I had to know what it was.

Turning slowly, listening for the sudden *whooshing* of a tail or wing, I saw Uxi sweeping down from the opening in the roof, a beacon of white light in the darkened room.

"Uxi," I said, confused and dazed, blinking.

He took little notice of me, soaring towards the dragon who sat alert, tense. It was almost laughable, the visceral reaction such a large beast had to one so small. But in some strange way, I could understand it. Both were winged creatures, and at its heart, the dragon was an animal, of sorts. Easily distracted by the new arrival of a living thing.

Distraction.

I glanced from the dragon to Uxi, who was diving and circling around the great icy head, moving in close and then spiralling away at the last moment before the jaws clamped down. Uxi was small and agile, unlike the great hulking dragon. He could take care of himself.

I took a few slow steps to the side, testing to see if it would notice my exit. Then, when I was sure it was deeply engaged with Uxi's distraction, I bolted for the door.

Relief hit me almost as strongly as the cold wind. The doorway led to a narrow ridge between mountain peaks. Ahead of me, slightly to the left, was the highest, blessed peak I'd come in search of.

I fell to my knees and cried beneath the stars I loved so dearly. Ever since those red lights had shone in the sky, since those Ør scouts had stalked us into that forest, since I'd decided what I needed to do, I'd been dreaming of this moment. Dreaming of reaching this very place. Now that I was here, it didn't feel real, and I wanted to clutch at my surroundings in case I woke up. In case my mind ripped it all away from me and I awoke back in Neska, doomed to die.

I rose and moved across the ridge, no longer feeling the bite in the wind that whipped against my body. I couldn't feel pain or cold. I could only feel a joy, a relief, so intense I didn't know if I could stand it. It wasn't over yet, far from it, but this peak before me, this tower of stone reaching up towards the stars, was the first, bold step in seeing this journey through. It was like crossing a stream, just wide enough to not know whether even a running jump would be enough, or a few confident strides that proved my legs were longer than I thought would get me to the other side. A step towards saving my people.

At the end of the ridge was another doorway, through which I moved gingerly.

I turned to take in where I was, and my breath left my lungs. I was *inside* the highest peak, in a rounded room that had no roof. The curved walls swept up towards the sky and then ended in a series of wild, jagged points, beyond which the stars were visible. A light, cool breeze came down to meet me, but it wasn't that biting cold wind from outside. It was gentle, almost refreshing. Around the walls were strange, beautiful inscriptions – and I recognized them as the Ploughstyle writing Ivar had shown me. Curved lines rising up and down, with meanings that were lost on me.

In the centre of the room was a raised stone slab – an altar, I thought. That was all it could be.

But perhaps the most notable thing about the room was how it *felt*. My body tingled, like the feeling of sparks from a fire kissing my skin. The very air I breathed was different, so pure and clean I could feel it in my lungs. Being here, ragged and worn as I was, felt disrespectful.

I took a few steps towards the altar, which was carved with a grace I was sure could bring even the Ør to their knees. I'd heard of altars before – used mostly for sacrifices – and the words of the king echoed back to me. *We will drain you of your blood and present it to Her on an altar.* Somehow, being here now, that didn't seem right. This was a place of beauty and peace. Blood and sacrifice didn't belong in here.

Slowly and deliberately, I took in a long breath. It washed through my body, bathing my soul in peace. No, angry and violent as the snow people were, their bloodshed didn't belong here.

When I studied the altar in more detail, my eyes fell on a little groove near one end, the perfect size to rest a head in. I moved to sit, inspired, but hesitated. If standing on the floor of this room felt disrespectful, touching the altar was something else entirely. And yet, my instincts urged me on. It felt right, like I was meant to do it, like it was somehow the point of this entire journey to the mountains.

Chapter 30

Ivar had given up trying to quiet his mind days ago. Now, instead of sleeping, he'd lie awake most of the night, thinking of everything all at once. He thought of Ósa in the mountains. What was she doing? Had she reached the peak? Was she still alive? He thought of the Ør. Were they on their way to shore? How many of them were there? He thought of Móri. Why had he not refused to let him go? Why had he let the boy out of his sight during the battle?

Ivar lay staring at the roof, one arm draped across his stomach and the other behind his head. It was just days ago that he and Ósa had both been trapped in here during the storm, reading scrolls and making plans and listening to the howling wind. Now she was Goddess knows where, doing hell knows what. That was wrong.

Different. Since they were children he'd always had at least some idea of where she was, what she was doing. This kind of physical distance between them was too real, made him too helpless.

The door opened. Ivar sighed and closed his eyes. Peace and quiet. That was all he wanted.

"You can't stay in here for ever, Ivar."

His mother. He rolled on to his side and eyed her where she stood.

"You will feel better if you keep your mind occupied." Freja wasn't usually home during the day, or even late into the night, when things were normal. She taught children how to knit and weave and doubled as a carer when their mothers and fathers fell ill or were otherwise occupied. It suited her. She'd always been a good mother, and now that Ivar was grown, he didn't need her around as much.

When she spoke, Ivar had a hard time arguing with her, especially not when he felt the way he did now. Sighing again, he sat up and yanked on his boots and wraps. Sitting around here thinking wouldn't help a soul, and right now, a lot of souls needed helping.

"You are right, as always," he said, crossing the room and kissing her forehead. "I'll be back later."

He shoved some food into his pockets and left the village behind.

There was blue sky overhead. The trees stood tall, the snow deep. All the things he'd always loved about

Skane, about their frozen little world, were still here, yet somehow their magic had disappeared. The once cheerful blue sky seemed less vibrant, the once glistening white snow looked dull. He kept his head down as he walked, feelings of foolishness playing with his mind. How could they think this wouldn't happen? Why should they be any safer here than in Löska? Looking back, these events seemed obvious, unavoidable. But until that run-in with the scouts in the forest, it had never crossed their minds.

He hadn't planned where to go, but once Neska had fully vanished behind him he found himself heading north, and climbing. His path led him close enough to the water to hear the crashing waves in the distance, though mostly the only sounds were his footsteps crunching through the snow.

Ivar had been up here, and many times before, to hunt or to find nearby caves with Leiv or his father. Sometimes it was with Ósa, for no other reason than their chores were done and her father had gone out on the sea. These were some of his most cherished memories, traipsing through the snow and trees with her, or finding cliffs over the water and sitting down to watch the stars come out. It was always the same one that shone first, high overhead and bright as a bonfire against the dark.

An hour after he'd left the village, he stopped to catch his breath. He hadn't been much further north than this but once or twice. The furthest he'd gone this way was last year with a group of villagers tracking a boar. They'd found it hiding in a thicket perhaps fifteen minutes from here, and it served as a feast for the mid-year—

Footsteps.

He was on his feet again in a second, the single small hunting knife in his hand. That dreadful sense of someone approaching him, of someone watching him, seeped into his mind in the same way it had that day in the woods with Ósa. They drew nearer, nearer...

His father emerged from around a bend in the path. Ivar's shoulders fell and crisp air once again filled his lungs.

"Why did you follow me?" he asked, releasing a breath through his teeth.

"You shouldn't leave the village alone," Sigvard replied, crossing his arms and taking in the area. "You know that."

"I always leave the village alone," Ivar replied. Then he realized. "Mother sent you, didn't she?"

"She told me you'd left. She worries, as I do. You haven't been the same since... Since it happened. Neska can't afford for you to let this consume you. Skane can't afford that. You can mourn when all of this is over."

"How could I be the same?" Ivar breathed. "How can I carry on as usual knowing that a boy of thirteen years is dead, when I could have saved him? Eldór has no feelings for anyone, but how can *you* carry on?"

"Móri knew the dangers he was facing, Ivar. He knew what could happen and he went anyway. If you had been his age, you would have done the same thing. I cared for him deeply. You know that. But his death was only one. If we keep our heads, we can save hundreds."

Ivar turned away and picked up a rock from the snow, then hurled it into the trees. "His life should have been saved."

"His life *could* have been saved," his father corrected. "You can make yourself suffer for his death until the end of your days, but it will not change the fact that it happened. Móri is gone, but you are still here. I am still here. Ósa. . ." He trailed off.

"Ósa is still here."

"Perhaps."

Ivar closed his eyes and breathed. The logic of his father's words made sense in his mind, but accepting it meant reconciling himself to Móri's death, and he wasn't ready for that. Not yet. It was far too soon.

But.

Sigvard was right. If everyone didn't work together, Móri's death would be just one out of hundreds. Most of Isavik had already been lost. The least they could do was try to save everyone who was left. If the Ør weren't stopped, all of their deaths would have been in vain. All future deaths would be in vain. They deserved to be avenged. They deserved to have died for something.

When he turned to face his father, he said nothing, only nodded.

Sigvard let a moment or two of silence slip by before asking, "Where are you off to?"

Ivar shrugged. "I want to see the boats from up high." He didn't remember making that decision, but now he was certain that was why he'd come. "I'm looking for a better view, so I can see when they move on the attack."

"Mind if I walk with you?"

Ivar shook his head.

Their pathway led steadily upwards. They spoke from time to time, about little things, like a white hare that ran across their way. As the way grew steeper, they had to slow their pace, and when at last they reached the top of the hill and a cliff that looked out over the ocean, Ivar nearly collapsed out of breathlessness into the snow beneath them. It took him a few moments before he could focus enough to look out over the water.

Cold air swept in from the sea as they both stared, silent. A long, thin line of dark boats stretched away, about two boats deep.

Further out to sea, boats were steadily making their way to the others from the horizon, streaming down from the north in an endless line. So many he couldn't even count their numbers. It made sense the more he thought about it. He and Ósa had killed their first scouts, and then he and the others killed the next five. Since they'd never gone back to spread the word about who and what was on the island, they didn't know what to prepare for. They were waiting to attack until more support came. But there were so many, far more than they'd ever need.

A quarter of those boats would have been enough.

"We should go and tell the others," Ivar whispered.

Sigvard didn't reply, just stared at the sight far below. The Ør had back-up arriving.

Chapter 31

I approached the altar and laid myself down, slowly, carefully. An intense wave washed over me then, realization of so many things. I stared straight up at the open roof – which perfectly surrounded the constellation of the Goddess. It made sense. It all made sense. Why I had to come here. Why Her stars never moved. Why there was such an otherworldly sense in this room. There She was, staring back at me expectantly, waiting, Her face wholly encompassed by the jagged stone edge of the peak.

My throat constricted. What would I say? Could She hear me? In the hundreds of times I'd imagined this moment, I was always sure of my voice. Sure of my choice of words. Yet now, faced with the prospect of actually doing it, words abandoned me.

Something overhead caught my attention. Orbs of light, a small handful of them, were descending from the open roof. They floated down at their own speed, not carried by the breeze, and the sight of them tickled within me a sense of familiarity. I'd seen them before. I recognized them. How? They'd played no part in my life until now, not in my childhood, not in the village...

The plain. With a sudden ferocity of confidence, I knew they were the lights that had brought me through the storm. They were the ones, somehow, who'd led me across the plain and delivered me to the safety of that cave where I'd awoken, confused. My handwriting played in my mind.

Then came the lights. I don't know what they were or where they came from. I lost consciousness for a time, but I know they led us to this cave.

That meant, then, that they were the very same lights from Gregor's story. The ones that led his ancestors through the storm to safety.

They belonged to the Goddess. Did Her bidding. If She couldn't directly interfere with us mortals, then perhaps the things at Her command could.

This moment, it was the pinnacle. It was the very reason I'd come, the very reason I'd endured the wind and cold and fear until this point. But somehow, everything I'd seen and everything I'd heard and everything I'd feared paled in comparison. This room, this altar, those orbs, they instilled in me a kind of bone deep chill that encouraged me to run away.

But the village.

Father.

Anneka.

Ivar.

I saw their faces, saw their fright and despair, I saw the plague shattering them into sparks and the Ør coming for the survivors. *Why had I let myself speak such cruel words to my father?* Anneka might have hated me. My father might not have loved me. But no one deserved to die like that.

Slowly, the orbs began to climb again, towards the opening of the peak.

"Wait," I said instinctively. They froze. "Please, wait. What are you?" I paused, waiting for some form of response, but again they started to rise away from me. "Stop!" I screamed.

Stillness. Silence. The orbs stopped ascending.

"Stop. Whatever you are, if you're sent by the Goddess, then please stop and help me. I've come so far for answers. I can't leave without them."

The lights made a small movement closer to me, and then paused again.

"I need to know why," I said, distantly aware of tears running down my face, into my hair. "I need to know why this is happening." I moved my eyes from the orbs to the Goddess beyond. "I need to know why you sent us the red lights when we could do nothing to save ourselves. I need to know why the Ør are on their way to butcher us after so many years of peace. I need to know why the plague keeps terrorizing my people. I need to know why we deserve it. And I need to know how I can stop it."

More orbs descended from overhead. They circled around me, dancing. My voice seemed to beckon them, to encourage a response.

"Tell me what I must do and I'll do it," I pleaded, not moving my eyes from those bright stars shining so starkly above me. "I'll do anything. We can't survive the plague and the Ør. We can't."

I paused, breathless despite having only said a few words. As I lay there, staring into the face of the Goddess, I finally realized how wholly exhausted I was, like I'd never slept a night in my seventeen years. Every word took a little more out of me, until I was certain I'd have nothing left.

The lights started to ascend again. Pure, searing fury burned through me, and a store of energy buried somewhere deep inside burst out through my tongue.

"Stop!" I screamed again. "Don't you leave me! I have travelled through snow and wind and mountains. I have left my family behind. I don't even know if they're still breathing. I nearly lost my life crossing the plain. I had to fight a monster I never thought I'd live to see. I left the only home I've ever known to come to the one place I was taught harbours nothing but death. And I would do it all over again if at the end it meant I would get answers. I've come in search of answers. I *deserve* answers."

The lights had surrounded me again, swirling about me before clinging to my body. Somewhere in the back of my mind I knew my voice sounded different, but I was so enraged, so full of emotion that I couldn't stop to process every thought.

"I couldn't save Skane seventeen years ago. I couldn't stop babies from burning to death. I couldn't stop elderly couples, married for most of their lives, from having to watch each other go mad with fever and die. I couldn't stop my own mother from leaving me alone as a baby." The stars overhead were blurred by tears. "She should have lived. I should have died." I blinked to clear my eyes, but more tears fell. "And I couldn't stop any of it. But I'm here now, and I want to stop this. Just tell me how. Just tell me what to do and I will do it."

I realized as I fell quiet what had been different, what I couldn't quite place earlier.

My words were no longer words. I was speaking in song. I felt sharply different than I had moments before, when every second I could feel energy seeping from my body. Now, with every passing word and every passing second, I renewed, charged.

"Show me how to save my people. Show me how we can defend ourselves. Give us the power to win."

It was my song, they were my pleas, but there was another voice, another song that I could understand.

"Ósa."

The voice was so pure I was afraid to raise my own again. "Yes," I sang softly.

"Ósa, you have not the room in your heart to learn how you can save your people."

I faltered, tried to reply, and then failed. *I don't have the room in my heart.* I couldn't make sense of it, no matter how hard I tried to.

"I don't understand."

"Why do you want to do this?"

I closed my eyes and pictured home. "They all deserve to be saved. Even my family. Especially my family. I want my father to forgive me." My throat tightened as I sang the words.

"That isn't so. You want your father's forgiveness, but you do not need it. And you know that."

Tears streamed from my eyes, turning cold against my skin. I knew my answer before I sang it in a whisper. "I want my mother to forgive me."

The Goddess was silent for a moment as a sob erupted from my core, but my view began to change. Light gathered against the sky at the opening of the peak and a face eased into clarity. I didn't have to ask who it was. A new rush of tears fell from my eyes and on to the altar.

"Ósa," the woman said. Golden hair, as I'd imagined. Green eyes. A sweet smile, not unlike Anneka's, if she ever used it. She reached a gentle hand towards me, and while it didn't appear to reach me, warmth caressed my cheek.

"Mother," I said. "I'm sorry. I'm sorry." I continued to repeat it until another sob choked out my voice.

"Ósa," she repeated. I never wanted to stop hearing her voice. So soft and beautiful and full of a kind of love I'd never experienced. "You have nothing to be sorry for. You did nothing wrong. You were only days old, and so much stronger than I. You had the will to fight that I didn't, and you still do. I can see it in your eyes, behind your tears."

"I hurt Father and Anneka so deeply. I want them to forgive me, but I don't think they ever will."

She quietly hushed me, and again I felt that comforting warmth on my cheek. I wanted to hold it there, to never let it leave. "You don't need their forgiveness, Ósa. Their bitterness cannot command your life. Do not hold on to this guilt. It has plagued you for far too long. Lighten your heart and leave room for good things. You defied the odds and fought to survive as a baby, and you won. You were given a life just as fairly as your father and your sister. Never forget that."

The warmth faded, and I instinctively reached out for her.

"Don't leave me," I said in a rush. "Don't go."

"This journey is not about me, Ósa. And it is not yet finished. There is more to be done."

"Please," I whispered.

"I love you, Ósa. Hold that in your heart."

She began to fade away.

"I love you too, Mother."

My heart ached as she disappeared, but it also felt lighter, as though the weight I'd been carrying for seventeen years had suddenly been removed. The stars of the Goddess came back into view, and again Her voice permeated the room.

"When the time comes, you will know how to save your people. You will know how to defend yourselves. You will have the power to win."

With that, the lights and the voice began to fade away. "Wait!" I shouted, nearly rising from the altar. "There's something I must know." Some of the lights remained, and I still felt that sense of Her presence nearby. "Why does this happen? The red lights? Will it ever stop?"

There was a long pause, silence reigning in the room while I waited with bated breath. She certainly didn't have to answer, and more than likely wouldn't, but I couldn't live with myself afterwards if I didn't at least ask. Try to understand. None of this would matter if the past was doomed to repeat itself over and over again. The children and grandchildren of the people we might save this time would only die the next time the red lights showed. It was a pattern, a cycle of destruction that offered little room for hope.

"Once," said the voice, so soft and gentle that the beauty of it could bring a person to tears, "long, long ago, when they were still the only beings to walk the world, a god and a goddess fell out over an island. She saw in it a beauty, a chance for a people and a world all its own. He saw only a chance for dominion, a land to rule. So the two of them did battle, and while her powers were stronger and chased him away, it was not before he cursed the island to a death that would repeat itself irregularly, unable to be stopped by the goddess. Since she could not break the curse, she exiled herself to the sky, where she could watch over the island eternally. The sky and all things in it are at her command, but the island she cannot touch."

I gazed at the stars, open-mouthed. Something painful tugged at my heart, and I realized I felt pity for the Goddess. Pity for a darkness that was beyond her control. Pity for the death and destruction she was forced to witness over and over again. One day, either by the hand of an Ør or in my own bed at the age of one hundred, I would die, but she would still be here. She would have to watch it happen again.

"The plague," I said. "I came to ask for help. To ask you to keep it away. We could not handle the fever and a fight with the Ør. But . . . you said that you are unable to stop it."

She was quiet for a moment. "The Ør are a battle you must face, for they are even now massing at the shoreline, but I can help you fight. Meet them head-on and you will see what I can do. But fight you must, and I cannot guarantee the outcome. The plague ... the plague is different. It is something I have no power to destroy."

A long silence slipped by, and then her voice, soft, as though she wasn't really saying it to me, said, *"The curse now placed upon the land, undone by no immortal hand, steeped in blood it now shall be, once or twice a century."*

Though the words were quiet, they resounded in the room like a song. I didn't know who'd written them or where they'd come from, but they meant something more than our simple poems and songs back home. These words were tied to something ancient, a curse rooted in the very beginnings of Skane.

"The power of the curse is strong, but the power of the stars will always be stronger," She said, and again I wasn't sure whom She was addressing. "My immortality prevents me from bringing that power to the land, but you are different. If you can command it, if it can touch these shores, it can push aside any curse or any power lurking beneath the snow. Harness that power, bring it to life, that it may chase away the darkness haunting these lands."

The words spiralled around, jumbling together until I didn't know one from the next. None of this made sense, and even less so the more I thought about it. *If you can command it. Bring it to life. Chase away the darkness.*

She paused again, then said, "Hurry, Ósa. Time is against you. When the moment comes, you will know what to do." I waited, hoping that She would speak once more, but then all sound vanished from the room. The lights that had clung to my body began to fade, yet I felt nothing. My ears rang with the sudden quiet, and drying tears stung my eyes. She would help us! I sat up, slowly, shaking. All the lights had disappeared.

I stared at the stone floor, thinking of everything and nothing. The past few minutes, they might have been a dream, might have never truly happened, and I worried that if I stood up, it would undo everything. I might find myself back home, rising from my cot in the corner, beneath a sky bleeding red, helpless and small. But there wasn't room for fear. My body flooded with a hope so intense it nearly pulled my mouth into a smile. I focused on my senses, on ensuring I was here, in this room, on this stone, feeling its coolness beneath me.

Glancing up to the sky and drawing in a deep breath, I tensed.

Something was changing overhead.

The stars of the Goddess shone brighter than I had ever seen them. They fairly near pulsed: pulsed like the rhythm of my heart, an optimistic voice in my head making itself known for the first time. I ran to the door. Something inside me knew that when I stepped on to the ridge, back into the clear, cold night, things would be very different.

I passed through the doorway and took in lungfuls of the chill air. Above, the universe was changing. The stars that formed the Goddess were moving, gliding through the night sky further towards the south. Within moments, none of them any longer remained directly overhead, directly over the peak in the part of the sky where they'd sat since eternity began. Now, in the spot where I'd always looked up to see Her, to where I'd always turned my head when I needed that drop of comfort from above, there was only darkness. But not entirely, I realized with a start. Where they'd previously been close to invisible in contrast to the Goddess's brightly shining stars, there were new stars.

Faint, small stars that I didn't recognize, but something within me seemed to understand. There were small empty spots in other constellations, insignificant, easy to miss stars that only someone like myself or Ymir were likely to notice. And there they sat, in the wake of the Goddess's sudden move. Around us, other constellations were changing, moving, shifting. The entire sky seemed to be transitioning. In the west, the Warrior and the Immortal slid towards the northern edge of the sky, yet a single star from each was travelling away much faster. They streamed across the sky towards our mountain, and within moments had joined the fainter stars in the newly-made emptiness. To our left in the northwestern sky, the Giant was changing as well. He was moving, further towards the west, but only subtly. Something else about him changed, which was far more apparent. The stars within the constellation were moving, and as with the Warrior and the Immortal, individual stars moved to join the space overhead. I realized, after a few more thundering beats of my heart, that he was kneeling.

From far and wide, stars were moving, coming closer and joining the new set that was growing, while the ones left behind spiralled north, then west, then south to get out of the way. I was reminded, though on a much grander level, of the eddying pools of the tide along the coast. I pulled my attention away from the other constellations and watched as an image began to form. They spun and shifted, taking a shape my eyes fought to understand. Words began to rise in my chest, but they weren't mine. They were unbidden, yet dying to come out. I couldn't contain them. Couldn't stop them. They erupted in song.

"You have come to me selflessly, with the hope of saving those whom you love, and for that, you are blessed. You carry within yourself the power of the stars, the power of the sky. Go and fight your battle, and the power will go with you. The mountains and all within them are at your command. Speak, and they will listen."

When the voice left me, I fell to my knees gasping for breath. A wave of unnatural warmth crashed against me on the open ridge, despite the bitter cold of such a height, of the dead of night. It wrapped and curled around me, a blanket of comfort that renewed my soul. A light sparked in my mind. I could see it inside me, like a candle behind my eyes. There was such an intense energy within me I could have run all the way back to Neska.

When I stood, I wasn't the same girl. I wasn't the Ósa who'd entered that room such a short time ago. Everything was new, fresh. Ready. I looked to the sky once more, where the stars had stopped moving. Where the Goddess had been only minutes before, sat the new form of a girl. She was smaller than the Goddess, but every bit as bright, and twice as fierce. Like the sky was a mirror, I knew who it was.

It's you, said a voice from within.

Chapter 32

The sails remained at sea, lurking, waiting, watching. Ivar stayed at the coast as much as possible, observing with a group of others until well into the night, when his eyes refused to remain open any longer and he would soon fall asleep on his feet.

"Go home," one of the men instructed him, with a friendly pat on the shoulder. "They'll be coming whether you're standing here or not."

"I want to know when it happens," Ivar replied, his voice breaking. "I want to see it for myself." A yawn interrupted their conversation and the stars began to blur into one hazy point of light. "But you're right. I'll be of no use without rest." If they did come just then, he'd likely pass out from exhaustion before he could remove a knife from his belt.

Excusing himself, Ivar fought to stay awake long enough to get home, where he collapsed by the fire and slept until a couple of hours before dawn. His sleep was dreamless, a single expanse of darkness unbroken by anything, until a knock on his door jarred him to reality. Still shirtless, hair prickling his eyes, he opened the door.

Damn it. Anneka. He considered closing it again, but she spoke.

"Ivar," she said softly. "I don't know where else to go. I can't speak to my father and Ósa's ... gone."

She was lying, or at least mostly. Ósa's absence almost certainly had little to no bearing on Anneka whatsoever. She was playing to his emotions, saying what she knew he would want to hear, and that bothered him more than anything. He said nothing, just stared at her, waiting.

Her eyes darted up and down his body before she went on. "I'm terrified," she said, and her jaw quivered slightly. Ivar couldn't tell if it was genuine or not. "I don't know what to do."

He closed his eyes and tilted his head up to the roof. What was it going to take for her to understand?

"Are we all going to die?"

"I don't know."

"That means yes." Despair washed over her face, lines of worry pulling this way and that.

"That means I don't know."

"Can I come in for a bit? I've been alone for days on end. I can't bear it."

He chewed on his bottom lip for a moment, then opened his door wider. She smiled and brushed past him as she entered the house. Anneka didn't strongly resemble Ósa, something Ivar found mildly relieving, only for the fact that he'd never got on well with her. Where Ósa's face bore angles well and had a sort of well-balanced construction that gave her an air of dignified grace, Anneka still resembled a girl. Round features. Close-set eyes. It was a wonder they were related at all. He'd never known their mother, was only three when she'd died, but he liked to think she'd resembled Ósa more than Anneka.

"Make yourself at home," he said as he pulled on a shirt. She watched intently, and then looked away. "But you'll be alone here as well."

Her mouth opened quickly. "Where are you going?"

"Back to the coast."

"Can't you stay, just a few minutes longer? Please, Ivar, I need someone. We all need someone, right now." She crossed the distance between them and wrapped her arms around him. "I'm lonely. I think I've been lonely for years without realizing it. Father is always out at sea or with the village leaders, and Ósa... Well, you know. She's always gone somewhere, with you, or alone in the woods or at the beach or the Goddess knows where. I was only a child myself when Mother died, but I believe she was my last true friend. I know much of your time is spent with my sister, but I like to think that in some small way you care for me too. Your presence has been such a warm and welcome one in our family for as long as I can remember. When I see you, I feel at home."

Somehow, her words managed to chip away some of the ice that had been building up on his heart since she'd arrived at his door. It felt like a time to let go of the past, to let go of all the wrong she'd done Ósa and to simply comfort another frightened human being. Slowly, he pulled her arms from around his waist and held them gently but firmly. There was an unmistakable spark of light, of hope and expectation in her eyes when she looked up at him. His resolve to say something kind and reassuring began to disappear. The way she looked at him – the way she had *always* looked at him – meant something. Something that would never happen.

She smiled, a small, shaky smile that didn't quite reach her eyes. "These days, the thought of you is the only thing that gives me any hope. I don't feel so scared when I'm with you." She took his hand gently, tenderly, moving closer while her gaze darted from his mouth to his eyes. "I might not make it out of this alive, so I think you should know how I feel. How I've felt for a while."

"I'm in love with your sister."

The words erupted from his mouth with certainty and force, permeating the air and repeating over and over again in his mind. It was surprising, even for him, yet never before had he been more sure of anything in the world. He hadn't planned to say it, yet she'd driven it out of him with her words and looks. If he didn't say it now, he might never get another chance.

Anneka's mouth fell open, and she took a step backwards, dropping his hand. He crossed his arms and held his elbows as the silence closed in around them. She looked everywhere but at him. She cleared her throat, and tried to smile, but it faded away almost instantly.

"That's. . ." she started, but stopped. "I thought you viewed her as a sister. I'm sure she thinks of you as a brother." Another pause. "I should go."

Without waiting for a response, she left.

Ivar stared at the door. What had he just said? It was the truth, there was no doubt about that, but he'd been so careful, so cautious in what he said and did. Ósa wasn't a romantic. Those kinds of feelings just weren't in her nature, or if they were, she chose to conceal them, and he'd always tried to respect that. Despite their being close, she'd always managed to keep enough distance between them to keep her comfortable. Except for that one time. . .

Everything with Ósa's family, with what happened to her mother, were things that she still had to face. Still had to deal with. There was no place in her life for him – not in that way. Not right now. But—

Shouting reached his ears. He jolted back to the

present and yanked on his boots before stumbling out the door.

"What's happened?" he yelled to the nearest person to him, a woman hurrying from house to house. A baby's cries from within the last house followed her out through the open doorway.

"They're in boats!" the woman shouted back, terror running rampant on her face. "They're coming ashore!"

A lump formed in his throat, cutting off his air.

No.

The wait was over. They'd had almost no time at all to prepare, yet it had felt like for ever since they'd begun to watch the waters, waiting for the day that the Ør would come. Waiting for the inevitable. Yet it had always been something that *would* happen. Something that would *eventually* come. It had never been so immediate, so present. Like how in the winter, they knew *one day* it would be warm again. *One day*, the air wouldn't bite the skin from their bones. *One day*. Now that day was here, and all he wanted was just a bit more time.

"Grab a bow and get to the water!" Eldór shouted at him as he ran past him in the street. Spinning on his heel, Ivar ran into the house and grabbed his bow. In a repurposed fishing net, a makeshift quiver, he retrieved the fire arrows that had been prepared.

Chaos flew through the village on a wind of doubt and fear. The hurried plans of the previous days fell apart into a maelstrom of opposing wills. Many of the children were being rushed towards one of the fortified underground storerooms, their little faces pale and some streaming with tears. Most of the others, he was vaguely happy to see, were running towards the water armed with an array of the weapons the villages had been working so hard to prepare. Knives here, bows and arrows there, even spears and darts. Some, particularly the younger ones, carried slingshots with bags of stones. What little use they'd be in such a fight, but bless their souls for the thought. Despite the harsh words that had been thrown around, despite that frightened man who'd hung himself, somehow, these people were coming together, and it was exactly what Skane would need.

How many of them, he couldn't help but think as he hurried to the sea, would be gone by the end of the day? All of them? Half of them? He knew what he ought to think, that given what they knew of the Ør, there wouldn't be a single villager who could still draw breath in a few hours' time, but that thought was too defeating, too overwhelming to contemplate.

He turned his eyes towards the northwest where only trees and snow and sky sat quietly. No sign of Ósa. No sign of the hope he'd been resting so heavily upon. That letter she'd sent; she'd reached the mountains. What had become of her since? If only he could send her his thoughts, cast them out into the void and see if hers were still out there. Would she ever know how this fight would end?

At the coast, it was a grim sight indeed, despite the darkness. In the moonlight, wide, bulky wooden boats, so unlike Skane's long, narrow ones, were coming ever nearer across the water. They moved quickly, too, much more quickly than any row boat Ivar had ever seen. Perhaps it was that kind of strength, paired with much larger boats, that gave them the power to make it through the wild White Water to the north. Or maybe the danger just didn't deter them. Maybe they did it regardless of how many lives they lost.

Ivar darted his eyes nearer to the coast on the water. Three boats were coming back to the shore, and one man waved a hand wildly in a signal. They'd done it.

"Eldór!" Ivar called to the man who stood a few metres away. In his hand was a torch.

Eldór hurried over while Ivar proffered the soaked tip of his arrow, and it was ablaze in seconds. It took him a moment to stop the shaking of his hands before he could properly take aim. It wasn't so much fear that wracked him as a sudden understanding of an event that had recently seemed so distant.

Taking a high aim so it would be sure to travel such a distance, Ivar drew in a slow, steady breath before letting the arrow fly. It soared into the windless sky, a signal of their first hope against the coming onslaught.

Without ceremony the arrow plunged into the water, swallowed by the ink-black waves. Just as Ivar began to think about readying a second arrow, a blue glow became apparent at the arrow's final destination.

A few of the villagers cheered as the oil spread atop the water went up in flames. From a distance, where the oil wasn't clearly visible, it looked as if the ocean itself was ablaze, the sight blindingly bright in the darkness. Despite the gravity of the situation, Ivar allowed himself a small smile when the boats carrying the Ør ground to a halt. A mist of spray from their shuddering oars rose around the fleet. It wouldn't put them off for long and the fire would soon burn out, but any way to throw off their attack and perhaps set them on their guard, especially if they feared fire, was welcome.

The flames burned a dull red. They were like liquid coals, petering out into a thick black smoke that obscured the stars and the ships. Ivar wished more than anything that they would sail their boats straight into it and burn to death, every single one of them. What a sight that would be. But they remained still. They had travelled such a great distance to do this; they wouldn't be put off so easily. They would wait the fire out, and then continue their invasion.

The men who'd spread the oil were dragging their boats inland now, readying for their second set of tasks. The second step wouldn't do much, no doubt. It would only stave the Ør off for a few more seconds or minutes, but that extra time, time between now and their last breaths, was all they wanted.

Here and there, where the water was moving in and out the fires were dying down, and holes were forming in the wall of flame. Already the Ør were making for those gaps. The first one to make it through unscathed made Ivar's skin prickle. They were so close now, so huge and monstrous.

When the first of the boats were just nearing the shore, grinding on to the pebbles beneath the surface of the water, Eldór handed him a second flaming arrow. The villagers began to draw back, intimidated by the sudden closeness of the Ør and the menace of their appearances.

Ivar shot the second arrow on to the ground just at the edge of the beach.

It was thick with oil, and this time caught the flame much faster than on the water. Now, the only way forward for the Ør would be through it. There were so many of them, though. More than he could have imagined. Once the first Ør fell, the others would be able to walk across their fallen bodies and reach the villagers in no time – if they treated their comrades with such contempt. Ivar hoped that wasn't the case. Those who were already at the shore hung back, leaving a small gap of water between them and the blaze.

"For those of you with bows and arrows, your time is

now!" Ivar shouted, fixing a regular arrow to his bow. He took aim at one of the brutes directly across from him, but realized they were more heavily armoured than the scouts. Their necks were covered in hardened leathers, which had been the one place he remembered they were the weakest. *Where else?* he thought quickly. Their arrows were fairly weak, not reinforced with stone or metals. It was unlikely they would pierce their skull.

Then he saw it.

Taking aim, he let the arrow fly in the monster's left eye. It sank in deeply, so deeply it had certainly reached his brain. The monster shrieked, stumbling and yanking the arrow from his face. Shooting it had been one thing, but seeing the Ør pull the arrow back out, dripping with blood and leaving a hole where it had pierced, turned Ivar's stomach.

"Aim for their eyes!" he shouted to the other archers. Within second, a small hoard of arrows was zipping through the air towards the monsters. Only a few of them made their mark, but those few hit were knocked off their feet, and some directly into the fire. Before they could move to stand, they were ablaze. For those whose eyes hadn't been pierced, some had been nicked in the arms or legs, and some missed altogether.

As Ivar moved to string another arrow, he caught sight of a familiar figure to his right, half-hidden in the trees. Anneka. She gripped a small knife tightly with both

319

hands, her eyes wide. He caught her gaze for a moment before she shrank back.

With a sudden deafening cry, a large group of the Ør charged through the fire, moving so quickly it didn't have time to fully set them aflame. While a few fell, clawing at small flames licking their feet, most of the oils that had stuck to them were soon wiped off by the wet rocks of the beach. From that single point, it spread down the line of fire until hundreds of them were pouring through. Any unease over the flames they'd once felt had vanished. Now they were ready to fight.

Sigvard, Eldór and a few others were forming a solid group armed with swords and large knives. On a shout from Ósa's father, they charged into the fight.

Something above caught Ivar's attention and he glanced up. The lós were faintly visible overhead, but – it couldn't be the lós. He craned his neck, as if it would give him a better view. Sure enough, they were waving, moving lights, just like the lós, but...

They were gold.

Smoke carried to Ivar on the breeze, along with screams from the villagers and shouts from the Ør. But something else was carried along with it. Something faint that reached his ears despite the shrieking of the devils.

The beat of wings.

Chapter 33

Outside the Goddess's temple, the dragon stood waiting. I understood without asking: at the instruction of the Goddess, it would take me home. It bowed its head to allow me room to climb his shoulder, where I gripped its ice-cold neck with all my strength.

The ground fell away and the sky embraced us as the dragon took flight, soaring far above the mountains towards the foothills and the plain. My head swam as we rose higher and higher, and my heart couldn't help smiling at the beauty. It was a view of my island I'd never seen before and perhaps would never see again.

Something moved below – a small figure clad in white, waving its arms, and a few notes of song teased my ears.

"Down!" I exclaimed, sitting up and staring. I knew who it was even before we landed softly in the snow.

Sejer.

"Let me fight with you," he said, placing a hand on the crossbow strung across his back. "There is nothing left for me here. Let my weapon serve you."

I answered with a smile.

How small everything looked, everything that had once seemed so monstrous. The mountains shrank away, the foothills were little more than mounds in the snow, and the plain was a blanket of white as we passed by in silence overhead. It was the closest I'd ever been to the stars, and while their beauty didn't escape me, my hurry to get home clouded my mind.

The trees streamed by. The River Horn. Everything below turned familiar, and in the distance, I saw the shimmering surface of the lake. And then we were over my village, seemingly devoid of life – and shouting reached my ears on the breeze. Smoke and fire rose from the beach. My stomach clenched as I leaned as far forward as I dared, straining for a better look.

We soared on to the beach and the fighting around us paused as everyone glanced up at the newcomers. I couldn't waste time, but I also couldn't stop my eyes from roving the beach, searching for those few beloved faces I longed to see. It was instinct, almost; against my will, my eyes searched for my family. For Ivar. But the Ør didn't let themselves be distracted for long. Again their blades were raised in the air, seeking a victim to sever in two. Already, bodies littered the beach.

Whose were they?

I sang to the dragon and he kneeled, giving us a way to slide down. Sejer jumped into action, the crossbow already off his back and in use. I snatched the knives from where they hung at my waist and let one fly into the face of a nearby Ør. Thank goodness for all of those lessons with Ivar, growing up. The Ør howled and fell backwards, tripping over the body of a villager. I swallowed vomit. I might have known that person. As I ran to retrieve my knife, I chanced a glance at their face. Unfamiliar, yet my heart still ached. They were one soul I hadn't been able to save. One out of the many who lay motionless around me.

A shriek sounded from behind, and I spun just in time to dive out of the way of an Ør blade that crashed to the ground where I'd been standing. The Ør howled and raised the knife once more, but I danced away, drawing back my hand to throw my own blade again. It surprised me, though, by charging forward and knocking into my body so hard that I hit the ground. All the air left my lungs in a burst and I opened my mouth, gasping, but they couldn't seem to refill. Tiny rocks and shell shards from the beach tried to cut through my clothing. Silhouetted against the dark sky, I saw the Ør raising its blade, and for a terrifying moment, I thought that was how it would end, gasping and breathless, beheaded by a monster who stood framed by my beloved stars.

The muscles in its arms tightened as it made to swing the blade down, but a whisper and a thud left an arrow protruding from one of its eyes. It screamed and snatched at it, pulling the arrow out with the eyeball attached to the end of it. I cringed and looked away as the beast thudded to the ground, writhing in pain.

And Ivar was there, running across the beach towards me, a bow in one hand. I couldn't hear the fighting for a moment, couldn't see anything else but that beautiful, familiar face coming for me. His heart still beat, his eyes still saw. Something poured down my face, and while at first I vaguely thought it might be blood, I realized they were tears.

"Ósa." He crashed to his knees and grabbed one of my knives, hurtling it towards an approaching Ør. Then he took my head where I still lay breathless on the ground and cradled it, saying my name over and over again. "You made it," he said into my ear. "You made it, Ósa."

I knew we needed to rise, needed to get back up and face the fight raging around us, but this moment was so perfect, so filled with comfort and beauty that I couldn't tear myself from it. I wanted every second to drag into a moment, to wrap myself in his familiarity and cherish it like I'd never done before. I buried my face in his clothing, allowing myself a few more seconds of being able to hide from the death, from the danger that lurked only paces away. I'd faced so much of it alone, faced so many fears and terrors without him, suddenly seeing his face and hearing his voice left me drowning in relief.

"Come," he said, standing and taking my hand. "We can fight together."

I drew in a breath, my lungs still fragile from the blow to my body, and used him as leverage to pull myself to my feet. The sound of the fight, the screaming Ør and shouts from my people, closed in all at once, a deafening amalgamation of fear and anger fighting one another beneath a starlit sky. I took it in for a moment, took in the bloodbath happening around us. Villagers were being cut down, and while some had managed to overpower a few of the monsters, the odds were stacked firmly against us.

"Ósa!" Ivar shouted. Two of the Ør were running towards us so fast I barely had the time to draw back my hand to throw a knife before they were upon us. They swept their arms out wildly, their blades looking for any body part to lodge into. I darted away but the tip of the knife caught my clothing – just my clothing, I hoped. I was too focused, too full of energy to feel any pain.

Ivar ran back a few steps, drawing away one of the attackers and giving himself enough time to string his bow. His quiver only bore one more arrow after the one he'd just strung.

He missed the shot. "Damn it!" he screamed, running further and reaching for the last arrow.

I couldn't watch. My attacker was growing tired of me evading it, and all around us there were the sounds of people dying. I took one of my knives and let it fly through the air, but in a surprising show of agility, the Ør used its own blade to knock it away. It clattered on to the beach too far away for me to be able to reach it. One more knife, that was the only weapon I had left.

I followed Ivar's example and turned, running away to allow myself enough room to throw. When I span back around to face the Ør, it was close behind me. There wasn't time to focus, to aim, so I just let the knife fly and prayed for luck. It clipped the left side of its head, taking his ear off completely, and then sank into the ground behind him. There was a sickening moment of silence from the monster as its eyes went wide and it reached a gnarled hand up to its severed ear. Then it erupted in a piercing scream that overwhelmed all other noises on the beach. I ran to my right, towards the knife it knocked out of the air, but it followed me. I reached for the knife, grabbed it, and whirled just as a blade was coming crashing through the air towards me.

Further along the beach, something caught my attention. An Ør was making for a villager – one I recognized – who seemed to be unaware of its approach. Anneka. I screamed her name, but my voice drowned in the noise. I'd never reach her in time, but I started to move anyway.

Just as I began to run, another figure joined her, slashing into the monster's neck. Ymir. My mouth opened in shock and joy. I'd hardly seen the old man move in recent years, let alone fight. Not far behind him, Gregor – the leader of Išavik – swung a sword with the agility of a much younger man.

It warmed me, somehow, seeing the two older men fighting together. If they were going to die, they wanted to die defending their country. I couldn't help but respect that.

Ivar rejoined me, throwing another knife as he did so. I gripped my own knife, ready to engage it once more, but the sight of another villager being cut down stopped me. The Ør slashed at the man's neck, nearly severing his head from his body, and then turned to find another victim.

Arvid, the man who'd loaned me the horse.

I swallowed bile.

I thought, then, as I watched the villagers being cut down, as more of the monsters poured on to the beach, as a hint of dawn began to glow on the horizon, of what had happened on the ridge. *You carry within yourself the power of the stars, the power of the sky.* I didn't understand then, and I didn't fully understand it now, but it *meant* something, of that I was certain. As Ivar shot the single arrow he'd retrieved, as screams and cries continued to echo around us, I looked up. The stars shone overhead, silent and peaceful as ever. They were all there, just like I'd left them on the mountains. The kneeling Giant, the fearsome Wolf, the Horse with that majestic horn. They were watching us, I realized, though I didn't know how I knew it. I could feel it, perhaps. Sense it. But watch us, they did.

Even with our numbers, we were all going to die if I didn't do something. We were all still in danger.

Go and fight your battle, and the power will go with you.

Overhead, there were faint traces of the lós glowing against the stars, only instead of blue or green – or red – the lights were gold.

Reawakens something old.

The words filled every corner of my mind, echoing and bouncing. Something *was* reawakening.

A shiver ran through me, heavy with power and spark: a shiver of snow and sky and everything that made Skane the fierce and beautiful island it was. Everything around me – the snow, the ice, the sea – seemed to flood me with its strength, its power, until I was brimming with an energy so intense it awoke every fibre of my body.

A song began then. It started in my core, in some unknown point deep within me, and grew from there. Words and notes carried themselves almost unbidden out of my throat, off my tongue and into the frozen night air in a burst of white. I kept my eyes on the stars, no longer hearing the fight around us, no longer thinking of anything but the sky and my song.

The words were foreign, even though they came from me, but a small part of my mind understood what they were, even if I didn't understand what they meant. It was an ancient language, long forgotten, if it was ever truly known at all, but it was one that the stars understood. The language of the Goddess. Somehow, I knew it. It held a power, a power that even now they were beginning to respond to. The constellations began to shine more intensely than they'd ever done, like each individual star was exploding. They grew brighter and brighter as my voice carried louder and louder, and within moments, they began to move. To the west, the Horned Horse shook its head as it came to life, its mane rippling in a breeze I couldn't feel. It wasn't just a set of stars any more. It had legs and a head and a tail, and a wind of light and song seemed to carry it to Skane. It landed on the ground, taller and stronger than any horse I'd ever seen – and as its hooves touched the earth, a ripple fanned out around it, a wave that swept through everything and everyone and vanished in an instant. Words rang out in my mind once more. *Bring it to life, that it may chase away the darkness haunting these lands.*

Its coat glowed white in the dim light, illuminating the air around it. Tearing forward, those powerful legs raising thunder, it flew across the beach until its horn, as long as my arm from shoulder to wrist, plunged through an Ør's armour and out of the other side, dripping with blood.

All around us, the constellations were coming to life. The Warrior descended upon us, landing in the water just off the beach with a splash. He was tall, taller than the Ør, and his body was hung with armour. In his hand was a sword, the sword we could see in the sky, but though the entire blade was the length of my body and caught the light from the stars. He charged out of the water, his long hair tied behind him.

The Wolf swept down from above, running before his feet had even touched the ground. He was huge, easily the size of the bear I'd encountered in the mountains, and under his fur I could see his muscles rippling.

"What did you do?" Ivar asked beside me, his voice rife with disbelief.

"I brought the stars to life," I replied, looking at my hands as if they'd worked the magic themselves. "The Goddess gave me a power, but I didn't understand it until now." This was what it meant. What it had all meant. The new constellation. The others moving around. She was giving me her power, channelling it towards me, a power that could control the stars themselves. The gold lós, the reawakening, it all pointed to Her, and that ancient, Goddess-like power coming to life. In Gregor's story, the gold lós must have foretold of those lights that would carry them to safety. The same lights I saw in the mountain peak. The same lights that had led me across the plain. All of it was Her way of communicating with us, of helping us in whatever ways She could from Her place in the heavens.

Ivar's mouth hung open, and he stared at me like I was a stranger. That pained me, almost. Pained me because until this moment, Ivar had known everything about me. There was so much to explain, but I'd have to do it later. For now, I ran to collect my knives and charged back into the fray, newly energized and with the stars on my side. With the stars on your side, the universe stands with you.

The fight continued to rage on. Nearby, Sejer shot spider webs at the Ør, immobilizing them as a villager finished them off with a knife or a bow. I took a running leap and launched myself at the back of one of the monsters, my knife digging into its jaw. When it crashed to the ground, taking me with it, I saw whom it had been attacking.

My father.

We both stood still for a moment, an entire conversation of unspoken words passing between us, and then he shook his head. It was dark, and I couldn't be certain, but the left corner of his mouth seemed to move slightly. I smiled then, too, as widely as I could as a laugh rose up from within me. I didn't know why, didn't know what amused me at such a moment, but it was the kind of uncontrollable laugh that leaves one out of breath. How utterly out of place it was, how wholly inappropriate, but so right. He was still alive. Still fighting. I reached a hand towards him, almost without thinking, and he took it. We both wore mittens, but I imagined feeling the comforting warmth of his hand in mine. I couldn't remember the last time he'd held it. Not as far back as I could remember. Now, in the midst of death and battle, he gripped it so tightly, it was as if he was making up for all the years he'd never done it. Making up for seventeen years of wrongs. In his own way, by holding my hand on this frozen beach filled with screams and smoke, he was saying sorry.

He turned away, dropping my hand, and I turned my attention back to the fight too. The dragon flew down in a crystalline flash, incinerating a group of the Ør where they stood. I remembered that heat, that burning sensation in the mountains, and shuddered. The Horned Horse fought close by, facing an onslaught of Ør who seemed determined to take him down. He had that sort of strength about him, that power that told them they should remove him from the fight. Taking the large blade from the hand of the Ør I'd just killed, I charged forward and grabbed hold of the Horse's mane, swinging myself on to his back. He ran, then, ran along the beach while I swept the blade from one side to the other, making quick work of a large handful of the Ør. When we stopped and turned, I looked to the water, where many of them were returning to their boats. Throughout the whole of the beach, there was a general movement towards the water, and a few of the boats were already being rowed back out to sea.

The Ør were retreating.

My breath caught as I watched, urging the Horse forward. I had to find Ivar. The Wolf took the head off a monster in one gruesome bite, a growl strong enough to shake the earth rising from its throat. A group of villagers were overpowering one of the Ør together, and the Giant was plucking them from his back, flinging them away like flies until their bodies broke against the ground. The Warrior severed two of the monsters nearly in half with one swing of his sword.

But many of the Ør were running.

"They're leaving!" Ivar shouted, his mouth open with elation. "They're running away!"

Something between a cheer and a cry of victory rose from a few villagers, and it spread like fire through kindling. The sound reignited them with life, replacing whatever energy they'd lost as they fought harder, stronger, chasing the monsters across the beach until they were clambering back into their boats. The Giant snapped one of the boats in two, sending its occupants crashing into the icy water.

I swung down from the Horse and lowered my knife, hands shaking with exhaustion and joy. The fighting was over – the Ør were leaving. They didn't belong here, and they never would – Skane was our home, our sanctuary after they ran us out of Löska. We'd fallen then, but we wouldn't do so again. All around me, villagers had become warriors and fear had given way to courage. Skane wasn't ours – we had to share it with others, and more than we'd previously thought, but this cursed little island stuck into the Grey Sea was worth defending, and we'd done it. We'd done it, and the pride running through my veins was a feeling I wouldn't soon forget.

Overhead, faint bits of light clung to the sky, fighting against the approaching dawn. I stared, a smile tugging at my mouth as I was bathed in a relief so intense I dropped my knives. Against the lightening sky and the fading stars, the lós shone green.

All is well.

As their boats sailed away, I caught my father's eye further down the beach. In the dim light of early morning, tears of joy glistened on his cheeks, and his lips curled into a faint smile.

On a cold beach riddled with blood and the bodies of monsters, my father was more human than he'd ever been before.

After

As the sun climbed ever higher in the sky, peace at last reigned in the village. The stars had been swept back into the sky, where they'd been since the beginning of time, like they'd never left. The dragon had vanished to the mountains with a few beats of those powerful wings, and for the most part, everything seemed as normal as it had been before all of this started.

Save for the bodies on the beach.

They would be burned in due course, but for the moment, no one had the heart to do it. A period of mourning would soon start, as we honoured their lives and sent their bodies to the sky in flames. To some who'd lost family, it didn't feel like a victory, but it was, though hard won. The Ør had left Skane. The plague was nowhere to be found.

That was a victory.

Most of the village was busy celebrating – Sejer amongst them – their faint cheers and relieved voices reaching me now and again on the breeze. They'd called for me to join them – cheered my name over and over – and I would go soon enough. But after the noise and violence of the night, my mind sought calm.

I stood in the trees, staring at a lonely form on the beach. He'd been there all night, sometimes helping to collect the bodies, sometimes searching for more wounded, and sometimes, as he was now, shooting triumphant arrows he'd plucked from the battlefield out towards the horizon, where hours ago, the boats had disappeared.

Not far off, Ri – who had safely found her way home – and a few other horses were helping to haul broken weapons and debris from the beach.

Ivar released another arrow. It soared in a wide arc over the water, then disappeared beneath the waves. I took in a deep breath, looking down at the scroll in my hand. Soon I'd leave the village and trek into the woods, to find a cave with a wall that I could call my own. After a lifetime of seeing runes and hearing their stories, I wanted to add my voice to their ranks. I wanted to leave something behind, something hopeful, that frightened souls in the future might take comfort in. Sometimes, when the world seemed shrouded in darkness, words could offer light.

On a branch beside me, Uxi's head spun to look behind, just as I heard gentle footsteps in the snow.

"I searched the village for you."

I turned and found my father standing there. His face was pale and tired, but his eyes shone with light. He stood with one foot resting atop a rock, hands behind his back. I'd seen my sister earlier, but only for a moment. She'd opened her mouth to say something, a look gentler than I'd ever seen softening the usual harshness of her face, but whatever words she'd been about to utter, she'd decided against them. I'd never know what they were, but the hard lines of disgust that had always haunted her features were nowhere to be found, and that was enough to make me smile.

"Skane is peaceful again," I replied, turning back to the beach. "I wanted to hear the silence."

A few heartbeats slipped by. I saw Ivar kneel to close the eyes of a villager on the beach.

"I. . ." My father's voice trailed off, as if he weren't quite certain how to proceed. I faced him as he cleared his throat. "I haven't thanked you. For everything. We, all of us, owe you so much. I should have put more faith in you than I did, and for that, I am sorry. I should have known you were a fighter. If that plague didn't take you, nothing would." He shook his head and looked at the snow at our feet. "You should know that it wasn't your fault. None of it. Petra — your mother. Her death. It wasn't your fault. I think I've always known that." His lips pursed and the last few words carried so much emotion that my own eyes burned.

He shook his head again and turned away, unable to continue.

I didn't give him the chance to collect his thoughts. I crossed the short distance between us and wrapped my arms around him. It didn't come naturally. I'd dreamed of doing this for seventeen years, but it would take time for it to become my normal. In that moment of pain and forgiveness, words felt powerless, yet there were two that pressed against my tongue. Two that I'd always wanted to say, if this moment ever came.

"Thank you."

*

I waited until Ivar left the beach and was part way home before I approached him. He heard my footsteps and stopped, his face unreadable. The trees surrounded us, their presence as comforting as it had always been, and nearby, birds sang softly. My heart rejoiced at the stillness. The sun had chased away the dark of the night and it warmed my soul.

"I don't know why," Ivar said when I was a few paces away, "but I'd let myself give up hope for a while. After I got the note from Uxi, I never heard anything more and I tried to hide it, but I stopped believing."

I said nothing, only drew in a breath and nodded. He took a step closer.

"I kept remembering all of those times when we were younger, when you'd prove me wrong any chance you could. When you'd prove anyone wrong. But I told myself this was different, that this wouldn't be like those times and that it wouldn't be your fault."

I swallowed a lump in my throat as he reached out and gently touched my hair, dark blue eyes shining in the cold.

His voice shook as he said, "I've never been so happy to be proved wrong, Ósa. I've never felt as whole as I did when I saw you alive."

Something tickled my cheek and he wiped it away. A tear.

"There was a time in the mountains," I said, pressing his hand to my cheek, "when I thought I would die. There were many times, but one in particular, I saw your face and all I wanted was to kiss it before I died."

He swallowed, and the quiver in his lip hinted at suppressed tears of his own. "But you didn't die," he said softly.

"I didn't die," I repeated.

"Do you still want to kiss me?" he asked.

I didn't let myself stop to think, I only answered by rising on to my toes and pressing my lips against his.

"How did you do it?" he asked, when the kiss had passed and we just stood in the trees with our foreheads touching, breath intertwining in the cold air.

"Do what?" I asked, without opening my eyes.

"She helped us with the Ør," he said. "The constellations, the dragon, all of it. But how did She stop the plague?"

I took a step back and looked up to the sky, remembering my time in the temple, surrounded by those lights and voice and the unmistakable feeling of Her presence. "She didn't," I finally replied. His head twitched to the side, confused. "She couldn't do it," I explained, shaking my head a little. "It's part of a curse on the island, placed here by a god who said that no immortal hand could break it. She could do nothing."

"I don't understand," he said calmly. "Then, will it still come back?"

I shook my head again. "I'm not immortal," I said, and remnants of disbelief over what had happened still clung to my voice. "*The power of the curse is strong, but the power of the stars will always be stronger.*' That's what she told me. So I brought the stars to Skane." The words sounded strange when spoken aloud, but they were true in every sense.

"The stars," he repeated distantly. "There was a wave that ran through the air when they came down. You must have felt it."

"I did."

"*You* brought the stars down, Ósa. *You* did something that even gods and goddesses can't do." He took a step closer, wide eyes searching mine. I always loved how they looked in this light, the bright snow reflecting off their steely blue.

"I was given the tools," I told him, but a spark of pride danced in my heart.

"But it was you," he said again, resting both hands on my shoulders. "*You* did it. *You* wielded that power. *You* saved Skane."

I nodded, heart quickening as I turned his words over in my mind.

"You did it," he said again, quieter this time. Then,

in a whisper, "You did it."

This time when he kissed me, I let the spark I'd spent years trying to quench grow into the blaze I'd always wanted.

*

Skane was built on superstition. Always enter your home right foot first. When you sneeze, someone who bears you ill will has just spoken your name. Don't whistle while looking towards the sun or you might bring on rain.

Mostly, the superstitions were about the lights.

But not any more.

ÓSA'S POEM

Red are the lights that darken the stars
And cold are the days that follow.
Frightened are those who have seen a red
    sky
That means there won't be a tomorrow.

Fear is a beast that haunts darkest of
    nights
And swallows our minds one by one,
But hope is a light that takes root in the
    heart
And can grow to be strong as the sun.

Thank you to:

My wonderful agent, Silvia Molteni, and my fabulous editor, Lauren Fortune. Without you both, this book would not be what it is today. Thank you for your hard work and dedication to helping the true story shine through. Thank you also to Olivia and the whole team at Scholastic, who have been amazing from the start.

Thank you to Dad, Mom, Cynthia, Rebekah, Diana, Heidi, Chase, Camden, Zoey, Chris, and William. You are the best and most supportive family a girl could ask for. (A more specific thank you to Diana and Heidi, the very first readers of the book, and essentially the reason I kept writing it.)

My longtime friends: Schuyler, for literally everything, and Reina, for all of the good times and the writing support.

Alex, my dear friend and an early reader of the book. Thank you for your time, effort, and feedback.

My Team Maleficent girls: Claire, Katherine, Krystal, Leiana, and Samantha. Samantha, especially, for your help and kind words.

Phil, Ruth, and Erin Catterall. I lucked out in the in-laws department. And to all of our extended family members. You all mean the world to me.

So many people have touched my life and inspired me in countless ways; any omissions are entirely my fault.

And to Thomas. Thank you for loving me and supporting me every single day, and for encouraging me to never give up. I love you.

A *Shiver of Snow and Sky* Pronunciation Guide

While the accent marks may be familiar, I have taken some liberties with how they are used in the world of *A Shiver of Snow and Sky*.

Ósa – OH-sa

Ivar – ih-VAR

Eldór – EL-door

Anneka – AW-neh-kuh

Móri – MORE-ee

Ør – Or

Löska – LOW-ska

Lós – (as in low)

Isavik – ICE-ah-vik

Jōt – YOT

Sjørskall – SYORS-kall

Sejer – sigh-YEAR